SNAKE OIL

SNAKE OIL

A SAXON MYSTERY

LES ROBERTS

ST. MARTIN'S PRESS · NEW YORK

SNAKE OIL. Copyright © 1990 by Les Roberts. All rights reserved. Printed in
the United States of America. No part of this book may be used or reproduced
in any manner whatsoever without written permission except in the case of
brief quotations embodied in critical articles or reviews. For information,
address St. Martin's Press, 175 Fifth Avenue, New York, N.Y. 10010.

Design by Stephanie Bart-Horvath

Library of Congress Cataloging-in-Publication Data

Roberts, Les.
    Snake oil : a Saxon mystery/Les Roberts.
       p.   cm.
    "A Thomas Dunne book."
    ISBN 0-312-04424-0
    I. Title.
PS3568.023894S6 1990
813'.54—dc20   89-77951

10 9 8 7 6 5 4 3 2

To DOMINICK ABEL,
TOM DUNNE, and
RUTH CAVIN—
The Master Builders

SNAKE OIL

1

The six-foot-seven-inch black pimp was named Suede—or at least that was his *nom de mec*. He had a gleaming shaved skull and a diamond in his nostril, and as I waited to make the left turn off Hollywood onto Ivar Avenue, he was sauntering along in his jogging clothes, heading toward Vine. Over his arm in a plastic dry-cleaners bag he carried two of his more elaborate pimp outfits, one in orange and one in passionate purple. When you stop to think about it, pimps have to go to the cleaners too. Just another morning on Hollywood Boulevard.

It was eight thirty A.M. the Monday before Thanksgiving, the beginning of that rather dreary six-week stretch known as "the holidays," and I was on my way to my office, just around the corner from Hollywood and Vine. When I become emperor, I'm going to outlaw all holidays. They have outlived their usefulness. They once afforded people the opportunity to take a day of rest, recharge the batteries, and relax with family and friends. Now they just reinforce feelings of loneliness and tend to make one look back over the past year of nonaccomplishments with regret and frustration. Holidays are a pain in the ass.

November in Los Angeles is gray and drizzly. The palm trees mock with the false promise of endless summer, and people like me who drive with their convertible tops down get a face full of self-delusion, refusing to admit that the weather in Southern California is really no better than any-

1

where else in the world, just a different variety of rotten. November in Los Angeles is what you'd wish on the third grade bully who used to beat you up every day and steal your lunch money.

I live in Venice, several miles to the west of Hollywood and Vine, and two blocks from the Pacific Ocean, but my office is in Hollywood because more people seem to be in need of a private investigator there than at the beach. Hollywood, as far removed from the glamour of the movie industry as Allentown, Pennsylvania, is colorful these days, to say the least, a mixed bag of grinding poverty, flourishing drug traffic, and street crime, with a sprinkling of Iowa tourists with their heads down trying to find Gary Cooper's star on the Walk of Fame.

Jo Zeidler was already there at her desk in the too large reception area. Jo has been my assistant and friend for five years now, and I can count on the fingers of one hand the times I've gotten to work before she did. I don't know what I'd do without her. Starve, probably, because she's the one who remembers to pay the rent and the phone bill and to send out statements to the slow-pays that make up the bulk of my clientele.

"Good morning," she said perkily. Jo is one of those perky women. "Have a good weekend?"

"Terrific," I said. "I read three whole novels, cooked two gourmet dinners I ate all by myself because Marvel was off with the guys, cleaned out the rain gutters, and when I asked my kid to wash the car he told me that I was lame and probably didn't have any friends. And thanks for asking."

"Don't be such an old bear," she said mildly. "It's just the beginning of the holidays."

"That's what I'm afraid of."

I went into my private office and began making coffee, filling the pot with Sparkletts water from the cooler and grinding in my coffee mill the whole beans I keep in the office freezer. Jo doesn't make coffee. She's not that kind of assistant.

She came in after me and said, "Don't forget your nine o'clock meeting."

I glanced down at my appointment book, which Jo always leaves open on the desk for me each morning. On the 9 A.M. line she had written *Geo. Amptman*. He had called the day before and asked to see me first thing in the morning. "Did he say what he wanted when he called?"

She shook her head as she placed my checkbook face open in front of me, with several checks already made out and awaiting my signature. "No," she said, "but he sure could use a few lessons in telephone etiquette."

"Why?"

"He kept calling me 'young lady.'"

"Wait another twenty years. You'll buy someone a present to call you that."

"Well, anyway, he sounds like a real snot."

I winced as I signed a check for the monthly rental of the copying machine. That's not one of my favorite words, and Jo knows it. I was to find half an hour later, however, that it fit George Amptman like a second skin.

He was around fifty, had sandy-colored hair that he combed not very artfully over his male pattern baldness, and a little volleyball paunch that tattled of too many rich dinners and not enough physical exercise. What seemed unusual to me was that such a wimpy-looking man would be wearing an eight-hundred-dollar suit, alligator shoes, and a beige silk shirt with a sixty-dollar tie, and would have an attitude befitting a medieval duke waving to the peasants from the carriage route.

"Shall I have the young lady bring you some coffee, Mr. Amptman?" I said loud enough for Jo to hear me outside in the reception area. She slammed a drawer shut in acknowledgment.

"No," he said, settling into my visitor's chair. Not "no thank you" or "not right now, thanks." Just no. "I want to get down to business. I don't have a lot of time." His speech had just the slightest trace of Texas hanging on the edges. The business card he handed me read *Amptman Developments, Mimosa Beach,* and he passed it across my desk as though it explained why he didn't have a lot of time. I suppose he had to rush off and develop something.

"I imagine you're wondering why I came all the way up here to you, why I didn't contact an agency closer to home."

I wasn't wondering at all, but I had a sneaking suspicion he was going to tell me anyway.

"I'm very well known in the Mimosa Beach area, and it would be very embarrassing to me if my private business was to get around to my friends and associates. So I decided to find an investigator who wasn't from my neighborhood. I'm a real estate developer," he said, "one of the biggest in the South Bay."

"Congratulations," I said. I can be something of a snot myself.

He flushed, sharp enough at least to catch the sarcasm. "I'm sure you think I'm your enemy, Mr. Saxon, just because I'm rich. Don't be that way. Rich people have problems, too, just like poor people. Sometimes the problems are worse. I wouldn't come to you if I didn't need you." He hesitated. "I have reason to believe my wife is . . . having an affair."

"What makes you think so?"

"A husband knows," he said. "She has a kind of rosy glow that makes me suspect something is going on." He lowered his eyes. "A kind of glow about her I've never seen before." Then he looked up at me almost angrily, as if I were the one who was putting the roses in his wife's cheeks. "I don't suppose a man like you could relate to that."

The fellow was really getting my back up, without even trying. Imagine if he really made an effort. "What do you mean, a man like me?"

"Well," he said as if it were the most obvious thing in the world, "you're young and good-looking, you act on television and in movies. Women fall all over you, I'd imagine."

"Not recently," I said, thinking of my lonely weekend

just past, "but thanks for the 'young' part, anyway. How do you know about my being an actor?"

"I made some inquiries about you."

"What'd you find out?"

He almost smiled and then remembered at the last minute that smiling was hazardous to the health. Quickly composing his face back into the supercilious sneer, he said, "Positive things, obviously, or I wouldn't be here."

"I still don't know what you want from me."

"I'd like you to confirm or deny."

I pushed his card around on the desk like a checker I was deciding whether or not to move. "Mr. Amptman," I said, grateful for all the speech and diction classes I'd taken over the years that allowed me to bend my tongue successfully around a consonant cluster like *m-p-t-m,* "we don't do much of this sort of thing in California anymore, what with the no-fault divorce laws."

"That's all well and good," he said, "but I still have to know for sure. Wouldn't you want to know if your wife was cheating on you?"

"That would depend on how I felt about my wife."

He examined his fingernails, fingers apart and palm facing out. Popular mythology says that's the feminine way to do it; real macho men make a semifist. "I want to keep my marriage intact, if that's what you mean."

I nodded. "And what if your wife *is* involved with someone? What are you going to do about it?"

"I don't see where that's any of your concern."

"I'm sure you don't, Mr. Amptman," I said, "but if I go poking around in your wife's personal affairs and you decide to kill her on the basis of what I find out, I'm going to be very unhappy."

He scoffed. "Perhaps your profession leads you to jump to erroneous conclusions, Mr. Saxon. I am not a violent man."

"No one is ever violent until they get violent. What *are* you going to do, then?"

"Why, put a stop to it, of course."

5

"How would you go about that?"

"I'm a rich man. I pay for what I want."

"I don't understand."

"When I find out who the fellow is, I'll simply make it worth his while to—find a new hobby."

"What if he's a rich man too?"

"I'll deal with that if and when the question comes up. But I know Nanette. She's not likely to risk the financial security I've given her for some other middle-aged man. She's more likely to have found a young, vigorous one, a man who's on the way up but hasn't yet arrived. So I doubt whether anyone she'd be . . . attracted to, would be immune to my generosity."

"And your wife?"

He shifted his shoulders sadly under the expensive linen suit. "I believe she is addicted to a certain standard of living which few other men could provide her. There won't be any trouble, and it will all be forgotten."

George Amptman might have been hell on wheels as a developer of real property, but what he didn't know about the human heart could fill several shelves at the public library. He hadn't thought ahead to those shimmering rages, those unexpected moments when the heart takes a roller-coaster ride to the feet and stays there for a while, to the pain knifing through the gut when he would see a piece of his wife's underwear in the hamper and wonder whether she'd worn it to see her lover, whether the lover had slowly and tenderly pulled that particular pair of panties off her body, exposing willing flesh beneath. It had probably never occurred to him. Amptman looked like the kind of man who compartmentalizes everything in his life into neat little pigeonholes, taking the elements out and looking at them only when the necessity arises. He was in for a rough ride. I finally shoved his card back across the desk at him. "I really don't like to get involved in situations like this, Mr. Amptman. Peeking through keyholes goes against my grain. I'm sorry."

"How much do you normally charge, Mr. Saxon? I asked

the girl on the phone about your rates, but she said I'd have to discuss it with you."

"The girl? They don't like it when you call them that anymore."

"Nevertheless. What are your rates?"

"Since I'm not interested in taking your case, I don't see where that's pertinent."

"I'll pay you five hundred dollars a day, plus expenses, with a three-day guarantee. I think you'll agree my offer is more than generous." His innate delusions of superiority glowed in his voice. "There are a lot of men in your position who would jump at such a chance."

Annoyed, I said, "I suggest you go talk to one of them, then; I'm not much for jumping," and gave his card a little nudge in his direction.

"But I told you I've made some inquiries, and you've been highly recommended for honesty and discretion."

"By whom?"

He folded his hands over his little belly, a balding, myopic white Buddha. "That doesn't matter. Look here, I appreciate your forthrightness with me, but I really need you. If I made it seven fifty a day . . . ?"

"I'm not trying to negotiate with you."

"Then let me negotiate with *you*, Mr. Saxon. I am, as you see, not a prepossessing-looking person. From the time I was in high school I was—well, we didn't have the term back then, but I believe nowadays the expression is 'a nerd.' I've never been much for the social graces. I concentrated on my studies, got an M.B.A. from the University of Texas." He made it sound like studying medicine at the Sorbonne.

"I went to Illinois myself," I told him.

"I know. I've checked your background more carefully than you might think. At any rate, I came out to California about twelve years ago and got into the real estate market at just the right time, and I've made a lot of money. A *lot* of money. And when I finally had the time to relax and enjoy it, I realized that my life, my personal life, was rather barren. I began looking around for someone to share it with. It

7

was difficult for me. I don't claim to be at ease with women. I have trouble meeting and relating to them. So I finally put an ad in the personal column of one of the better magazines here, and that's how I met Nanette."

"When was this?"

"Six years ago. She answered my ad, and we arranged a meeting for dinner." George Amptman was the kind of person who spoke of a blind date with a beautiful woman as "arranging a meeting for dinner." I sighed. He said, "I took one look at her and knew she was the person I wanted to grow old with. I proposed marriage on our second meeting." He took a white envelope from his jacket pocket and removed a studio color portrait from it, which he handed to me gravely. "Can you blame me?"

She was pretty, all right, but not really my type. In her middle thirties, her hair was the kind of blond that lived in a bottle, and though her mouth, smiling in the photo, was full and sexy, there was a hardness and a cynicism around her eyes that would normally send me running for cover. But even if she'd been a knockout, there is more to marriage than a pretty face and a well-turned ankle—something they never bothered teaching Mr. Amptman at the University of Texas. I said, "Is this a recent photo?"

"About eight months ago. She still wears her hair that way." He took off his glasses and rubbed his eyes. "Oh, she was no angel when I married her. She was twenty-nine, after all, and she didn't spend those twenty-nine years in a nunnery. I've been able to deal with her past well enough. But it eats me up alive to think of her being with someone else now and then coming home to me."

Amptman shared the anguish of most cuckolds, and despite his lousy attitude I couldn't help feeling some sympathy for him. I said, "What is it you want me to do, Mr. Amptman?"

He inhaled raggedly. "I'm going out of town this afternoon, to Dallas, and I won't return home until Thursday morning. I want you to watch Nanette. Monitor her movements, and let me know where she goes and with whom.

Make careful note of anyone—any man—who visits my house in my absence. Find out who he is, his name and address. I'll expect a report from you on Thursday afternoon. Don't worry about interrupting my Thanksgiving dinner."

"What about my Thanksgiving dinner?" I said. I was just being contentious. I didn't have any holiday plans. Jo and her husband Marsh had invited me to share turkey with them and another couple, but I was between relationships at the moment, and I am not fond of being a fifth wheel.

"I think seven hundred fifty dollars a day should ease the pain of any holiday inconvenience," he said.

I didn't like the feel of this, but I couldn't think of any concrete reasons to turn down more than two grand for a simple job like this one. "All right, Mr. Amptman," I said. "I'll go to work for you."

He took a checkbook and a gold Cross pen from his inside pocket and wrote me a check for the full amount. He tore it out carefully and passed it over to me. It was a business check.

"I'll need your home address," I said, and he jotted it down on a piece of paper from the notepad on my desk, along with his home phone number.

"My plane leaves at four o'clock this afternoon," he said, "so I'll be leaving the house at about two thirty. That will be time enough to begin your . . . surveillance." He stared down at his lap and shook his head. "I don't feel good about this, Mr. Saxon. It's like pissing on something holy."

I folded the check and put it in my desk drawer. "What happens," I said, "if I find out nothing? What if this is all in your imagination, and your wife doesn't make a single false move in the next three days?"

"You think I'm suffering from paranoia?"

"I'm not a psychiatrist. But what if I discover your wife is as pure as Ivory Snow? It's entirely possible, you know."

"In that case," he said, a small and bitter smile playing about his lips, "it's a small price to pay for peace of mind."

2

I filled Jo in on the details of the Amptman case so she could write it up for the permanent files, and then I went home for a good meal and a rest. Surveillance jobs like this one, although rarely taxing or dangerous, tend to stretch into hours of cramped boredom in the front seat of a parked car, and if I was going to be up all night I wanted to be rested for it.

Venice, where I've lived since I was invited by the management to vacate my apartment in Pacific Palisades, is a seaside community just below Santa Monica. It got its name because of its intricate system of canals, modeled after the Adriatic port city in Italy, which were designed by a man named Abbot Kinney as a tourist attraction at the turn of the century. The idea didn't take, and the canals fell into disuse and disrepair; in the sixties the city itself became a mecca for drug addicts, hippies, speed freaks and derelicts, and despite a recent resurgence it has remained the kind of community that respectable button-down types with fashionably aproned wives and 2.5 cute kids drive through on their way to the beach very quickly so they won't have to look at the darker tones and coarser textures of the California experience. But I like Venice, because of its proximity to the ocean, its inhospitality to marauding hordes of ethnic street gangs, movieland phonies, and upscale social climbers, and because its restaurants tend toward honest and forthright food and drink, unlike the soulless, noisy, trendy, pink-and-gray neon-lit eateries that infest the remainder of West Los Angeles like anthills, with their meager portions of duck sausage and arugula.

I parked my gold-colored Le Baron convertible in the garage of my leased bungalow and, stopping for a few seconds to listen to the birds chirping in the tall grass, let myself in through the back door. I stumbled over a football shoe that hadn't quite made it to its intended destination in the corner, and my forward motion propelled me into the kitchen. I would have to talk to Marvel about that.

Marvel—accent on the second syllable, please—is my son. You might not notice a familial resemblance—he is black and I am not, for one thing—because he is not my biological child. I scooped him out of a pretty ugly situation about a year and a half ago and am now in the process of adopting him legally, which involves me in official dealings with more social workers and child welfare people and government paper-pushers than I ever before knew existed. No one is quite sure how old he is, but the best we can figure is around sixteen, which we arrived at due to his voracious appetite and his antipathy toward cleaning his room. We commemorate his birthday on mine in July, which makes it easy to remember and gives me an excuse to celebrate a day that had for some time previous only served to remind me that I'm no callow youth anymore. Marvel is a great kid, with a good ear for early bebop, a sense of humor somewhere between Don Rickles and Ghenghis Khan, an awesome sinking curveball, and a predilection for Pepsi that borders on mainline addiction. He is hopelessly love-struck over the girl who lives down the street, Saraine by name, who is about a year older than he and pretends she doesn't know he's alive, which is eventually going to send him around the bend. His only flaw is leaving his size-eleven shoes all over the house, and one day somebody is going to be seriously injured falling over one of them. Probably me.

Marvel was at school, as it was almost eleven o'clock in the morning, so I set my alarm for one thirty and tried to nap, but it didn't work. I had only gotten out of bed a few

11

hours before and I just wasn't tired. I switched on the television set in my bedroom and began watching a soap opera in which Hilary was trying to tell Dexter that Emily wasn't really his baby because she'd had an affair with Jason who never knew she'd become pregnant; I was asleep in five minutes. Don't let anyone tell you daytime TV doesn't serve a useful purpose.

I awoke to the clock radio alarm, heavy metal rock which I loathe so cheerfully that the sound immediately propels me out of bed to switch it off, fixed myself some weisswurst and eggs and washed it down with a John Courage, and put on my silver Los Angeles Raiders jacket over a pair of black sailcloth slacks and a gray shirt. I made some coffee and dumped it into a thermos, in case this took longer than I hoped, and took a box of granola bars, to which Marvel had also become addicted, in case I got hungry during the vigil.

I went into Marvel's room, a journey with a fairly high risk factor, and waded through the dirty clothes on the floor to the closet, from which I removed his Raiders cap, putting it in my pocket. I look like the king's fool in any hat I've ever plopped on my head, and the very thought of wearing one all day gives me the shivers, but people in hats are harder to identify, especially if, like me, they have a full head of gray hair. Then I printed a note for Marvel to read when he returned home from school. When he first came to live with me he knew the alphabet and could recognize words like *dog* and *cat* and not much more, but his progress in school since then has been remarkable. The problem of functional illiteracy in the United States really comes home to you when you try to leave a note telling your teenager you're going to be late for dinner and he can't even read it.

It took nearly an hour to drive down to Mimosa Beach from Venice on the Pacific Coast Highway, a route that unavoidably plunges you into the backwash of Los Angeles International Airport's nightmarish traffic and makes you wonder why you don't move to a small town in Kansas. Los Angeles becomes harder to live in each year: the smog gets worse, violent crime is on the rise, the cars on the road seem to multiply like rabbits on fertility drugs, the streets fall into disrepair, and there's hardly a store or gas station where the attendants speak enough English to figure out just what it is you want.

Mimosa Beach, nestled in the crescent of the South Bay, is divided by social custom into two groups of permanent residents that are known by the postapocalypse sobriquets of "tree people" and "sand people." Sand people live within two blocks of the beach and tend to be youthful, fair-to-look-upon, sexually adventurous party freaks with a remarkable amount of discretionary funds to feed and nurture their hedonism and purchase Bud Light by the case. Once in a while you'll find an older guy among them, somewhere in his early forties, who thinks that proximity to the young and the reckless will restore his own lost boyhood, who likes the firm, tan beachflesh of the bikini girls, and who is only tolerated because of his seemingly bottomless supply of hash and coke. Tree people, on the other hand, tend to be older, more affluent, more sedate, and live on the slopes of the hills overlooking the ocean. They have three-bedroom homes with VCRs and hot tubs, drive Beemers and Volvos equipped with cellular phones, buy the wines of Mendocino and put them down in art-nouveau plastic racks until they have matured, and use designer drugs.

The Amptmans were, not surprisingly, tree people. I wound up a hill designed by a sidewinder rattlesnake for his cousins and found their house in a wide cul-de-sac. It and the three neighboring homes were done in a Bauhaus-modern style, with lots of wood and glass on the outside forming angles at once dramatic and pleasing to the eye, the type of house described in realtors' ad copy as "emotional." The Amptmans' place, which was the first one on the left in the half circle of the cul-de-sac, was the largest. In the carport was a new white Volvo sedan next to a fire-engine-red Mercedes convertible with its white rag top up. I slapped Marvel's cap on my head, glancing in the rearview mirror to verify how duncelike I looked, and parked in front of the house beyond, facing the Amptmans'. I was looking to the

east, where the November sky was the color of an un-
washed muslin bedsheet. From the situation of the house on
the hillside I supposed that the back yard afforded a view of
a good bit of the South Bay communities of Redondo Beach
and Torrance, and I reflected on the folly of building an expensive home up on a hill, six blocks from the ocean, facing
inland.

At about two thirty a white Cadillac stretch limo pulled
into the crescent driveway and a uniformed chauffeur got
out and went to the entrance of the house. Before he could
ring the bell, the door opened and George Amptman came
out, dressed the way I'd seen him at my office in the morning. He said something to the chauffeur, who went inside
and reemerged a few seconds later juggling two matched
pieces of Gucci luggage, which he stowed quickly and expertly in the trunk. The driver waited by the open rear door
of the limo while Amptman went back into the house for a
few minutes, then came back out carrying a briefcase that
matched his luggage. He said something over his shoulder
to someone inside. Then he climbed into the limo as the
door to the house was closed behind him. The big car
moved quietly around the driveway, out into the street,
heading past me and down the hill. George Amptman was
on his way to Dallas.

Things were quiet for a while after that, and I unscrewed
the thermos and poured some coffee into the top. I slumped
down in the seat to wait. I had exhausted my coffee supply
before I had anything else to look at.

Shortly after five o'clock Nanette Amptman emerged
from the house. She didn't look quite as hard-edged as her
picture had led me to believe. Her platinum hair was pulled
back from her face and held by little gold barrettes, and the
straight white skirt she was wearing was slit high enough
up the side to expose a trim, long leg. A beige cashmere
jacket covered but didn't conceal a bright red blouse. She
was carrying a small makeup case and her purse. I couldn't
tell anything from her facial expression. She locked the door
of the house, got into the Mercedes convertible, and backed

out onto the street. She was moving pretty quickly, but since the house was on a dead end there wasn't much danger from passing traffic.

I started up my own car as she turned and headed down from her hilltop. There wasn't much chance of losing her on the winding hill road, and I didn't want her to know she was being tailed, so I kept far back out of sight until she reached Highland Avenue, where I came around a curve just in time to see her turn north. We were driving along the beach, Vista Del Mar Road being the demarcation line between the sand on the left and the big oil refineries on the right.

I kept about a quarter mile behind her and took care to keep at least one other car between mine and hers. We went through Manhattan Beach and El Tercero, and when she reached Playa Del Rey she turned off onto a side street. I slowed down a bit and followed her.

Driving as if she knew exactly where she was going, she pulled into the visitors parking lot of a condominium complex half a block from the beach, built on a finger of land that jutted insolently out into the water. I stopped about a hundred feet before the driveway and cut my engine. I saw her get out of her car, carrying the makeup case, and head for the row of modern town houses. They had been built in the late seventies in a vaguely nautical design with a lot of rough-hewn, splintery timbers that didn't even remotely resemble those of a sailing vessel but imparted the sea-going feeling, anyway. Each unit had a large round window facing the sea to give the impression of a giant porthole, and the wood treatments on the doors and the windows were blue. Nanette walked halfway down the row, stopped at one of the units, and rapped on the door. She opened it with a key and went in before anyone had time to answer.

I gave it five minutes before I got out of my car and strolled up the inclined driveway and down the row past the unit she had entered, noting a large metallic 5 on the turquoise door. I continued on down to the end of the row, peering intently at each unit so anyone observing me would

15

think I was looking for something, then came back. The curtains on the windows of Unit Five were drawn, but there was a light inside, warm against the oncoming twilight. I went back to the driveway. From the tarmac a well-tended lawn rolled up to an iron gate that led into the grounds of the complex, the tennis courts, Olympic pools, saunas and Jacuzzis and common rooms. At the gate a menu board listed the tenants by name and number; Unit Five was occupied by a P. D'Anjou. I wrote it in my notebook with the address and returned to my car.

On the way I had noticed a 7-Eleven store at the corner, and I made a U-turn and drove back to it. Since anyone coming from the condos would either have to pass that corner or drive into the ocean, I knew I would see Nanette Amptman's car if she left before I got back. It was almost seven now, and damp and chilly November darkness had fallen on the South Bay, with a thick mist drifting in from the sea. Two cars and three pickup trucks clogged the parking lot, and about fifteen teenage boys wandered around carrying candy bars or half wrapped sandwiches or Slurpees, probably taking a break from playing the electronic video games inside the market. Next to the door were two wall phones. I looked in vain for a directory, but they had long ago been trashed or stolen, so I dialed information and asked for a listing on a P. D'Anjou on Rambla Way in Playa Del Rey. The operator told me when he came on the line that his own name was Michael, apparently confusing me with someone who gave a damn. After playing with his computer for a while he found a Peter D'Anjou at that address and a metallic voice came on and gave me the phone number. I wrote it in my notebook.

Then I dialed home.

"Yo," Marvel answered.

"It's me," I said.

"Wha's up?"

"I'm on a job, and I don't know what time I'll get home. Did you get my note?"

16

"Man, you lef' it on the lid of the john! How c'd I miss it?"

"I wanted to make sure you saw it. There's a TV dinner in the freezer," I said. "Throw it in the microwave."

"What kind?"

"I think it's lasagna."

"Man," said Marvel with that upward inflection he always employs to express disapproval. I'm fairly adept in the kitchen, and Marvel has grown spoiled by my tri-tip roasts or lamb chops in orange sauce or braised Szechuan prawns, but on nights I'm not there to cook he feels that a pizza with everything but anchovies is somehow his Divine Right.

"Did you do your homework?"

"Yes-s-s-s," he said, his exasperation with me growing by the minute.

"Okay," I said. "If you want to wait up for me I'll bring home some ice cream."

"I'm a growin' kid," he said. "I need my sleep." It is the normal pattern for those citizens between the ages of thirteen and eighteen to say and do the diametric opposite of whatever their adult guardian says, even when it involves ice cream. Sisyphus would have been a lot more sanguine about rolling his stone up the mountain had he ever tried rearing a teenager.

"Well, I'll bring some home and eat it myself."

"Whatever," he said. "Hey!"

"Hey."

"We doin' a fiel' trip next week to the Whatchimacallit Tar Pits, and you got to sign a paper."

"La Brea," I said. "Okay, leave it out for me."

"I'll leave it on the toilet lid," he said.

I smiled as I hung up. I wasn't sure where he had developed that wicked wit, but I secretly hoped I'd had something to do with it.

I dialed Peter D'Anjou's number. It was entirely possible that Nanette Amptman's visit was innocent, occasioned by an ongoing Scrabble marathon, and I wanted to be sure of the facts before making my report to her husband. Then again, people usually don't have keys to the homes of their Scrabble partners. It was more than likely they were screwing their brains out in Unit Five while I stood in a damp, chilly, 7-Eleven parking lot watching a bunch of greasy-haired acne sufferers throw Slurpees on each other. I heard three rings and then an answering machine clicked on. The voice on the tape sounded young and intelligent.

"This is Peter's machine. You know what to do: wait for the beep and leave a message and I'll get back to you. Thanks."

The machine didn't prove anything except that whatever Nanette and D'Anjou were doing in there, they would brook no outside disturbance. A well-played bout of Scrabble takes a certain amount of concentration.

I hung up without leaving a message. I'd been on the job for more than four hours and had consumed a thermos full of coffee; I had to make a pit stop. I went across the street to a bar with a lot of walnut paneling and hanging ferns and used their rest room without ordering anything, which earned me a dirty look from the bartender, and then drove back to my spot in front of D'Anjou's. The red Mercedes was still in its berth, nose out facing the street. They were certainly taking their time about it.

I slouched down in the seat. It wasn't pleasant sitting alone in the chill outside an apartment where I knew two people were boffing each other silly, but at seven fifty a day I could live with it. I consumed two of the granola bars. I hated the damn things, but I couldn't very well cook an osso buco in the front seat of my car, and I didn't know when I'd get to eat a real dinner. Bored, I attempted to read a paperback by flashlight, but I guess I lacked young Abe Lincoln's thirst for the printed word, and after a while my eyes started aching, so I just sat back in the seat and relaxed. After another three and a half hours I would be so relaxed I could hardly move.

But that's how long I had to wait before the door to Unit Five opened and Nanette Amptman came out. It was too dark to see her properly, but when the light behind her turned her into a momentary silhouette I noticed her hair was done in a slightly different way, pulled up at the back of her head in an attractive haphazard tangle. Something or someone had apparently messed it up during her stay at D'Anjou's. Scrabble can get rough.

I followed her Mercedes back down to Mimosa Beach. When she made the left turn to go up her hill, I figured she was going home. Since it was about ten thirty in the evening, that sounded like a good idea for me too. I made a U-turn on Highland and headed back up to Venice, stopping for ice cream at an all-night market on the way.

Every light in the house was on when I pulled into my garage. Marvel figured that the manumission of the slaves had absolved him of the responsibility for turning lights off when they weren't being used, and if I wasn't home to act as light monitor the bungalow was usually ablaze as if for a Christmas party.

When I walked into the living room, stepping carefully over the football shoes, Kelly Lange was describing a warehouse fire on the Channel 4 news, and the stereo was overriding her with a jazz cassette. Marvel was sprawled across the sofa, sleeping with his mouth open. Three empty Pepsi cans stood on the floor between him and the coffee table. I looked down at him. He had grown since he'd been living with me. When I'd found him he'd been pretty much of a runt, but sixteen months or so of good food, regular exercise at school, and the absence of fear and stress had filled him out a bit. He was almost five foot ten, his shoulders had broadened, and the shadow of a youthful mustache darkened the café au lait of his upper lip. He was a good-looking kid. A good kid. Whatever social or financial hardships I had suffered since his abrupt entry into my life have been more than offset by the certain knowledge that if I hadn't taken him off the street and out of the hands of the vicious people who were exploiting him, he would surely be dead by now, or strung out on drugs or ravaged by disease. He was also a lot of fun to talk to—some of the time.

19

I turned off the stereo and the quiet woke him up.

"Where you been?" he said, rubbing his eyes.

"Hanging around with the guys down at the 7-Eleven. You eat?"

"Lasagna," he said, as though it were strychnine.

"Dessert," I said, and tossed him the sack with the ice cream in it. He caught it easily and took it into the kitchen, where I could hear him clanking around getting down two bowls. I glanced at the TV. They were showing highlights from *Monday Night Football*. Despite my Raiders jacket, I have little or no interest in football. Baseball is my game. The custom-made jacket was a gift from a long-lost admirer, and I wear it because the silver matches my hair. I stripped it off and tossed it and the cap onto the sofa, where they landed on top of Marvel's sweater.

"Any calls?" I said when he came back in with the ice cream divided carefully into two portions.

"Not for you."

"For you? Who called?"

He just smiled. "I said not for you." That meant it must have been Saraine. He landed heavily on the sofa, skillfully balancing his bowl. Marvel doesn't ever sit down; he lands.

I went into the kitchen eating my ice cream and picked up the phone and dialed Jo's home number. Her husband, Marsh, answered. "I've been meaning to call you," he said. "Got an idea I want to bounce off you." Marsh Zeidler works as a waiter in a trendy Westwood restaurant and writes screenplays in his spare time. Since he is a transplanted New York intellectual, his writing tends to be arcane, and in the five years I've known him he hasn't had even a nibble for his efforts. But hope dies hard in the creative soul. "How's this? We have a family, Mom and Dad around forty, who were hippies during the sixties. Like most of them, they've gone straight since they grew up, and now they have kids, almost grown, who are as uptight and establishment as you can get. They can't understand the kids, and the kids can't understand them."

"Yeah, go on," I said.

"That's it. What do you think?"

I sighed. "Marsh, have you ever seen a TV show called *Family Ties*?"

Silence. Then, "Oh. Oh, yeah, that's right." I sensed him swallowing his disappointment. In the wonderful world of show business the taste of disappointment is as familiar as steamed rice in a Chinese restaurant. He said, "You want to talk to Jo?"

"If it's not too late."

"No, we were going to watch Carson. Hang on."

In a moment Jo's voice was spreading cheer through the phone line. "Hi. What's going on?"

"Well, I think Mrs. Amptman is doing deeds of darkness. I need to use your car tomorrow, and you can drive mine. Somebody might have seen me hanging around today, and I'd like to have a different set of wheels when I go back."

"Okay. You want to meet me at the office?"

"No," I said, "I'll drop by your place at about nine o'clock."

"I'll even buy you breakfast," she said.

I went back into the living room with Marvel and finished my ice cream. "How was school today?"

"Fine."

"That good, huh?"

"Oh, man, they was talkin' about the Revolution. Those dudes Jefferson, Sam Adams, Ben Franklin, them. They had the stones, man."

"How do you mean?"

"When they try to start they own country, they was puttin' they asses on the line with the British every day."

"That's what it's all about, Marvel. Someone once said— Emerson, I think—that man is like a tortoise, who never takes a step forward without sticking his neck out."

He nodded. "That's some heavy shit."

"They were heavy dudes."

He scratched himself luxuriously. "Who you say say that about the tortoise?"

"I think it was Ralph Waldo Emerson."

He looked at me for a few seconds and then burst out laughing, pounding the sofa cushion beside him in helpless mirth.

I said, "It seems like everyone's having a good time but me. What's so funny?"

He wiped his eyes. "Waldo," he said. "What a dork name! Waldo!" He let his laughter run its course and then put his dish down on the coffee table and stood up, stretching. "Me for some Zs," he said.

"Listen, Marvel, I almost broke my ass tripping over your shoes in the front hall today."

"Tha's cool."

"And this living room is a disaster area. Vacuum when you get home tomorrow, will you? It'll take you five minutes."

His eyes rolled back in his head as he moved loose-jointed toward his bedroom. "Man . . ." he whined. Nature abhors a vacuum, and so does Marvel.

3

I was crumpled up in the front seat of Jo Zeidler's Ford Tempo, just down the hill from the Amptman house in Mimosa Beach. It was ten thirty in the morning, and a fine cold mist was collecting on the windscreen of the car, part of the "early morning low clouds" Los Angeles is famous for. Day two of the Nanette Amptman confirm-or-deny operation. Now that I knew the way the streets were laid out, and that no one could enter or leave the cul-de-sac without driving right by where I was parked, I saw no reason to sit in full view of the house anymore, and after my vigil of the previous afternoon I thought it might be interesting to sit and stare at somebody else's house. The dwellings on the down side of the hill were older, of the architectural type real estate ladies describe as rustic, their wooden facades and their feel darker in hue. They were practically hidden behind thick bottlebrush and eucalyptus and jacaranda trees, deluding their occupants into thinking they were really plain, quaint country folk living off the land in some leafy woodland glade, getting up almost at sunrise to fire up the Jacuzzi for hot water and going out to the barn in the chill dawn to milk the golden retriever.

I seemed to have a lot of time on my hands on this job, and I used it to think about the blessed union of George and Nanette Amptman. There didn't seem to be much passion involved in his decision to make her his wife, at least not at the beginning. I wondered how he had worded the personal ad he'd placed, but knowing George I imagined it had made some reference to his wealth and from his comment about Nanette's enjoyment of the life-style he provided her, I assumed she had concluded that fun and games were all well and good in their place but it was time for someone rich like George to take care of her. Sexual chemistry apparently never entered into it.

Maybe that's why I never married. A marriage negotiated like a business merger is too cold for me to even consider. Most of my past loves have been women who inspired passion and fire and nurtured the boylike romantic in me. But all of them seemed to come complete with a full set of problems and hang-ups of their own. There are no guarantees, of course, but I guess I'm searching for a relationship that is hassle free. I realize that is akin to hunting snipe, but hope springs eternal.

A few minutes before noon Nanette Amptman's convertible turned the corner and snaked past me down the incline. I counted to twenty and then followed her.

Her destination was the Mimosa Beach Village Mall, a sprawling complex of department stores, shops, and restaurants on the Pacific Coast Highway. It was as crowded as it always is, but on a Tuesday morning there were a few parking places to be found within hiking distance of the shops, so I had no trouble keeping her in sight.

Her first stop inside the mall was a lingerie boutique. Picking up a little something for her next Scrabble session with Peter D'Anjou? I could think of no way to go into the store without being conspicuous, and I really didn't care what she was buying. She came out with two packages, however, and didn't notice me lurking across the concourse in front of a cutlery shop. I followed her down to the mall's one bookstore, and I browsed among the mysteries while Nanette headed for the pop psychology section, which featured tomes about women-who-hate-men-who-love-girls-who-like-dogs-who-are-hung-up-on-their-mothers-who-fear-commitment. Apparently she didn't find anything that provided new insights into her current situation, because she left without making a purchase. I noticed a Marcia Muller mystery I hadn't read, but this was no time to be adding to my home library. I hurried out into the concourse after Nanette.

As it turned out I had plenty of time to go back for the book I fancied, and to read half of it, too, because the Amptman woman's next stop was the beauty salon. I watched from a distance as the rather theatrical shop owner greeted her, kissed her on both cheeks as though he were presenting her with the Croix de Guerre, and handed her over to a smock-clad young woman who had obviously decided to show up for work that day as the bride of Dracula, a white streak down the center of her spiked black hair and eyes circled with kohl. The Transylvanian émigré whisked Nanette back into the bowels of the shop, where two lines of glum women sat imprisoned under dryers like heretics chained in a dungeon awaiting the next visit from the Grand Inquisitor. Nanette was relieved of her suede jacket and issued a pink plastic smock with little gray flowers all over it, matching those of her fellow prisoners. The last I could see of her, they had bent her over backward and were sticking her head in the sink. They play hardball in those beauty salons.

One thing makes this mall unique in the wonderful world of indoor shopping in Los Angeles: there are no fast-food stands to dispense brownies and yogurt and quick-fix sandwiches, as if the affluent foodies of South Bay are above a hot dog and Orange Julius on the run while spending their money on clothes with the labels worn on the outside. So I couldn't grab a bite and keep my eye on the beauty shop. However, I figured Nanette was going to be there for a while, and the thought of another sumptuous repast of peanut butter granola bars was intolerable, so after I went back to the bookstore and bought the paperback, I popped into a Mexican restaurant that services the lunch crowd of conspicuous consumers by day and turns into a Dionysian pickup spot as soon as the sun sinks into the sea about a mile to the west. I ordered tamales and a margarita and read my book for a while. Then I had coffee, used the rest room without guilt, and spent the next hour strolling up and down the concourse waiting for Nanette Amptman to finish her hair appointment. I had left the Raiders jacket and cap at home today and looked more like myself in a pair of blue slacks, a tan corduroy sport coat, and a dark blue shirt open at the neck. It was a wise choice, because people who hang around the Mimosa Beach Village Mall don't wear football jackets and billed caps unless they're making a delivery.

Nanette was finally bowed and scraped and hugged out of the salon by all the people she had just tipped lavishly. Her hairdo was softer than I'd seen it before, or would be when the quart of hair spray wore off, and when she walked through the concourse it was with the specific confidence of a beautiful woman who has just been done over by experts and knows how good she looks. I followed her out to her car, one among the vast multicolored automotive sea in the lot. She put her lingerie purchases on the seat next to her and she backed a bit recklessly out of her parking spot, causing an equally elegant lady in a BMW to lean out her window and call her a cunt. It didn't seem to bother Nanette, though; she drove straight home.

This time when I got up into the tree people section of Mimosa Beach I eased Jo's car into the same spot I'd been in yesterday in my own Le Baron. And I waited.

It was going to be a long wait. The sun went down, the evening fog rolled in wet and chilly, and my eyes nearly crossed with boredom. It was more than my own moral repugnance that kept me from taking too many jobs like this, spying on adulterous spouses and reporting their various comings and goings and comings. It was certainly less hazardous than a lot of other things I am sometimes hired for, but a good bit of the job involves waiting for someone else to do something they often fail to do. There isn't enough excitement or intellectual stimulation to ward off brain death.

At about seven thirty Nanette came out of the house, dressed in a clinging white jersey number that molded itself to her long thighs and lower abdomen. Her dress and her walk advertised her sexuality like a sandwich board. I could see she'd probably be more than a handful in bed for poor old George Amptman. She got into her car and zipped off down the hill, and I didn't even need to keep her in range to know she was heading back to Playa Del Rey for more Scrabble by the sea.

We replayed the tape from the night before. I stopped before I got to the driveway of the condo complex and watched her leave her Mercedes in almost the same spot. She swung out of the car and headed straight for unit five again. I noticed that this time there was no light behind the curtains. Once more she knocked and then let herself in with her key, and I settled back to give my imagination free reign as to what they might be doing inside. Another long dull evening was boding, for me if not for Nanette.

I watched as the light went on behind the shade over the big round window next to the door. Thirty seconds later another light illuminated one of the windows upstairs. The fog was billowing in with authority now, the lacy cobwebs of early evening mist sucking and clutching at each other and then merging to form solid pockets. It smelled of sea salt and was thick enough that it made seeing anything through the windows of the condominium complex almost impossible from where I sat at the curb. I wondered how I was going to stay awake until George Amptman's wife had enjoyed her multiple orgasms and was ready to call it a night. It was too dark to read, and if I listened to the radio too long I'd wear out Jo's batteries. Besides, listening to the radio isn't something you do when you're bored; it's something you do while you're doing something else. Not like the old days of *Inner Sanctum* and *The Shadow*.

I decided to work on my Bogart impression. It isn't something I get a lot of requests for, but I've always wanted to leave an outgoing message on my answering machine saying, "Of all the gin joints in all the towns in the world, why'd you have to call this one when I'm not here?" and I figured I might as well sound right. I ran that one by a few times, and when I was fairly happy with it I did "Nobody puts one over on Fred C. Dobbs!" for a while. I had just started on "When a man's partner is killed, he's supposed to do something about it," and was getting Bogey's soft *s* down pretty well when the door to Unit Five opened and Nanette Amptman emerged and shot across the parking area as if a pack of hunting hounds was baying at her ass. I slumped down low in the seat as she looked around with quick, sparrowlike head movements. Then she jumped into her car, started the engine, and backed out with a squeal, leaving a two-inch thick strip of rubber on the driveway as she peeled out past me. It was very foggy and she was driving awfully fast, but from the glimpse I got of her it seemed to me her face was several shades whiter than normal. She sacrificed some more tire tread when she got to the 7-Eleven corner, and then the roar of her engine was swallowed by the night.

My first impulse was to follow her. That was, after all, what I was getting paid for. But she'd only been in D'Anjou's condo for ten minutes, maybe less, and she'd been a hundred times more anxious to leave than she'd been on the way in. The skin on the backs of my hands started to prickle, which usually foreshadows bad things. I got out of the car and walked up the driveway through the fog. I rang the bell four times, trying to peek in through the partially open door, and waited, but there was no sound from inside. I gave the door a little nudge with my knee, and it swung open.

The living room was on two levels. The lower one was ringed with shelves stuffed with books, records, and audio and video cassettes. I scanned the spines of the books quickly: lots of best sellers, a few biographies, and an entire shelf on the petroleum business. An expensive stereo system complete with compact disc player stood against one wall, next to a twenty-four-inch television with a VCR on top of it. Peter D'Anjou had all the yuppie toys he needed. I was sure there would be a Cuisinart, a pasta maker, and a rice cooker in the kitchen. Up seven steps was another level with a small love seat and an apartment-size dining room set in blond wood. A paperback copy of *The Control of Oil* by John M. Blair was open face down on the table. Beyond was a big kitchen with the lights off. An open stairway rose up from the second level, the kind you could stand beneath and look up women's dresses if you had a mind to. After checking the kitchen for occupancy I headed upstairs. There were two bedrooms up there, and the doors to both were open. One of them, the one with no lights on, had been converted to an office, with a desk, a chair, a filing cabinet, and a compact computer table with a Leading Edge PC and a Panasonic printer. The lid of the plastic box of diskettes next to the computer was open; so were both drawers of the metal filing cabinet, and they looked as though they had been rifled.

I moved to the door of the other bedroom. The overhead light was on, so I could easily see Peter D'Anjou, if that was indeed who it was, lying on the bed, his head on one of the pillows. He was long and slim, with thinning blond hair and an aquiline nose, and blue eyes that were at the moment almost bulging out of his head. He was in his middle thirties, I estimated, and he wasn't ever going to get any older. He was wearing a black cashmere pullover sweater with no shirt under it, white sailcloth pants, and white deck shoes on his sockless feet. The skin on his face was black and mottled, and the foul smell in the room was explained by a quick glance at the crotch area of the white pants, which was stained with urine and feces. That's what tends to happen to you when someone knots a length of silk scarf around your neck and twists it until you die.

4

Joseph Anthony DiMattia sat massively behind his desk, his hands flat on the surface and his elbows cocked, looking wide and hard, an old fighting bull who'd survived the arena and been put out to stud. There was shiny pink scar tissue around his left eye, and a vertical scar on his upper lip just to the left of center, and word had it there was a scar from a knife wound about two inches under his heart from when he'd gotten careless with a coked-to-the-eyeballs Chicano junkie suspected of robbing and stabbing a liquor store owner over near Pico and Alvarado. Joe had brown eyes that twinkled more with malice than merriment, and his oft-broken nose slalomed down his face. He carried a little more stuffing under the swarthy skin around his jowls than when I'd first met him about five years earlier, when a secretary at Paramount Studios I'd dated casually, Marie Vitale, introduced me to him at the bar at Nickodell's as her new bridegroom. Marie had been thirty-two and Joe forty-six, and it never ceased to torment him that I had once seen his wife naked, and so I found myself with a mortal enemy.

He'd been Sergeant DiMattia then, but when he'd started to put on a little weight the Los Angeles Police Department had given him a gold lieutenant's shield and kicked him upstairs to a job that was mostly administrative. He'd squealed like a warthog when they'd assigned him to personnel, and finally, just to shut him up, they'd put him back in homicide, Culver City Division. Joe DiMattia liked the new gig; it gave him a chance to work out his mental muscles.

And now he had drawn the D'Anjou case. Had the murder occurred a few miles to the south in El Tercero it would have been their police department's headache, but officially Playa Del Rey is a part of Los Angeles. It was too early for there to be a formal file on the D'Anjou murder yet, as the investigating officers had not gotten around to completing their endless paperwork, but Joe had some notes in front of him. He ran his hand over his face as he looked at them and then up at me.

"It's eleven o'clock at night and I have to look at you, Saxon. God damn it! Why is it every time the shit flies, you're hanging around someplace? There must be ten thousand married broads in this town getting some strange dick on the side, but the one *you're* watching wraps a scarf around her boyfriend's neck and causes me *dolore*. How does that happen?"

"It comes from having an inquisitive nature, Joe."

"That's your trouble," he said. "Or, just one of your troubles. How long you been trailing her around?"

"Since yesterday afternoon. She spent the evening in D'Anjou's condo yesterday, then went home. Today she did a lot of shopping and got her hair done, and then she went back over to his place. I don't think she's guilty."

"Thank you, Judge Wapner, for the verdict," he said. "You saw her go in, she stays ten minutes, comes out and runs like she's on fire, then you go in and there he is, dead. Who you think did it? The Phantom?"

"Doesn't the method of the killing make you stop and wonder, Joe? It's not a woman's MO. They don't strangle their lovers. They shoot them, they stab them with a barbecue fork, they bop them over the head with a Ming vase or a bottle of Smirnoff in the heat of anger, or they slip them a dollop of arsenic in the béchamel sauce. And they don't get their hair done and doll up in a slinky white jersey

31

dress to do it, either." I rubbed my stiff neck. "And they don't rifle their filing cabinets."

"Why'd she run then, smart ass?"

"She was having an affair, for God's sake. She probably thought she could get out of there and her husband would never find out. Any woman would do the same thing."

His eyes glittered at me, his Italian machismo burning a hole in his guts. "You know all about women, huh?"

I shook my head. I hadn't seen Marie in so long I barely remembered what she looked like, with or without her clothes, but Joe DiMattia was still living in feudal Sicily, and it was getting tiresome. "Joe, it's late. Don't start with me, all right?"

"Start, you fucking *cimice*? If I ever start with you I'll have you singing 'Ave Maria' in about ninety seconds." The corners of his mouth turned up just thinking of it.

"Someone was looking for something, and killed him to get it. I don't think it was Mrs. Amptman. It doesn't add up."

"Who gives a brown rat's ass what you think? We place her at the scene by a credible witness—that's you. She was putting out for the guy, again according to you, so we can dig up a probable motive. He was seeing another woman, he wanted to break it off with her, or maybe he couldn't get it up anymore. What's the difference? Even a moron like you can fill in the blanks." He rubbed his hands together like Hansel and Gretel's wicked witch. "Oh, the DA is going to love this in the morning, it's so clean and neat. And I get to close the file before it starts getting yellow with age, which makes me look like a *genio* to the precinct commander. So I've got no eyes to start poking around when I don't have to. You ever hear of a cop who needed to look for trouble? Now haul your ass out of my office and let me get some real work done. It's starting to smell like dead meat in here." And he buried his head in his paperwork. I knew it would go hard with me if I were still there when he looked up.

It wasn't far from the station to my place in Venice,

maybe ten minutes. But it left me plenty of time to replay the events of the evening. I had called the police from D'Anjou's kitchen, and they started arriving within minutes. First came a couple of uniforms in a black-and-white, looking lean and tough and younger than springtime with their razor-cut hair and mustaches and starched blues, trying not to vomit when they saw the victim's blackened face and tongue and wide, staring eyes. Then two tired-looking detectives showed up, their suits off the rack from a discount house someplace and their eyes dull and marblelike from seeing too many bodies for too many years. Next was the crew from the forensics lab, and finally the cranky medical examiner, who examined Peter D'Anjou and delivered the official and not exactly startling verdict that he was dead. After the two suits took my statement at the scene, they called in, somebody got a warrant, and they picked up Nanette Amptman on suspicion of murder. Then they invited me to follow them back to headquarters to talk to their boss, Joe DiMattia. I'd been no happier to see him on this Thanksgiving eve than he was to see me.

I found out while in DiMattia's office that Peter D'Anjou had been a petroleum engineer, thirty-five years old, most recently unemployed and formerly with Gamble Petroleum, one of the California oil giants with lease holdings all up and down the coast from Mexico to Oregon. One of their biggest fields was located right next to their company headquarters in El Tercero, which was almost walking distance from D'Anjou's place in Playa Del Rey. Not that my lieutenant friend had volunteered any of the information, but while I was giving him my statement, various underling cops had popped in and out and told him things I couldn't help overhearing. It was none of my business anyway. Murder was a police matter, and with Nanette Amptman in custody, I didn't even have a client anymore. It was just as well. Spying on a cheating wife or husband pays the bills sometimes, but it doesn't make me feel too terrific about myself. I was sorry for Nanette and her supercilious husband, but I was out of the picture and glad to be.

The next morning I went back to the office and Jo and I exchanged car keys again. I dictated a report on the Amptman investigation for the files, and while Jo typed it up I looked through the stack of mail, but there was nothing exciting. There rarely is. When I was a kid, waiting for the mailman was a big deal, because maybe there would be a letter from a friend who'd moved away, or a note from your grandmother, or some sort of premium you'd sent away for off the side of a cereal box. But with the advent of long-distance direct dialing, letter writing has become a lost art, and the U.S. Postal Service has been reduced to delivering junk mail that nobody wants. I don't know how I get on some of these mailing lists: psychics who want to tell me what the future holds, financial whiz kids who want to share with me the secrets of their success for only $79.95, scam artists who tell me I've won either a car or a color TV or a steam iron if I'll only return the card with my check for fourteen dollars, and the ubiquitous magazine sweepstakes with Ed McMahon's picture on the envelope. The arrival of the mail isn't much of an adventure anymore.

So I sat by myself and drummed two pencils on the edge of the desk and tried not to think about Peter D'Anjou's bulging eyes and distended tongue and the ugly bruise where the silk scarf had bitten into his neck, and tried not to think about Nanette Amptman in a holding cell wearing her sexy white jersey dress for the edification and amusement of the lice-ridden bag ladies and twenty-dollar hookers and diesel dykes and mainline drug addicts who were her roommates. As I mentioned, it was no longer my concern.

At about ten thirty my commercial agent called. Henry Hiscock is a slim, elegant seventy-year-old with a slight British accent and a Rex Harrison incisiveness, which holds him in good stead when he's talking to the twenty-five-year-old children who run the television commercial production houses in Los Angeles. He probably doesn't do as much for me as he could, because he rather resents my cavalier attitude about the acting business in general and TV commercials in particular. But every couple of months I take him to lunch, and within two weeks or so he sends me out on a call. I get maybe three commercials a year, usually for local companies rather than the big national brands, and average three or four acting jobs annually for movies or episodic TV, secured for me by my other agent, Bernie Silverman, who wouldn't touch a commercial with lead-lined gloves. Since my acting assignments are so infrequent, I have learned not to count on them and pretty much live on what I earn through Saxon Investigations. Any income I get from acting I consider fuck-you money.

"I'm glad I caught you in," Henry said. "I was afraid you'd be out peeking over somebody's transom somewhere."

That stung. "They don't make transoms anymore, Henry. They went out in nineteen thirty-seven. Isn't it time you joined the rest of us in the twentieth century?"

"Poetic license," he said. "You want to read for something this afternoon?"

"Why not?" I said. "I have nothing better to do."

"It's for Glendora Bank. Think you can look like a loan officer?"

"A loan officer," I said. "I thought I was a leading man, not a heavy."

"It's the gray hair. I've been telling you for years you ought to color it."

"You color yours first," I said. It was a spot of gratuitous cruelty, since Henry was bald as an egg.

He gave me the address of a studio in Hollywood and told me to be there at three o'clock. "And wear a tie," he said before he hung up.

That's why I always keep a tie hanging in the closet in the office, for last-minute emergencies like this one. It was one of five wearable ties that I own. I have a few more extra-wide ones in my closet at home, dating back to the late sixties and, although like new, as out of style as a Nehru jacket. In Southern California, unless you're a lawyer in court or a stockbroker or a sales rep for IBM, ties are something you wear to funerals. I guess loan officers in Glendora wear them too. The one in my office closet is a sort of tan number with little red things on it, neutral, to go with anything. I was wearing a blue blazer and gray slacks with a medium blue shirt, so it didn't look too bad. I scooped a picture and résumé out of the bottom drawer, standard equipment for any actor, and at about two thirty I told Jo where I could be reached. "After that, I'm going home," I said.

"Hey, are you sure you don't want to come over tomorrow?" she said. "We've got plenty."

"Thanks, Jo. But Thanksgiving is kind of a family deal, and I don't have a family."

"Yes, you do, you louse!" she said. "What about Marvel?"

I didn't answer her. I was feeling too guilty about what I'd just said. I've been a bachelor so long, it's often hard for me to remember that now I have parental responsibilities. Even though the mailbox in front of our bungalow says Saxon-Watkins, I still think of myself most often as a loner.

"He's probably spent most of his Thanksgivings on the street," Jo went on. "Don't you think it might be nice for him to have a traditional turkey dinner with some friends?"

I ran my fingers through my hair. "You're right as usual, Jo," I said. "Nobody said being a father was easy."

"Four o'clock," she said. "And don't be late, or the turkey will dry out." And then she smiled. A big one. Jo was a really cute woman, and when she forgot to be severe and maternal and businesslike with me and smiled, the cuteness turned radiant. Next to Marvel she was the most important person in my life.

"Jo, leave Marsh and marry me. You're the only one who's ever been able to keep me on the path of moral righteousness and solvency." The sad thing is I was only half joking. "And," I said, "I'd only make sexual demands on you the first and third Saturday of every month."

She got up and went to the file cabinet, pulling out the

36

accounts receivables. "It'd take you longer than two weeks to recover, sweet buns."

The TV studio was on a side street off Santa Monica Boulevard near La Brea, one of the less felicitous areas of Los Angeles. When I had first come out from my native Chicago it had amazed me that the movie and TV business, which was synonymous with glitz, glamour, and life in the fast lane, was invariably conducted out of grubby studios and rattletrap offices furnished in thrift shop modern and located in areas where no sane person would venture unless fully armed. I drove onto the lot after identifying myself to the guard, who checked my name off his list as carefully as if he were guarding atomic secrets. I think the tight security employed by the studios is solely for the purpose of deluding all of us show business insiders into thinking we are indeed involved in something special.

When I had wandered around the lot long enough to find the waiting room, I was chagrined to see that there were seven other actors, all close to fifty, all with gray hair and all but one wearing suits, sitting on rump-sprung sofas or tired metal folding chairs, holding their pictures and résumés. A few of them I knew by sight. All looked much more like the stereotypical bank loan officer than I did, and I began wondering what I was doing there in the first place. My impulse was to turn around and walk out again, as it always was on such occasions, but then Henry would be mad at me and would "forget" to send me out on calls for the next six months. So I sat down on a long sofa between two of my competitors, my documents on my lap, occasionally receiving a halfhearted smile from one of the other applicants.

As I sat waiting to be appraised like a side of beef, I couldn't help thinking how trivial it all was. Over the years I'd begun to feel more and more that acting was a silly profession anyway, full of frustration and rejection and blows to the ego. And after discovering a garotted body the night before, it was hard to attach much importance to looking like a loan officer for Glendora Bank and Trust.

When ten minutes had passed I was called into the inner office. Sitting in one of the chairs was a guy who looked a lot like a banker from Glendora, which is what he was. The other two men were, I supposed, the producer and the director of the commercial. Neither looked old enough to shave. We shook hands all around and I gave one of the grown children, the one with the most gold chains around his neck, my bona fides. He gave them a cursory glance and tossed them onto a thick pile of composite photos of other actors who looked like bankers.

"You have some nice credits," he said. "So! Tell me about yourself. What've you been doing to keep busy lately?"

"Well," I said, "I found a corpse last night."

I didn't get the job.

I stopped on the way home at my favorite west side market and bought some pork ribs, a tomato, a half pound of skinless peanuts, and some smoky chipotle peppers. I was going to blend up a genuine New Mexican chipotle sauce and cook Marvel one of his favorites, which I called Ribs Socorro, to make up for the frozen dinner the night before. When I got there Marvel was standing out behind the house on the edge of the canal, tossing stones at the ducks. What else would a sixteen-year-old kid do on a gray Wednesday afternoon?

"How was school?" I said.

"Okay."

"You catching on better to algebra?"

He shrugged.

"You want me to help you with it tonight?"

He laughed. I'm about as proficient at algebra as I am at ancient Semitic languages, and Marvel knows it. I blame all my mathematical shortcomings on Sister Concepta, the wimpled demon of Saint Aloysius High School in Chicago. I had been so terrified of her, of the sinister rustling of her starched skirts and the flexible steel ruler which seemed to be an extension of her right hand and which descended across the knuckles almost without warning, that I couldn't concentrate on what she was saying. Many have been the nights Marvel and I sat at the dining room table scratching our heads over X and Y. But I can tutor him in English, and I'm proud to say he was doing quite well in that subject. He and I had been given a B minus on the first report card of the term.

We tossed rocks together for a while, not really wanting to hit the ducks but only to annoy them, and then as darkness fell I went in and started preparing the meal, involving a lot of food processing and the use of too many bowls and pans. I can really trash a kitchen when I get to cooking, but there is a satisfaction that comes from creating a memorable dinner that can't be dimmed by a massive cleanup afterward. I did notice that the living room, at least, had been vacuumed.

"Thanks for doing the floor, Marvel. Nice job."

"Yo," he said.

We had dinner, and I opened a bottle of gray riesling to go with the ribs. I poured Marvel a glass. I don't allow him to drink any hard liquor, but I figure one glass of good wine at dinner isn't going to hurt his growth, dull his senses, or turn him into a wino. We talked of the Lakers, who were currently favored in the coming NBA season, and I came to realize why professional sports are so popular in this country; it is the only conversational subject that is a possible common ground between a teenager and an adult in which the teen doesn't feel rank is being pulled on him, in which his knowledge is generally superior.

"I'd still rather have Larry Bird on my ball team," I said. I had never watched a pro basketball game all the way through before Marvel came into my life, and I still only paid attention out of the corner of my eye while he sprawled in front of the TV set in the living room, so I had no idea what I was talking about. But I knew my ill-informed comment would bring a salvo from Marvel, and

39

getting him to open up about anything with enthusiasm is worth showing my ignorance.

"You shittin' me?" Marvel said. "Magic have guys like that for breakfas'. Larry Bird ain' gonna know he in the *league* nex' to Magic, man." And he nattered on about someone named James Worthy, who probably was. At the end of the meal he even allowed as how the Ribs Socorro were better than the last time I'd made them. It was taking Marvel just as long to feel safe and at home with me as it was for me to realize I was the father of a half grown black kid. Each of these conversations we had, no matter how trivial, was a stepping stone toward mutual understanding. The respect was already there, and it went both ways.

We were just finishing dinner, mopping up the peanut chipotle sauce with hunks of Monterey sourdough bread, when the doorbell rang.

Doorbells make me nervous when I'm not expecting company. At the very best it will be someone trying to sell me something I don't want, or to collect funds for some religious mission. And in my business it could be a lot worse than that. I opened the door with some trepidation.

"I hope I'm not disturbing your dinner," George Amptman said, framed in the doorway.

"As a matter of fact, you are. I don't do business in my home, Mr. Amptman. I'd rather see you in the office."

He said, "My wife has been arrested for murder because of you."

"Hardly because of me," I said sourly. "All right, come on in, as long as you're here."

He walked past me into the living room. His suit was creased and the collar of his white shirt was going gray. He looked tired and drawn, and the furrow between his eyebrows had deepened since I had seen him last on Monday morning. "Marvel, this is Mr. Amptman," I said. Marvel nodded, picked up several dirty dishes and went in to deposit them in the sink.

Amptman sat down on the sofa and glanced toward the kitchen. "I have to speak to you confidentially, Mr. Saxon. Can you send the nigger kid home?"

A hot steel band of anger tightened around my head. "He *is* home, George," I said, "and you use that word again, you'll find yourself in the canal."

He put his fingers under his glasses and rubbed his eyes. "I'm sorry. I'm exhausted. I flew in from Texas this morning and went directly to police headquarters. It's taken my attorney the better part of the day to arrange Nanette's bail. They set it at a quarter of a million dollars. It's been a difficult time for me. I'm sure you understand."

"I understand that you're going to watch your mouth when you're in my home."

He sort of threw his hands up in the air and then slapped them down on his thighs. "I'm in shock."

"Do you want some wine?" I said.

"Do you have anything stronger?"

I nodded and went to the bar that separated the living room and dining area from the kitchen and fixed him a Jameson on ice, figuring that was the closest I could come to a Texan's kind of drink. I poured myself the rest of the wine. Marvel looked at me across the countertop, shook his head, and rolled his eyes ceilingward. I'm sure he'd heard the word before lots of times on the street. I'm also certain that that didn't make it hurt any less. I gave him a conspiratorial smile and a wink.

Amptman didn't say thank you when I handed him the drink, he just sucked it down. "More?" I said.

He shook his head and set the glass down on the coffee table, expelling his breath loudly. "She didn't do it, Saxon."

"For what it's worth, I don't think she did either."

"Tell me . . . what you found out."

"I'm not sure it's important anymore."

"Perhaps not," he said heavily, "but I've paid for that information and I want it."

I shrugged. I learned a long time ago not to ask questions I might not want to hear the answers to, but apparently

41

George Amptman had been too busy developing that which developers develop to have acquired that particular bit of wisdom. "I followed your wife to Playa Del Rey on Monday evening at about five o'clock. She stayed in Mr. D'Anjou's condo on Rambla Way for four hours; then she went home. I have no way of knowing for certain what they were doing in there, but I called and no one answered. On Tuesday afternoon she had a hair appointment, did some shopping for lingerie at the mall, and went home. Tuesday night she went to D'Anjou's at nine o'clock. She'd been inside for just ten minutes when she came back out looking extremely agitated and got into her car and tore out of there. She'd left the door open, so I went in. I found D'Anjou's body and called the police. The coroner fixed the time of death at about nine o'clock, so that leaves Mrs. Amptman in a rather difficult position."

"She didn't do it. She told me she didn't."

"That doesn't necessarily make it true."

"But she said—" His eyes got red and damp and he studied his shoes. He could have been sitting for a portrait of misery. "She said she wouldn't have killed him because she . . . loved him."

Marvel grabbed a Pepsi from the refrigerator and tiptoed into his bedroom. He didn't want the best part of George Amptman. Neither did I.

"I'm really sorry about your troubles. But I couldn't very well not tell the police about your wife being in D'Anjou's condominium."

"I understand that. But now I need your help again. And I'm willing to pay for it. At the same inflated rate," he sneered.

I sat down in the chair opposite the sofa and waited.

"The police seem to feel they've found their killer, and my lawyer has been informed that the district attorney's office will press for an indictment." He shifted uneasily on the sofa cushions. "Needless to say, when this all goes public I am going to look like a fool."

I nodded. A cuckold's horns don't look good on anyone,

although I thought it curious that Amptman's dignity was more important to him than his wife's vindication.

"What can I do?"

He took his glasses off and wiped them with his handkerchief, then put them back on. "Nanette's only chance is if you find the killer."

"I don't get involved in ongoing police investigations, especially of capital crimes. It's against the law, and it would cost me my license."

"But this isn't an ongoing investigation, don't you see? The police are closing their books."

"I think you need a good criminal lawyer, not a private investigator," I said. "I'm sure your own attorney knows someone. If not, I can give you the names of a few defense lawyers I trust."

"My own attorney suggested this, Mr. Saxon."

I didn't answer him. This had started out as a particularly ugly marital triangle, and Peter D'Anjou had been killed in a particularly ugly way. I had no delusions that if I went back to work for Amptman things would get any prettier.

"You shit! Do you want me to beg?" Amptman said, his voice an E-above-high-C quiver. "No matter what she's done, I love Nanette. I'll do anything or pay anything I have to in order to save her." I knew this wasn't easy for him. Rich people often have difficulty asking anyone for anything.

"No, Mr. Amptman, I don't want you to beg," I said. "I'll look into this for you if you want me to. But I'm not putting either my license or my ass on the line. And I'm not making any promises. I don't 'solve' murders. I'm required to report to the police that I'm acting on your behalf. I may get you enough to forestall an indictment, or at least a trial. But there are no guarantees."

He took out his checkbook. The alacrity with which he wrote checks was George Amptman's most endearing quality. "I'd think that at these prices there would be."

43

"It might seem so to you," I said. "But you're forgetting one thing that's out of my control. Or yours."

"And what's that?"

There didn't seem to be any nice way of putting it. I thought about it, took a deep breath, and just said it straight out. "There's always the possibility that Mrs. Amptman is guilty."

5

You notice that there's not a lot of going over the river and through the woods to Grandmother's house for turkey and homemade cranberry sauce and pumpkin pie on Thanksgiving in Los Angeles. There are no available woods, unless Grandmother lives tucked away up in some isolated canyon north of the city, and the Los Angeles River is just a concrete aqueduct running from above the San Fernando Valley to downtown. It's bone dry nine months out of the year, and for the other three months it handles the runoff from the dreary rains. The horse doesn't know the way at all, unless he happens to be plugged in to the highway patrol's radio traffic reports, besides which no horse with a lick of sense would venture onto the kamikaze killing ground that is the Los Angeles freeway system. There is no fresh snow on the ground, and there is no tart midwestern smell of woodsmoke in the air, because everyone in town who has a fireplace has stocked it with smokeless gas logs. When you live in L.A. you leave the traditions of childhood behind.

Marvel spent the morning watching parades from New York, Detroit, and Toronto and picking out the minor-league TV celebrities all bundled up in loden coats riding on the floats, asking me if I knew them personally. Then he settled in to watch a football game between Minnesota and Detroit. I had no rooting interest either way, so I puttered around the house watering my plants and putting plant spikes around the edges of the pots, cleaning out one of the kitchen cabinets and doing a few loads of laundry. I had asked George Amptman to start my new term of employment on the following day because I didn't see what good I could possibly do him on a holiday.

At about three o'clock we dressed for dinner. Marvel chose his one sports jacket, a light tan, with a black shirt and gray slacks. I had given him a gold medallion for our mutual birthday, and it gleamed brightly against the brown skin at his throat. He looked handsome and happy and seemed eager to have his first real Thanksgiving. I was glad Jo had talked me into coming. I wore a dark blue corduroy jacket with a royal blue shirt and gray slacks, and I grabbed two bottles of 1981 MacGregor chardonnay from what I laughingly called my wine cellar—a cupboard built in next to the mop closet in the utility room.

There's no really fast way to get from Venice to where Jo and Marsh live, so I breezed along Wilshire and looked at the video stores and men's sportswear shops and sushi bars along the way, wondering if anyone in their right mind would opt for tamago and maguro and futomaki as their Thanksgiving feast. In this town, though, you never know.

The Zeidlers' apartment is just south of Santa Monica Boulevard in West Hollywood. Four palm trees stand guard outside the double doors, and some wide-leafed tropical shrubs are planted next to the stucco building. At one time this was the area where the young wannabees from out of town came to live, stacked three and four to an apartment to wait out their big break in landing an agent or a studio contract, but in recent years West Hollywood has become a mecca for gays. Jo and Marsh were now probably the only heterosexuals on the block.

Marsh Zeidler had been in Los Angeles for several years now, but he still dressed as though he lived in Brooklyn Heights, dark pants and a white shirt, with a not as white undershirt peeking out at the neck. His glasses gave him an owlish appearance, and he was equally intense whether talking about his career, the troubles in Nicaragua, or the price of Bibb lettuce.

Their guests turned out to be a young, soft-looking man named T. Michael Sweet, who had something to do with the story department at Fox Television and introduced himself with a limp handshake as "T. Michael," and his girlfriend, whose name, I think, was Carol, and whose presence at the Thanksgiving feast seemed to hinge on T. Michael's inability to go anywhere without a date. She was long-legged and deep-chested with a kind of geometric haircut that was as trendy as it was ugly. From the way they talked during the evening I had the feeling he had picked her up in a bar no earlier than the day before.

Marvel had visited Jo's house several times. When I had to be away overnight I often asked the Zeidlers to look after him, and since they had made a well-thought-out and modern decision to remain childless, it was a form of dilettantism having a teenage kid on their hands. Marvel adored Jo as much as he could any adult, and thought Marsh was pretty "bad" too; like most New York intellectuals in California, Marsh remained loyal to the Knicks and could spew basketball statistics at a rate that even impressed my son.

T. Michael talked easily of how things were "on the lot," and dropped some pretty impressive names, like Bobby Duvall and Bobby De Niro, and I had the feeling he was desperately trying not to let us know he was only one step up from the mail room at Fox. He seemed to have appointed himself booze monitor and insisted on making whiskey sours for everybody. His date, Carol, spoke in monosyllables when she spoke at all and wore a glazed expression, as if everyone else were talking Rumanian. Poor Marsh Zeidler probably thought T. Michael was someone significant, thus the invitation to share the holiday groaning board.

I went out to the kitchen to make the salad for Jo. She was wearing a frilly apron over a pretty blue-and-white dress, and looking at her while I struggled with a tube of anchovy paste and two kinds of salad oil, I pondered how nice it might be to live like normal people, with a wife who cooked turkeys at Thanksgiving. That emotion didn't get to me very often, but holidays have a way of boring into the souls of the single like a wood-burning tool.

"I'm so glad you guys could come," she said. "I hated the idea of your sending out for a pizza or something."

"I'm glad you asked us," I said truthfully. "And it's always fun meeting new people."

She snickered. "You mean T.? He's something else. Marsh thinks it's an in for him at Fox, but I'm not sure T. Michael knows where the studio gate is. There hasn't been so much bullshit in one place since the rodeo left town." She shook her head as she basted the turkey. "I wish Marsh would just give it up and stop getting himself disappointed."

I carefully tore the romaine with my hands. "Don't even think like that, Jo. When we give up our dreams, something dies inside. Leave Marsh his."

"I know," she said. "But maybe the dreams aren't worth dreaming if they include people like T. Michael."

We began dinner with the Caesar salad I'd put together. My dressing turned out pretty well, and the croutons Jo had made earlier were tasty and crisp. We broke open one of the chardonnays and Marsh offered a toast about good friends being together on days like this, and dinner was progressing more or less smoothly between T. Michael Sweet's discourses on what was wrong with the movie business today. I couldn't make eye contact with Marvel because we would both have burst out laughing. Marvel might not be too swift when it comes to factors and integers and subtrahends, but he had come up through a far tougher school, the hard streets, and was more than savvy enough to sniff out a phony at fifty paces.

Finally, when he had run out of Hollywood anecdotes, T. Michael said, "Marsh tells me you're a private eye."

I flicked a glance at Jo, who knows how much I hate being called that. "I'm an investigator, yes."

"Fascinating," he said. "Must have a lot of great stories."

"A few."

"Why don't you give me a call Monday at the studio? Put

our heads together, you can tell me some of your more interesting case histories, and maybe we can make a few bucks getting a development deal for a picture." He smiled around a mouthful of Jo's chestnut dressing, which was delicious. "You're an actor; maybe you could play yourself in the movie. God, wouldn't that be a kick in the ass? Saxon as Saxon! Hey, yeah, give me a call next week and we'll sit down. Gotta explore every avenue in this business if you want to stay ahead of the game. Throw enough shit at the wall, some of it's bound to stick."

Not the metaphor I would have chosen to trot out at Thanksgiving dinner, but I supposed he had a point. Out of my peripheral vision I noticed Marvel's eyes searching the ceiling. I said, "I'm afraid I'm going to be busy next week. I'm working on a case."

"Oh yeah? Tell us about it."

"I can't talk about an open case," I said. "It has to do with that petroleum engineer who was murdered in Playa Del Rey the other night."

"Yeah? I think I read about that. So come on, give." He made some fluttering come-hither motions with his fingers. "There may be a movie in it."

"As I said, I can't talk about a case I'm working on. I really haven't gotten started yet."

T. said, "If you want to find out all about the oil business you ought to go see Billy Ledbetter."

"Who's he?"

"He's a hell of a character. Old-time wildcatter, up in his eighties somewhere, lives out by the beach. He's been a millionaire and a bum five times each, and he's fought some big battles with the majors. I took him to lunch a few times, thought maybe there was a movie idea there, but it never came to anything. He's got a real foxy granddaughter, too." He sighed wistfully. "That never came to anything either." He looked over at Carol. "Of course, that was before I met this beautiful, incredibly sensuous and delightful lady here," he added, and leaned over to cup Carol's chin in his hand affectionately. She was in the middle of a mouthful of food, and she stopped chewing and waited until he took his hand away, as if the act of mastication would damage the gossamer fabric of their meaningful relationship.

"The victim used to be with Gamble Petroleum," Jo said. "Does your friend know them?"

"Know them?" T. Michael said, loosening his grip on his date's face and renewing his attack on his drumstick. "The way he tells it, he and old Jesse Gamble were wildcatters together in the old days. They've been in and out of court about twenty times, and in between lawsuits they'd go out and get drunk together. Of course, Jesse's dead now, and his son Jason runs the company. But he's something, old Billy. Actually his name is Billy Ray Ledbetter, but he dropped the Ray because he didn't want people thinking he was some dumb hillbilly." He speared a gob of cranberry sauce and shoveled it into his mouth. "I wish *I* was as dumb as that old fart. I'd be running the studio." Apparently T. Michael was a wannabee too.

Jo looked at me. "Maybe you should go see him."

I waved the notion away.

Marsh Zeidler grinned. "I love it when you come over," he said to me, "and she has somebody else to nag."

"Jo's right," T. said. "Jason Gamble is a pretty important guy in the oil business, but I'll bet you Billy can get you in there with a phone call."

"I'm not sure I want to bother the chairman of the board of Gamble Petroleum," I said. "But tell me how to reach Billy Ledbetter anyway, just for the hell of it."

T. Michael wiped his greasy fingers on his napkin and reached into his hip pocket for his address book, which turned out to be one of those four-inch-thick, vinyl-covered organizers that give you the day, date, phase of the moon, tell you Robert Redford's birthstone, remind you of your grandmother's wedding anniversary, and do everything else but microwave popcorn. While he was thumbing through it, Marvel leaned over to me with a wry smile, his brown eyes twinkling. "So you gonna play yourself in the movies, huh?"

"I don't know," I said back. "Call me and we'll sit down." Marvel covered his face with his hand to keep his merriment from showing. Jo was shaking her head at my incorrigibility, Marsh was being, as usual, intense, earnest, and somewhat befuddled, and Carol sat looking straight ahead or at her food, as uninvolved with the rest of us as though she were dining alone in a downtown cafeteria. For all intents and purposes she might have been.

T. Michael found Billy Ledbetter's address and phone number in El Tercero and jotted it down for me on a paper ripped from the scratch pad in the back of his Daily Organizer.

"I'll get in touch with him," I said.

"He's a catankerous old man—is that the right word, catankerous? But if he'll talk to you, you'll have a ball with him," T. said. "And then afterwards, give me a tinkle. Maybe we can make some money."

The Zeidlers would not have the usual post-Thanksgiving problem of leftovers, thanks to Marvel's growing-boy appetite. He leaned back in his seat on the way home, the top button of his pants unfastened to make room for the three helpings of turkey and dressing and the entire third of a pumpkin pie he had consumed. It was pretty obvious the customs of traditional American family life suited Marvel like a tailor-made jacket. And I had done more than my share to deplete the turkey supply, too. I had that pleasant, stuffed feeling that is almost a national condition late Thanksgiving night. I was grateful to Jo and Marsh and felt stupid that I hadn't accepted their gracious invitation earlier.

Marvel turned sideways in the seat facing me and drew one leg up under him. It was one of those rare moments he wanted to talk. "This murder business you doin'," he said. "'Zit dangerous?"

"What we're doing right now is dangerous—driving a car in Los Angeles," I said. "No, it's no more dangerous than anything else, I guess. Except that someone has been killed. Deliberately. That makes it a bit hairy."

"Why you be a detective like that?" he said. "More fun bein' a actor, huh?"

"I don't do it for the fun."

"You make good bread?"

"Sometimes. Sometimes not."

He scratched his nose thoughtfully. "How come, then?"

"Take this case. The police and the D.A. think this lady killed somebody. I don't, so I'm going to try and prove she didn't."

"But you don' know. What if she did it?"

I laughed. "Then I'm going to look pretty . . . lame."

"Why you foolin' with it, man? None o' your beeswax."

"Marvel, most people are pretty decent. But some of them aren't—you know that. So it's up to the people that are to dig in their heels and see to it that the assholes don't take over."

"Yeah, but why you? You always gettin' beat up and pushed aroun' an' stuff."

"I don't know," I said. And that was the best answer I could give him.

6

The international headquarters of Gamble Oil had been built right across the road from the beach in El Tercero, just west of the airport. It was a sprawling cinder-block building resembling a federal prison and guarded with approximately the same complement of cadre. The uniformed man at the gate wore a .45 automatic on his hip in a leather holster with the flap unsnapped, and over his shoulder I could see a high-powered rifle with a telescopic sight hanging on a rack on the wall inside the sentry shack. Off to the right of the main building a working oil well was surrounded by a chain link fence, and the pump bobbed and rocked with rhythmic monotony like a pterodactyl at a water hole. It was not the only well on the sprawling property. It seemed a shame that such a scenic spot, not six hundred feet from the ocean, was given over to such unsightly business, but the U.S.A. measures progress in dollars, and all but the most rabid and outspoken environmentalists have given up the fight and are learning to live with the visual pollution of industrial concrete and steel and neon where once trees stood, flowers bloomed, and birds twittered the coming of the seasons.

"There's visitor parking around to the left of the building," the sentry told me. "Please park in the unmarked spaces *only*. The door to the main lobby is right there, you can't miss it." He ripped a pink form from a pad, wrote my name on it and the date and time of day, which was eleven thirty A.M., and handed it to me. Then he gave me a clip-on visitor's badge and told me to put it on before entering the building. "There'll be a guard in the lobby," he said. "Make sure you sign in, and he'll give you a pass."

I followed his instructions to the letter—with all his fire-power I was afraid not to.

The guard inside the lobby was big, black, and rather pleasant-looking. I showed him my visitor's badge and he told me to sign in. Under "firm name" I wrote *Victory Insurance,* which was the phony company name I had used to secure my appointment with the director of operations. Then the guard asked for further ID. I showed him my driver's license and my American Express card, and though everything in me wanted to show him my library card, my paid-up SAG card, and my membership in the Gourmet Singles Club, I decided that being a wise-ass at Gamble Oil was not going to get me where I wanted to go.

Where I wanted to go was an office on the fourth floor. I had phoned at eight thirty that morning, and the chief of plant operations, a gentleman named Mr. Tomita, had agreed to see me. On the way down the hall I passed by a medical office presided over by Rosario Soldana, M.D., the payroll department, and the office of the chief engineer, explorations, whose closed door told me his name was Rama Magdi Khali. It seemed Gamble Petroleum was running its own mini–United Nations. Other than that, the headquarters of a medium-size oil barony wasn't all that different from the offices of an insurance company or a computer chip firm or the William Morris Agency. It made me feel better about the choices I had made in my life; I'd last about twenty-five minutes working in a sterile environment like this before the little men with the white coats came to drop a net over me.

It finally hit me, up there in the quiet corridor, that there was hardly anyone around, and that the parking lot downstairs had only been about ten percent full. It was, after all, the day after Thanksgiving, a traditional day off for the troops. Only the workaholics, the lickspittles, and the truly key members of the company would be in the office.

I didn't know into what category Mr. Tomita fell. I entered his empty waiting room—his secretary was obviously neither important enough nor insecure enough to work on a holiday—and he called me into his inner office. He was no more than five feet tall, wore wire-rimmed spectacles and a gray suit with a narrow black tie, and was close to sixty years old, from the look of him. He stood up behind his desk—at least I think he was standing up—and bowed. I bowed back, being careful not to bend too low for fear he'd think I was mocking him. The whole Asian concept of face, the keeping and saving and losing of it—is as complicated as recombinant gene research, and I didn't want to offend him before I'd found out what I came for.

Mr. Tomita indicated the chair opposite his desk and seated himself after I did. "You spoke on the telephone of Mr. D'Anjou, yes?" he said. His clipped Japanese accent made it come out Don-Jew.

"I'm with an insurance company," I said, "and I'm doing some investigation into his death."

"A tragic happening. I read of it in the newspaper."

"I understood he worked here?"

Mr. Tomita nodded and lovingly patted a manila folder on the desk in front of him. "I took Mr. Don-Jew's jacket from the files after we spoke," he said. "The nonactive file. He has not been employed here for some six months."

"Was his separation from this company voluntary?"

"You ask if he was let go?" I nodded. Tomita opened the folder. "He was indeed terminated. Yes. Yes."

The word *terminated* was particularly grisly under the circumstances. "May I ask why?"

"That information is not available, sir," he said politely.

"How long did he work here?"

"For . . . eleven years and seven months, it is."

"That seems like a long time to work someplace and then be let go for no reason."

"I did not say for no reason, Mr. Saxon. I said that information is not available."

"Not available to me, you mean?"

He lifted his hands in a show of helplessness. "Like any other company, Gamble Petroleum has its confidential files."

"Do you have any idea what he was going to do when he left Gamble?"

He shook his head. "I was not personally acquainted with Mr. Don-Jew until the day he came here to clear the company."

"Clear the company?"

"When an employee leaves, there are certain items of Gamble Petroleum property he is required to—surrender."

"For instance?"

"His Gamble identification badge. Keys to his office and certain other offices that might have been issued to him. His parking lot card key. Other items. In Mr. Don-Jew's case, a company car."

I raised my eyebrows. "A company car? He must have been a pretty big cheese around here."

"Big cheese?" Mr. Tomita said. "I am sorry . . . ?"

"Important person," I explained.

"Mr. Don-Jew was assistant chief engineer in charge of exploration."

"Help me out, Mr. Tomita. What does that mean?"

Mr. Tomita smiled as if talking to a rather dense five-year-old. "Oil does not jump out of the ground and into our hands, Mr. Saxon. We have to look for it. It was Mr. Don-Jew's responsibility"—he pronounced that one very carefully, enunciating each syllable to make sure he didn't miss any—"to search out likely places where there might be oil reserves and to conduct whatever tests are necessary before making recommendations to the company."

"So his supervisor would be Mr. Rama—I'm sorry, I can't remember the name I saw on the door outside."

"Rama Magdi Khali," Mr. Tomita said. "An East Indian. Oil is a global business, and Mr. Gamble's staff reflects that.

We have people here from Iran, Saudi Arabia, Indonesia, Iraq, Mexico, Guatemala—and of course, Japan." And he gave me a little bow acknowledging that he was one of the globals.

"I don't suppose you have any knowledge of the project Mr. D'Anjou was working on before he left?"

"I am afraid that is not my area of expertise. I am the director of plant operations. I have little firsthand knowledge of the technicalities of petroleum exploration."

"Is that something I could discuss with Mr. Khali?"

"I suppose so. He is chief of the section to which Mr. Don-Jew was attached."

"Is he in this morning?"

"For most of the people here, today is a holiday, Mr. Saxon. But Mr. Khali should be in on Monday, if you wish to make a meeting with him."

"Was there anyone here at Gamble with whom he kept in contact after his—termination?"

Tomita smiled and bobbed his head. "That information also is not available."

"You mean again that it's not available to me."

"I mean, sir, that I do not know."

I stood up. "Thank you for your assistance, Mr. Tomita. I'll get in touch with Mr. Khali on Monday."

He got to his feet too and stood there looking up my nose. "Mr. Saxon," he said as though it were the beginning of a sentence.

I waited, but he didn't go on. I said, "Yes, Mr. Tomita."

When he finally spoke it was with the exquisite care of a man navigating his way through a minefield. "Oil business is odd. Like a fraternity in the college. Very—ingrown, yes?"

"Inbred, you mean?"

"Yes. Yes, inbred. They don't so very much talk to the outside persons."

"Why is that?"

He said, "I do not believe they trust."

"I see."

"In this matter of Mr. Don-Jew," he said. "His lady, I believe, they say she did this thing."

"Nobody has proved that, yet."

"But they say it is so. Mr. Saxon, this matter of Mr. Don-Jew, it has nothing to do with oil business. Gamble Oil, we do not wish to become so famous in the news reports."

"You don't want to get involved?"

"Involved, yes. Better you say what they say, that the lady did this."

"Better for whom?"

He shrugged elaborately. I looked down at him, at the top of his head; his hair was very black and full. "Are you telling me I should be careful, Mr. Tomita?"

His eyes lit up behind his glasses. "Careful. Yes. Yes, careful."

I had to stop at the guard's desk in the lobby to surrender my pass and sign out. "Terrible thing about that oil guy that got killed the other night," I said.

The guard didn't answer me or give any indication that he'd heard me speak at all.

"He used to work here, didn't he?"

"Yup," the guard said.

"Did you know him?"

He exhaled noisily. "Some." He must have gotten his dialogue from an old Gary Cooper movie.

"Nice fellow?"

Shrug.

"Who do you suppose would want to kill a guy like that?"

He looked up at me, and I knew the way offensive tackles must have felt getting down in a three-point stance head to head with Mean Joe Green. He said in a tone that could only be interpreted one way, "Make sure you give your visitor's badge to the man at the gate." Then he turned away from me and started writing something in a little notebook.

If the petroleum industry was full of good old boys from the wildcatting days in Texas and Oklahoma, quick with a laugh and a bourbon and branch water and reminiscences of gushers past, they had indeed all taken the holiday weekend off.

7

The woman's long brown hair flew more than a foot straight out behind her as she ran along the sand at the surf line. She had on a red sweat suit, not the fashionable kind with a designer label on the outside that most women of the west side sport when they go to the health club to work out and meet yuppie iron pumpers, but the serviceable type worn by those who take their running seriously. I admired her from a distance as I stood at the curb of Vista Del Mar across from the strand, which was separated from the highway by a twenty-foot strip of weeds, stagnant salt ponds, and the skeletons of gulls picked clean by sand crabs and water rats. As her lithe figure receded and faded into the gloomy overcast that hung over the beach, I turned and opened the cyclone fence gate and started climbing the pathway leading up the hill to a large weatherbeaten house. Railroad ties had been imbedded crossways in the path to form a set of crude steps, which was the only thing that kept me from sliding backwards down the hill in an avalanche of loose earth. The soil on either side of the pathway was dotted with patches of saw grass and couldn't quite make up its mind whether it was dirt or sand. The result was unfelicitous.

But the house had a million-dollar view. It was just high enough up the hill so that it could look out over the beach and the ocean beyond across the tops of the cars that used Vista Del Mar as a private speedway between Mimosa

Beach and El Tercero. A wide picture window had been carved into the weathered wood across the front of the house, facing west and a bit to the north so the broad curve of Santa Monica Bay was included in the vista. It must have been beautiful in the summertime, with the California sunshine coruscating on the water and the beach crowd with their bright suits, colorful blankets and umbrellas and ice chests, and their hard tan bodies dotting the sand. In the gray of November, however, the view was bleak, especially now that the runner had loped out of sight. About two hundred feet away a gravel road wound its way up from the street around the back of the building.

When I got two thirds of the way up the path the front doors opened inward and a bandy-legged little man came out. He was wearing a pair of weathered blue jeans, thick-toed engineer's boots, and a red-white-and-black plaid flannel shirt. His eyes were a bright pale blue, his shoulders and back were straight and square, and his chin and cheeks sported a two-day growth of whiskers the same sandy gray as his hair. Only the turkey wattles at his throat indicated he might be older than his late fifties. He stood on the porch just beyond the top step, his hands on his hips, and watched me struggle up the path. "You the one that called? Saxon, is it?" he said.

"Yeah. Mr. Ledbetter?"

"Call me Billy," he said a bit prematurely, as I was still about sixty feet from him. "Everyone does."

He waited until I had climbed the steps to the porch and stuck out his hand in welcome. His handshake, strong and firm, belied his age, but he didn't try to pulverize my fingers. Only guys who need to prove something do that; Billy Ledbetter was eighty years old, five times bankrupt and five times a millionaire, and he'd already proved all he needed to. "Come on in the house," he said. "This damn wet air out here's enough to rot your insides."

We went in through the wide double doors. The living room with the large picture window was spacious, open and airy, and the furnishings were expensive in a very sim-

61

ple way. All the other windows contained leaded colored glass. A startlingly beautiful R. C. Gorman oil hung on the wall opposite the window, dominating the rest of the room, and the hardwood floor had been covered with a big colorful Navajo rug. It was a nice, warm, lived-in space.

"I appreciate your taking the time to see me, Billy."

"Aw, hell, time's just about all I got. You said on the phone you're a friend of that T. guy?"

"T. Michael Sweet," I reminded him. "No, he's not my friend. I just met him last night and we got to talking, and since I need some background on Gamble Oil for a case I'm working on, he suggested I call you."

His eyes twinkled. "Glad you're not his friend. He's an asshole. His only excuse is that he's young. Lots of young fellows today are assholes. T.'s problem is that he's showing no signs of outgrowing it. Sit down, sit down, we're not formal here. You drink?"

"Whenever I can," I said, choosing a comfortable brown leather sofa.

He squinted at me, weighing all sorts of factors, and then made his decision: "You look like a Scotch man to me."

"You've got a good eye."

"You're a city guy, that's all. Can tell by the way you walk, the way you dress, just the way you hold yourself. Most city guys either drink Scotch or vodka, and since I was kind of hoping to like you I'm glad you're a Scotch drinker."

"What's the matter with vodka?"

He made a sound as if he'd just smelled something bad. "There's no taste in vodka. No finesse, no strength. It's a drink for people who don't like booze. I'm a rye man myself, but at least Scotch's got a taste. You look like a fellow who knows what's good."

He went into the next room and I heard him clinking around with bottles and glasses. He came out with two drinks, one amber and one, for himself, a darker brown. "I don't mess with ice cubes," he said. "I hope neat is okay."

"It's the only way," I said. I raised my glass to him, took a sip. "Wow! What is that?"

"Glenmorangie," he said. "Like it?"

"Sensational. I usually drink Laphroaig."

"That's good too. Well, here's to the next gusher." He gulped down half his drink, and when he brought the glass down his eyes were twinkling even more. He flopped into an overstuffed chair in front of the fireplace, in which a real log about eighteen inches around was crackling happily. "So," he said, "tell me what-all you're up to."

I recounted the Nanette-D'Anjou scenario as best I could, and he nodded sagely while I spoke. When I had finished he was silent for a bit. Then he said, "I'm glad to get the chance to meet you, but I'm not clear why you came to me."

"The people at Gamble Oil aren't being terribly helpful," I said. "I was hoping to get in to see Jason Gamble, but I know that won't be possible unless I can get a little help from you."

"Uh-huh. What I don't see yet is why you want to talk to young Jay."

"I don't know, to be honest with you, Billy. But if Mrs. Amptman didn't kill D'Anjou, I have to find out who did."

"How can anyone at Gamble tell you that?"

"It's the only lead I have."

He finished the rest of his drink, and I somehow feared he'd think ill of me if I didn't keep up, so I knocked back the rest of mine and he went in to get refills.

While he was gone the front doors opened and the runner from the beach came in, her face glowing from exertion, patches of sweat at the armpits and chest and back of her running suit. Her long hair hung wetly down her back. Her eyes, with the same twinkle as Billy's, were a delft china blue, and the pupils were unusually large and dark. They widened in surprise when they saw me, a stranger, in the living room. She was a small woman, no more than five foot two. She was about twenty-six years old.

I got to my feet and introduced myself.

"Hello," she said. "I'm Kim Ledbetter, Billy's grand-daughter."

She certainly didn't seem to be T. Michael's type. He had been only partially accurate in his description; she was indeed attractive, but not in a foxy way. Her mouth was wide and soft-looking, her face round and broad, and there was a sweetness about her that was at odds with the beach jock outfit she wore. She pulled a white terry headband from around her forehead and shook out her hair. It was beautiful, long and medium brown.

"Kimmie?" the old man called from the other room.

"Hi, Billy," she called back. She looked at me and smiled. "He's the only one in the world I let call me Kimmie."

"Is that a warning?"

She smiled. It was one of those open, no-holding-back smiles that light up medium-size cities. "Let's just call it a word to the wise, okay?"

Her grandfather came back with the drinks. She said, "Billy, how many is that?"

"Kimmie, get off the pot, will you? You don't need to be clucking after me like you were *my* grandma!" Then he looked sheepish. "It's only two. Well, we have a guest. I can't let a guest drink alone, can I?"

She shook her head. "'Course not, Billy." She excused herself and went off toward the back of the house. In a few minutes I heard the sound of a shower running.

Billy Ledbetter sat back down. "My son's kid. He died in an accident when she was four and I've practically raised her."

"You did a good job," I said appreciatively.

"Damn right. You know that gal has a master's in petroleum engineering from the University of Oklahoma? And it was her idea, too, I didn't even suggest it, but I'm naturally pleased as hell about it. And proud." He handed me my drink. "You know, there's something about oil. It's like railroading or baseball or working the land. It gets into

64

your nervous system and you can't kick it. Me, my son, my granddaughter—I guess we've got high-grade crude in our veins."

"I like family traditions," I said.

"To an old wildcatter like me it's more than tradition. Sniffing around for just the right spot, negotiating the lease, drilling, sinking the shaft, knowing how long to wait, and then hitting that gusher—that's the kind of high these kids today can't get out of a bottle or a needle or something they stuff up their noses. Kimmie grew up around oil and decided she couldn't do without it. So she went to oil college, and here we are. She works for Texaco now, in the research lab, but one of these days she and I are going to go dig us a hole someplace."

We worked on our drinks for a while and watched the sun struggle unsuccessfully to break through the haze over the water. He said, "Well, I can probably talk Jason Gamble into seeing you, if that's what you want."

"I'd sure appreciate it."

"Let me make a couple more calls too. I remember this Peter D'Anjou by reputation. Recognized the name right away when I read about him in the paper the other day. He was good, or that's what they say. Trained in Texas and worked all over the world for Gamble. I can't believe he was on the beach for six months without getting another offer. I still know some people around here; maybe I can find something out for you, if you don't mind an old man sticking his nose in where it doesn't belong."

"I'll take help anywhere I can," I said. "Gratefully."

Kim Ledbetter came back out. She had changed into a pair of khaki pants and a red-and-white sweater and had pulled her still-wet hair into a loose ponytail. She wore no makeup and didn't need any. She had the clear, healthy complexion of a five-year-old. On her feet were a pair of strange-looking wooden sandals, the kind that are sold only in natural vitamin stores and come with a six-page brochure.

"Has Billy been chewing your ear off?" she said.

"Mostly about you."

"It's all lies." She went back into the other room and came out with a glass of sparkling water. "So how's old T. Michael?" she asked, sitting on the sofa and tucking her legs beneath her.

"I've only met him once, so I have nothing to compare it to. But I guess he's fine. He spoke very highly of you."

She threw back her head and laughed. "I'll bet he did," she said. "I'm probably his only failure."

"He did mention that."

"A lot of girls fall for that eager puppy routine. I prefer men to puppies." She leveled a look at me, her pupils wide dark windows.

"Are you in the movie business too?" Billy asked.

"Sort of on the fringes. I pay more attention to my business than to acting, but whenever I can land a job . . ."

"Yeah, I thought you looked familiar. I don't go to the movies much, but I watch TV. Maybe it was on TV."

"It's possible. Right now I'm a lot more interested in who killed Peter D'Anjou."

Kim shuddered. "I read about that. Pretty awful."

"Murder always is," I said. "But what's worse is when the wrong person gets blamed."

"And that's what you're working on?"

I nodded.

"I wish you good luck. And the innocent man too."

"Actually, it's an innocent woman."

Her grin was impudent. "Oh."

"It's not like that," I said.

"Kimmie, you let the man be," Billy ordered.

"I'm sorry, Mr. Saxon, it's none of my business."

"Well, it could be," I told her, and immediately felt awkward. The china blue eyes twinkled. "You could give me some background on what a petroleum engineer does."

"They see to it their grandfathers don't drink too much." Billy made an impatient noise, and she said, "You mean besides that? I guess we're like those dogs they have at airports who are trained to sniff out marijuana. Only we do our sniffing for oil. We know where to look and what to look for, and we have ways of testing now so that we're hardly ever wrong."

"Takes all the fun out of it," Billy grumbled. "Science and fancy machines and chemicals and stuff, you need ten college degrees to even figure them out. Used to be more of a crapshoot. Just blind instinct, faith, and a pair of cast-iron balls. But when it paid off, it was caviar for breakfast."

"So Peter D'Anjou found out where there was oil and where there wasn't when he worked for Gamble?"

"That's a simplification," Kim said, "but yes. A good engineer is almost assured a job someplace. Although in the past several years some of the oil producing countries of the Third World have been home-growing their own."

"Like Rama Magdi Khali at Gamble?"

"He's an Indian," Billy chimed in. "From India, I mean. Not a real American Indian. Time was, you were either a Texan or an Oklahoman, and everyone talked the same language. Now you talk to oilmen, you can't even understand what they're saying. Guys with names like Hirohito and Gonzales and Rama-Lama-Ding-Dong . . ."

"Don't be an ugly American, Billy," Kim said mildly.

I said, "It's a dirty job but someone's got to do it."

"Let's have another drink," Billy said.

"Billy, you've had just about enough before dinner."

"Well, where *is* dinner?" Billy argued reasonably. "It's just about time for dinner. Mr. Saxon, why don't you stay and have it with us?"

I looked uncertainly at Kim, and her eyes were twinkling again. "It's nothing fancy. Just linguini with clam sauce."

"White or red?"

"White. Does it really matter?"

"No," I admitted.

"Good," she said wickedly. "I'll set an extra place."

I was shown into a small room, probably designed as an extra bedroom, that contained a desk and some files, an IBM Selectric typewriter, and a telephone, from which I called Marvel to let him know I wouldn't be home for dinner and told him to grab a bite somewhere in the neighborhood, maybe Rosebrock's Tofuburgers. That's a restaurant about the size of a large closet, near the intersection of Windward and Pacific, about three blocks from where we lived, the quintessential California fast-food joint. I suggested he ask Saraine to go with him, and that seemed to mollify him a bit. For Saraine, Marvel would even eat a tofuburger.

When I came back into the living room, Kim had disappeared into the kitchen to tend to the linguini. Billy switched on an ecru-shaded lamp to counteract the gathering darkness outside. "That's more like it," he said. "How do you like our little place? Cozy, huh?"

"It's a great house. Great view."

He nodded. "I bought it back in the fifties, before the real estate values in this place went screwy. When you've spent sixty years digging in the dirt like I have, it's kind of nice to be able to see the clean ocean. Not many parcels of private land left along this coast. What isn't a restaurant has been bought up by the big oil companies, and they dig wells and put up fences to keep the people out. They've really messed up the coastline for all time, haven't they?"

"That's a pretty strange observation coming from an old roughneck like you."

"Listen," he said. "We old-time wildcatters, we're from a different era. Sure, we took from the land, but we loved and respected it. We gave back, too, because we knew our kids would have to grow up in the world we left them. The guys running things now are like the Roman army, raping and looting and pillaging, leaving ruins and scorched earth behind them. They only know about balance sheets. Maybe it's because they've got no kids, and that's no wonder. At night they go home and dry-hump their computers. They've got fat bank balances, but it doesn't make them smile any. There's not much passion left in the world, my young friend." He sighed and stared out at the darkening sky for a moment. "I get to thinking about it, makes me

68

feel old. And God damn it, I don't like to feel old. I've already decided I'm going to live forever."

"Keep thinking it and you will," I said.

The linguini was marvelous, and so was the sauvignon blanc Billy opened. I noticed Kim didn't drink any but stuck to mineral water, and she noticed me noticing. "No, I'm not a recovered alcoholic, in case you're wondering," she said. "I'm a runner. I ran in the Long Beach Marathon last spring. I finished, too. No smoking, no drinking, no red meat. I believe in taking care of my body."

"You're doing a hell of a job," I said, and Billy stifled a guffaw. "Tell me more about your work."

"It's fairly boring," she said, "because mainly I do testing. You're more interested in the finding of oil in the first place. Right?"

"You tell me." I washed down a mouthful of clams with the sauvignon blanc. "Suppose a petroleum engineer said there was oil in my back yard and the oil company leased my land and sunk a lot of money into drilling a well. What would happen if he was wrong—or she? What if there was no oil?"

"You'd have a healthy bank account and one p.o.ed oil company."

"Do you suppose that's why Gamble let Peter D'Anjou go?"

"You'd have to ask Gamble Oil."

"I did that. They told me to mind my own business."

"Maybe Jason Gamble himself will be more talkative," Billy said. "He's not the man old Jesse was, but he's okay, he's oil people just the same. Functionaries are no good to talk to—they're too busy covering their own ass. You want straight answers, ask the man whose name is on the door."

"It's that way in the picture business too."

"It's the same business," Billy said, "since Gulf and Western bought that movie studio."

We went back out to the living room after dinner, and the rest of the evening was spent pleasantly, with Billy spinning stories of wildcatting days in Oklahoma in the late twenties, and Kim prompting him to "tell the one about the time you met Rockefeller, Billy." Their obvious affection and rapport filled the room like the smell of a gently burning pine log. He was a Norman Rockwell painting of a grandfather—funny, informed, sometimes cranky, at once as old-fashioned as a potbellied stove and as up to date as a microchip, and brimming over with delight at being one of the lucky ones to have been born on this planet. Billy Ray Ledbetter was a classic.

But eighty years—eighty-two, I found out during dinner—take their toll, and the Armagnac Billy poured both of us after the meal made him a little sleepy. I could see him struggling to keep his eyes open.

"This was delightful," I said, "but it's getting late."

"Hell, it's not late," he said. "Not for you youngsters. I'm gonna say good night, but you stay and keep Kimmie company for a while. It gets lonely for her, taking care of an old fart like me. Do her good to be with a good-lookin' guy closer to her own age."

I stood and shook his hand, meaning it, and remained standing until he had gone into the back of the house. Then I turned back to Kim, who was curled up on the sofa.

"Another brandy?" she said.

"No, I think I'm fine. Look, if you want to get to sleep too, I can—"

"No, Billy's right about being with someone younger."

"Well, I'm not eighty, but I have a few years on you."

"You wear them well, though."

I went and sat down on the opposite end of the sofa. "Don't you have any friends your age, Kim?"

"Not really," she said. "Most of the people I work with are older. But I think that gray hair of yours is a fooler. Did you start to go gray real young?"

"Younger than you are," I said. "It's a great conversation starter, if nothing else."

She appraised me almost professionally, then nodded. "It

suits you. Was that your wife you called before, to tell her you wouldn't be home for dinner?"

"No wife. Not in my business. That was my adopted son."

She cocked her head. "No wife, but you adopted a kid?"

"Well, I didn't go down to the orphanage and take him out of a cradle," I said. "He was a runaway, living on the streets. I ran across him while I was on a case, and I just somehow couldn't let him go back out there and die. It wasn't in my game plan, but there it is, and so far it's worked out okay."

"You talk tough, but you're squishy soft, aren't you?"

"I don't know about squishy. But I'd hate like hell to think I was hard. Half the time I'm dealing with great white sharks who sit behind desks in the entertainment business and the other half with scumbolas I meet on my cases. It'd be easy to get brittle, so I fight against it."

"Keep on fighting," she said.

"What about you, Kim? Is there a significant other in the picture somewhere?"

"No," she said. "Guys my age are real jerks, especially in California. I went with a guy in college, another oil jockey, but he didn't want to make any commitments, so it ended at graduation. I'm tired of guys who don't know what they want."

"Do you know what you want?"

"No. But that doesn't make any difference. I don't have to make any decisions until I grow up."

"And when's that going to be?"

"Another thirty years or so, I guess. I *hope* I won't grow up before then."

"We adults are pretty boring, aren't we?"

"What you mean *we*, white man? You've got a ways to go too. First of all, you're an actor, and all actors are big kids playing dress-up. And running around on a white charger being a private detective and rescuing the innocent

71

of the world hardly qualifies you for the retirement home, you know."

"You have it all figured out, don't you?"

"Not it. You."

"The side of the highway is littered with the broken bodies of people who thought they had me figured out," I said. Then I looked at those blue eyes of hers and knew I was going to do something silly. I leaned over and kissed her. Not a long kiss, nor a passionate one, but it was as nice a kiss as I could remember.

"Was that your big surprise finish?" she said. "I knew about four hours ago you were going to do that eventually."

"I'll have to think of something else."

"Don't go to any trouble," Kim said. "Sometimes what you expect is even better than a surprise."

8

They keep trying to upgrade the image of Hollywood Boulevard. The chamber of commerce stages cleanup campaigns every so often, and middle-aged volunteers with mops and brooms come out in force and make a big show of sweeping the cigarette butts and crushed wax Coca-Cola cups and used condoms out of the gutter. They've remodeled the Taft Building and reopened the Brown Derby, complete with the caricatures of movie stars whose names no one can remember hanging on the walls. It's right on the corner of Hollywood and Vine where the Howard Johnson's coffee shop used to be. They've even gone so far as to give a screenwriter, Phillip Dunne, his own star on the Hollywood Walk of Fame, as if to prove to the rest of the world that yes, people in Hollywood can *too* read.

But the shops on the boulevard still draw metal security gates across their facades at night, obscuring the going-out-of-business signs in the windows. The only people crazy enough to park on the street are motorcycle gangs, their "hogs" arranged in military precision outside the sleazy bars and taco stands. Two doors west of Vine is a twenty-four-hour porno movie theater, next to that a dirty bookshop with a live peep show and a full line of "marital aids," and winos and drag queens and bag ladies and stone junkies and fourteen-year-old boy hustlers with Mohawk haircuts still cruise the sidewalk right outside the Derby's front window, in case the diners eating Cobb salad get tired of looking at the caricatures of Wallace Beery and Brian Aherne.

However on this particular morning, the Saturday after the holiday, things were pretty quiet in Hollywood. The tourists were down at the western end of the boulevard trying to fit their shoes into John Wayne's cement footprints in the forecourt of the Chinese Theater, now called Mann's but in the hearts of movie fans everywhere still Grauman's. It was too early in the morning for the hard-core dope addicts, and most of the pimps were out of town, having opted to spend the Thanksgiving weekend at home visiting their moms.

Since Marvel and a couple of other kids his age who lived along the edge of one of the Venice canals had started a deadly serious basketball game in the driveway at about 9 A.M. and had been heard making plans to watch some rented movies in my living room during the afternoon, I had donned a pair of jeans, a Fighting Illini sweatshirt, and deck shoes and quietly slipped away to my Hollywood office where I could do some thinking in relative quiet. There is something about going into an office building on a weekend, even my own, that always makes me feel as though I am violating a sanctuary. Maybe I was. But when lives hang in the balance, as Nanette Amptman's seemed to, there's no such thing as a thirty-six-hour work week.

I flipped on my tape recorder and dictated notes for Jo to transcribe into the permanent files on Monday morning. I spoke of the previous day's meetings with Mr. Tomita at Gamble Oil and with Billy Ledbetter; I even included much of what Kim had told me about petroleum engineers. I omitted the kiss, and the fact that we had a date for dinner that evening. There were some things Jo didn't need to know.

I doodled on a yellow legal pad. If Peter D'Anjou had been as good at his job as Billy seemed to think, there had to be a powerful reason for his firing from Gamble after eleven years. And that reason might be tied in to his death. It was likely that Jason Gamble would know the reason, and if not I could ask Rama Magdi Khali, D'Anjou's immediate superior. I hadn't really convinced myself that Nanette Amptman was innocent, but I couldn't make a convincing case in my mind for her guilt. She may have indeed been in love with D'Anjou, but if Amptman read her right, she was not about to leave the comforts of marriage to a rich and socially prominent husband for the joys of a struggling existence with an out-of-work engineer. And that would mean that even if he had decided to break off the affair with her, she'd probably shrug it off, cry a little bit, and go back to her rounds of upscale shopping. Judging from the length of her stay in his condo Monday evening and the purchase of the sexy lingerie Tuesday afternoon, there had been no cooling of the relationship. She hadn't been inside on Tuesday night long enough to break up with him and then wrap a scarf around his neck, so she had either gone to see him with murder in mind, or she was innocent. The telephone rang. My first impulse was to let the machine pick it up, but getting a call in my office on Saturday was unusual enough to make me curious. I answered on the second ring.

"Saxon Investigations."

"Billy Ledbetter here."

"Good morning, Billy," I said. "I'm glad you called. I wanted to thank you again for a terrific evening."

"I guess that could have waited until you come to pick up Kimmie tonight," he said merrily, and I felt my ears warm. "I made those calls I said I would."

"Terrific."

"First thing, after this D'Anjou fellow left Gamble Oil he did some freelance consulting. Most of his work was for a wildcatter by the name of Don Stack, who bought up an old lease right next to Gamble's big field in El Tercero."

"An old lease?"

"Gamble worked that well, back in the fifties. It was never a great producer but it paid its way, until about fifteen years ago when it watered out."

"What does that mean?"

"Means there was no more oil. They pumped nothing

but seawater for about two months and then shut the well down. About five years ago the land reverted back to its original owner, and then about a year and a half ago this Don Stack bought the mineral rights and started drilling a new well. The rumor is he's got some pretty heavy investors around town and that he paid cash for the lease, about twice what it was worth."

"And what happened?"

"Damnedest thing," he said. "He drilled a new shaft. I don't know what magic he did, but he started pumping about five hundred barrels a day. Jason Gamble was fit to be tied, as you might imagine. Anyway, he's agreed to talk to you if you call him on Monday morning."

"Billy, that's great. Now, where can I get hold of this Don Stack?"

He paused for a moment. "His office is on-site in a little doghouse, but from what I hear, they have a pretty tight security setup at that well. I'm not sure it'd be such a good idea to go there."

"I'll call for an appointment."

"No phone, that's the word I got."

"How the hell can you run a business without a phone?"

"They've got an office in Inglewood, but it's just one room and a kid doing the phone answering. Stack's never there. He spends most of his time at the well."

"You think he'd be there today? Saturday?"

"Oil wells don't stop pumping on weekends," Billy said.

"Exactly where is this well, Billy?"

"About five miles north of my house there's a big field; you'll see the Gamble's sign. They've got about ten wells pumping there. Just beyond that there's a little unmarked fenced-in area with one lonely pump working. That's Stack's."

I thanked him and we hung up, and then I brewed myself a cup of coffee and drank it. Why would anyone pay good money for an oil well that was known to be watered out? And what miracle had brought back the flow of oil? It wasn't my business, really, but Peter D'Anjou had worked for Don Stack shortly before he died, and it was a question that might bear asking.

I called George Amptman at home. He sounded irritated when he heard my voice. "What is it?" he wanted to know.

"I'd like to talk with your wife," I said.

"What for?"

"I'm not sure what for, Mr. Amptman, but if I'm supposed to prove that she didn't kill Peter D'Anjou it might be a good idea if we chatted. I don't know what I might learn, but it's for damn sure I won't learn anything by not talking to her."

I heard him rustle papers. "I don't see the necessity."

"You may not, but I do, and that's what you're paying me for. If you want me to run this investigation you have to let me run it. If not, do it yourself and save your money."

"All right, then," he said grudgingly. "When?"

"How about five o'clock?"

"Today?" he said. "It's Saturday."

"And tomorrow's Sunday. I have to see other people during the week, but I figured if Mrs. Amptman was free—"

"Oh, Christ. Hang on a minute," he said, and he put me on hold. Not many people have hold buttons on their home phone. At least there was no Muzak playing in my ear while I waited. After a minute or two he came back on the line. "Five o'clock, then."

"Thanks."

There was a pregnant silence. He seemed to want to say something else, so I just waited until he was ready. "Look, Saxon, this has been very difficult for me. Don't add to my troubles."

"What do you mean?"

"Please don't take this wrong, but—I don't want you getting any ideas about Nanette."

"Ideas?"

He cleared his throat. "I know you're a bachelor, that you have a reputation with women—"

"And you don't want me to take that the wrong way?

Fuck you, Mr. Amptman. Seven fifty a day isn't nearly enough for me to swallow your crap."

"I didn't mean to insult you."

"Try again, then."

"Please—don't quit on me."

I didn't answer. I was too busy watching my knuckles turn white around the handle of my coffee mug.

"I'm . . . sorry," he said. "The strain is getting to me. I don't know what I'm saying half the time."

"That seems to be a recurrent problem with you. The next time you say something offensive you can start looking for another investigator, and I'm not kidding."

He apologized until I got sick of him and hung up. I had rarely met anyone who set my teeth on edge the way George Amptman did. It wasn't his money that made him obnoxious; he was just one of those people that was born with the knack of saying the most insulting thing imaginable in any given situation.

I finished my paperwork and headed home. As advertised, there was a contingent of adolescent males in my living room screaming at the TV set. The floor was a festival of potato chip bags and Pepsi-Cola cans.

"Hey," Marvel said, hardly looking up from the old movie. One of the other guys said, "Hey, Mr. Saxon," and waved. I waved back. On the TV, Dirty Harry seemed to be winning, but I knew my very presence put a damper on things, so I grabbed a John Courage from the refrigerator and took it into my bedroom. I showered and got dressed for my dinner with Kim Ledbetter. Most of what I had to do for the rest of the day was down in the South Bay area anyway, and I didn't want to make any extra trips.

"I'm out of here for the day," I told Marvel. "If you'd like the guys to hang around, I'll buy the pizza."

"All right!" one of the other boys said.

As I was giving Marvel money he said, "Wha's up?"

I said, "I have a date with a lady."

"Tha's cool," Marvel said. It was nice to get his approval.

I drove east on Venice Boulevard to Lincoln and turned

south, then west again on Culver until I got to Playa Del Rey. As I headed south along the ocean I couldn't resist a quick glance up Rambla at the condo complex where I'd discovered Peter D'Anjou's body. It wasn't a happy memory. No matter how many times it happens, seeing someone dead shakes me to my foundations. For a guy who won't even look at a dead dog in the middle of the highway, I suppose I'm in a strange business.

The oil well owned by Donald Stack was back off the road a bit and so well hidden that I passed it the first time and had to turn around in a driveway about half a mile south. A steel mesh fence encircled the well and the adjacent hill, and some ragged ivy plants had climbed most of the way up the chain link on the side facing the road, ivy not particularly indigenous to the beach area but planted there, it seemed, to shield the site from curious stares. There wasn't much traffic along the oceanside drive, and I had made pretty good time. I turned up the dirt and gravel access road and pulled my car to a stop by the padlocked gate. Off up the hill overlooking the lone oil pump, bobbing quietly in the grayness, was a portable shelter constructed of what looked to be light tank iron. The overcast was heavier here than inland.

I got out of the car and walked up to the fence, which was about ten feet high and sported four rolls of barbed wire across its top. Several signs warned me to KEEP OUT, that there was to be NO TRESPASSING, that it was PRIVATE PROPERTY, and that VIOLATORS WILL BE PROSECUTED. I didn't bother looking for a welcome mat.

I pushed the button marked CALL and walked the length of the fence as I waited. Someone came out of the doghouse and headed down the hill. I went back to the gate.

He was a huge man, about six foot four, with a chest like an oil drum under his black-and-white flannel shirt. His thick wrists and forearms were covered with a sprinkling of large freckles and hair the same reddish color as what was on his head, or as much as I could see of it beneath his hard hat. Sideburns reached to the bottoms of his earlobes, a length that had gone out of style in 1972. A cigarette dangled from one corner of his mouth, and its smoke caused a squint in one of the cinnamon brown eyes almost buried within flabby pockets of pale flesh. He didn't seem to be in any hurry to get down the hill. I might have felt better if he'd shown some agitation, but he was walking with a measured tread I didn't like at all.

"Don't understand English?" he said as he got to the fence. "Or is it that you can't read? This is private proppity."

"I'm here to see Mr. Stack. Don Stack."

"We don't want any."

"My name is Saxon," I said, and pushed one of my business cards through the mesh in the fence. The big man took it and dropped it in the dirt at his feet without looking at it.

"I don't care what your name is. No visitors."

"Is Mr. Stack in?"

"He's busy."

"It'll just take a minute."

"Can't you fucking hear either? He's too busy to see anybody now. Call up for an appointment."

"Why don't you just tell him I want to see him and let him make his own decision?"

"Don't make me unlock this gate," he said like a mother threatening an unruly six-year-old.

"Look," I said, "I'm not selling anything. I just want a moment of Mr. Stack's time. I'm a private investigator, which you'd know if you'd bothered to read my card. I'm not looking for any trouble."

"Well you found some, buddy, unless you make tracks out of here fast." He put one palm up on the chain link above his head. It was big enough to blot out the sun.

"Why the security?" I said. "You guys hiding something?"

"I'm gonna be hiding my boot in your ass if you don't move along."

"Kind of feisty, aren't you?" He looked at me in the non-comprehending way of the terminally stupid. "Feisty. Means, in this case, touchy, quarrelsome. Ill-tempered."

"I'm gonna count to ten," he rumbled.

Several witty remarks about it therefore not being necessary for him to remove his shoes flitted through my brain, and I wisely decided against any of them. I turned my back on him and returned to the car as if it were my idea. I didn't think he could get the padlock open quickly enough to do me any harm. But then he might be as much of a gorilla as he looked and scale the fence to come after me.

I had an hour before my appointment with Nanette Amptman, so I drove down to Mimosa Beach and parked in a lot and had a cup of coffee at an outdoor restaurant on the strand. The restaurant staff thought I was crazy to sit outside in this weather, but the view was just too tempting. By the time I'd been out there ten minutes I was chilled through but too proud to admit it to the young waitress who had reluctantly seated me.

I thought about Don Stack's oil well. I knew that oil people are a clannish lot, but Stack went to extremes to keep visitors out, what with the padlocks and the barbed wire and the unmarked, almost camouflaged site, and the gorilla in the hard hat. Eventually I was going to have to talk to Mr. Stack, with any luck at a time when he didn't have his pet monster on the premises.

I finished my coffee, collected my car from the lot, which charged me three dollars for parking near enough to the beach to rust my engine, and headed for the Amptmans' house.

I don't know why I expected a butler or a gray-uniformed maid to open the door, but Amptman himself answered the summons of the bell. He was wearing what were obviously suit pants and a white pinstriped dress shirt with no tie and the top button undone. That was apparently his idea of casual attire on a quiet holiday afternoon at home. He looked at his watch. "You're early," he said.

"Five minutes. Would you like me to drive around the block a few times?"

"No, come in," he said as though my question had been in earnest. He led me through an atrium entryway with black-and-white tile flooring and a couple of large potted palms flanking the door, and into a living room that showed the unmistakable slick touch of an interior decorator and reflected none of the personality of its occupants. The sofa was black with white cushions, the wooden tables were all lacquered in black, the rest of the accents and furniture were white. One of those ultramodern lamps with a long neck and several crazy angles loomed over the sofa like a giant praying mantis. Above the stone fireplace was an abstract painting done in varying shades of black and white and gray, with the barest splash of cobalt blue in the lower left-hand corner. People have strange tastes when it comes to decorating their homes. If I'd had to spend more than three hours in that room I'd be clanging my tin cup against the bars and yelling for the warden.

"Nanette is out on the sun porch," he said, pointing his chin at a large glassed-in area beyond the living room. "Come on."

"Mr. Amptman, I'd like to talk with her alone."

"Why?" His suspicion bristled like porcupine quills.

"Under the circumstances she's likely to speak more openly if you're not around." Behind his glasses his eyes flashed again, and I said, "Don't worry, I'm not going to try anything."

"Suit yourself," he said coldly. "I'll be in my study. Please come by and see me before you leave." He turned on his heel and left me standing there in the middle of what I'd begun to think of as the cellblock.

I made my way carefully over a llama-hair rug on the floor—I'll leave it to your imagination what color it was—and went through a sliding door onto the sun porch.

Nanette Amptman was huddled in a rattan chair with a big fanlike back, the kind you'd expect to find Somerset Maugham sitting in conducting a salon. She was sipping from a tall glass that looked like water and I was sure was something else.

"Mrs. Amptman?" I said.

She looked up dully. "Call me Nanette, please. Everyone does. You must be Saxon. My husband has told me all about you." She nodded at a wicker love seat across from her. "Sit down."

I did so, perching on the edge of it. There was no way I would ever be comfortable in this house or in this situation. "I know you have every reason to hate me," I began, but she put up one languid scarlet-nailed hand.

"You were doing your job," she said. "I don't blame anyone but myself for my troubles." She looked off in the direction of the rest of the house and added, "Well, that's not completely true. But I don't blame you. Do you want a drink?"

"No thanks," I said.

"What is it you want to know?"

"I'm not sure," I said. "But the easiest way to prove that you didn't kill Peter D'Anjou is to find out who did. I assume you're sticking to your story—that you didn't kill him."

She blinked her shining eyes. "Killing Peter was the furthest thing from my mind."

"Okay, then. You're going to have to give me some background. Some of this will be painful, or awkward. But let me assure you that none of it will get back to your husband unless it has a direct bearing on the murder. Deal?"

She looked half asleep. "I suppose."

"Now. How long had you been . . . seeing Peter?"

"Five months or so," she said. "Since the beginning of summer. I met him at Reuben's in Redondo Beach. Isn't that where most people meet their lovers in this neighborhood?"

"I'm not from this neighborhood."

"Well, it's a meet market. I used to go there once in a while—when George was out of town." She lapped at her drink and then looked up at me. "You think I'm a slut."

"No, I don't. We all do what we have to. And that's kind of an out-of-date word."

"It was what I had to do, all right. Look, I'd been around a bit before I married George. I did the bar scene, mostly up in the San Fernando Valley, where I used to live. And I was one of the few that liked it. It was fun, it was exciting, and it was a little dangerous too." She scrutinized me thoroughly. "I have the feeling you know what I'm talking about."

"I've been across the street a few times, yes."

"Well, then, you know. It gets old after a while. You want to settle down and start the meaningful part of your life. So I answered George's blind ad in a magazine. I'd answered a few other ads, too, but George's was the most appealing to me. Would you like to guess why?"

"Because he's rich?"

She smiled without mirth. "Shot in the dark, Mr. Saxon? Lucky guess. So I married him. I'd thought it out pretty carefully and decided this was what I wanted, the beautiful home, unlimited charge accounts, social position. The whole nine yards." She took a deep, shuddering breath. "Not the first mistake I ever made."

"I've heard that those who marry for money, earn it."

"You may have noticed George is something of a—how can I put this? A cold fish. You can imagine the way he is in bed."

I couldn't and didn't want to, but I nodded.

"After a while it seemed I was going to flip if I didn't do something about it. So . . . I did. And it was back to the same old shit as before I was married. A few drinks, a quick tumble, then put on your panty hose and go home. Until I met Peter." Her eyes and the end of her nose started to redden. I could see she was trying not to cry, so I waited until she got herself under control.

"How often did you see him?" I asked.

"Whenever I could. Whenever George was out of town, or during the day when Peter was free."

"He wasn't working, was he?"

"Not full time. He was a consultant for a few people, as I understood it. He didn't talk much about his work. We didn't have time for small talk." Her mouth twisted bitterly. "When you're committing adultery you make the most of every moment."

"All right. Nanette, this is important, so think carefully. Did Peter ever mention the name of anyone he was working for? Or any friends that he saw regularly?"

"I know he was working for an independent oilman here in the South Bay. Donald Stack."

"What did he say about him? Anything at all?"

"I can't remember. I know he didn't like him very much. Said he was a crook."

"What about the people at Gamble Oil?"

"He had left Gamble just before I met him."

"Did he ever mention anyone there?"

"Just Jason Gamble. Oh, and some Indian, the one who fired him."

"Khali? Rama Magdi Khali?"

"Yes, I think so." She frowned, concentrating. "I don't think Peter liked him very much either."

"Did he ever say why?"

She thought about that for a moment and sighed. "No, not really. As I told you, we didn't talk much about his work. All we talked about was us, and whether we had a future."

"The district attorney will probably try to make a case against you by inferring that Peter wanted to break off the affair and that you killed him because of it."

The tears came then, big tears that spilled out and rolled down her cheeks, and she made no effort to wipe them away. "That isn't true. We loved each other. Peter said that he was going to be coming into a lot of money, and that we could get married then."

"When did he say that, Nanette?"

She sniffed. "About a month ago, I suppose."

"What was the source of this windfall going to be?"

"He never told me." She shook her head. "You think I'm

just a round-heeled tramp, not wanting to leave George and marry Peter until he had a lot of money. Well, I suppose I am a tramp. But I was poor for a long time, and I decided not to be anymore. That's why I married George. I didn't think Peter would ever have been rich the way George is, but he had to get to the place where I wouldn't have to count pennies. It sounds cold, but that's just the way I am, and you have to give me some credit for knowing it."

"My only interest is that you don't go to prison for something you didn't do. The rest of it, that's between you and your husband. Or you and yourself. It's none of my business." She stared into her drink. "You're sure Peter never said where this money was coming from?"

"Just that it was coming soon. What's the difference now, anyway? He's dead."

"The difference is that this big money may have been the reason he was killed," I said. "And if I can find out the source of this money, I may keep you out of the penitentiary."

"I wish you luck, Mr. Saxon," she said, and drained her glass.

I felt I had been dismissed, so I stood up. "Nanette," I said, "I'm not the one that needs the luck."

9

Billy Ledbetter steadfastly refused to join Kim and me for dinner no matter how many times I asked him, insisting he could do fine opening a can of tuna or finishing the leftover linguini. I think he knew I really didn't want him to come. This was a date, after all, the first one I'd been on in quite a while, and as delightful as he was, I didn't want Kim's grandfather along for the ride. She was an attractive woman I wanted to get to know better, and the best way to do that is always one on one, with no distractions, no third parties, no colorful old codgers with tales of oil-drilling days in Oklahoma.

When we got out to my car Kim said, "From the way you dug into those clams last night, I get the idea you like seafood."

"One of my favorite things."

"There's a little place just up the beach a way. It's nothing fancy, kind of a neighborhood hangout. But they have fresh clams, mussels, oysters, just about anything you want. And about thirty different kinds of beer."

"You've made yourself a sale," I said.

Rusty's Sea Food was, as advertised, nothing fancy. It was built along one side of an old pier on a little promontory jutting out into the sea and resembled a fishing shack both inside and out. I imagine that on a clear day the view would be terrific. Over the door was one of those neon signs depicting a naked girl in a giant martini glass. It was that kind of place. The tables were covered with red-and-white checked cloths, and on each a candle burned in a red glass jar with plastic netting around the bottom. It was all one room, the bar along the back wall and the tables by a long window facing the sea. I was thankful there were no sporting events on television to drown out conversation; if I'd wanted to eat with screaming crowds and a banal play-by-play announcer in the background I could have stayed home and had dinner with Marvel. Instead the counterpoint to the meal was a vintage jukebox heavy with big band stuff and vocals by Tony Bennett and Lena Horne and of course Sinatra. There were even a couple of pure jazz sides, Bird doing "I'll Remember April," Brubeck and Desmond and Senator Eugene Wright's "Blue Rondo à la Turk," and some early rock classics by Chuck Berry and Little Richard.

There was nothing wrong with the food, either. We ordered mussels in garlic butter for openers, and I was glad to see they weren't the rubbery New Zealand variety served by most seafood restaurants in Los Angeles. The thirty brands of beer didn't include John Courage, but I ordered a Perrier for Kim and a Dortmunder for myself. It was not only an excellent beer, but it made me smile every time I thought of Donald E. Westlake's hapless crook of the same name. The garlic sauce was quite heavy on its main ingredient, and I usually avoid garlic when I expect to get kissed, but I figured since we were both partaking, it wouldn't hurt.

"Did I tell you what a terrific kisser you are?" I said, since I was thinking about it.

"No, you didn't, and I was waiting."

"I suppose you've heard that before."

She gave a little shrug of her shoulders, but there was nothing coy about it. "It does take two, you know."

I snapped my fingers. "Damn! That's what I've been doing wrong all these years."

For an entrée Kim suggested the baked clams. They chopped them, mixed them with fragrant chunks of garlic, some bread crumbs, crabmeat, and butter, covered them with paprika, baked them on the half shell, and served them with big hunks of sourdough bread. It was an excellent choice, and the Dortmunder tasted as if it had been brewed with that dish in mind.

We talked about a lot of things during the meal, all pleasant. I heard about what it was like being raised by an elderly grandfather, to be a pretty young woman in a field in which men predominated, and about running in marathons, where the main goal was not so much to win as to finish.

I didn't realize that I'd been doing all the listening until she said, "Enough about me. I want to know about you. Which do you like better, acting or detecting?"

"I'm not sure," I said. "I wanted to be an actor all my life, but the way the business is today it isn't very much fun. Most films are made with idiots in mind. I don't take it very seriously anymore."

"Do you take detective work seriously?"

"I have to. There's a lot more riding on it than on a savings and loan commercial or a movie of the week."

"But not for you," she said. "A lot more riding on it for other people."

"I'm self-employed, but my business is doing things for other people."

She nodded sagely, stuffing her pretty mouth with clams. "I think you really get off on it."

"I've worked for people I didn't like very much just because they waved a checkbook at me, but there are some things I won't do no matter how much they pay me. I think most of us are like that. We all draw the line at different places, that's all. And where we draw it is called integrity."

The pupils in her eyes were big enough to drive a large van through, and the irises were still the incredible blue of fine china. She caught me looking at her and smiled around her food.

I said, "Don't mind me, I'm just enjoying the scenery."

"You're supposed to be looking out at the ocean."

"It's prettier in here."

"You're going to spoil me."

"Come on, I'll bet all your boyfriends spoil you."

"Only until they find out I've got a master's degree. Then they tuck their tails between their legs and run for cover. Men in this town talk big about wanting to meet a smart, clever, independent woman, but they always wind up dating dumb gorgeous ones and marrying them. Then after a few years they find a bright one to have an affair with because they don't get enough mental stimulation at home. It ain't easy." She poured herself the last of her second Perrier and said, "I can't see you turning tail and running from any woman."

"I like women. I don't look at them as foes or conquests, so they don't intimidate me. Not even smart ones like you."

"If that's true," she said, "I'm going to frame you and hang you on the wall. A simple silver frame, to match your hair."

"An interior decorator too," I said. "Is there no end to your multitude of talents?"

"I can't cook."

"Don't pull that one on me; I had your linguini."

"Any fool can make a good clam sauce," she said. "But I can't *really* cook."

"I can. I like good food too much to open up a can or defrost something, so I learned. My specialty is Chinese; I'm hell on wheels with a wok."

"I'll bet you're hell on wheels in general."

"Is that a compliment?"

"You bet."

"Then thanks."

"Then you're welcome."

I ordered a Rémy Martin and two coffees, and we chatted about the world in general and the sometimes exciting and often dull world of a private investigator. She seemed really interested, not like a lot of people I talk to, who are disappointed that my days and nights aren't full of bourbon bottles in the bottom drawer and chesty blondes with deep dark secrets and a red neon sign flashing monotonously off and on from the cheap hotel across the street, but with the healthy curiosity that comes with intelligence. She was a good listener, and like most of us, when I speak about myself I'm not a bad talker.

There were sudden loud voices at the door and I turned to see what the commotion was all about. Four large men had walked in, and my heart moved into my throat when I saw that one of them was the big mean redheaded guy from Donald Stack's oil well. I turned back to Kim and saw that she was looking a bit unhappy herself.

"Damn," she said, and then she raised her eyes. I was aware of someone extremely large hulking over me.

"Hey, Kim," the big redhead said. And then he looked down at me and something markedly unpleasant came over his features the way a shadow slips over a baseball diamond when a cloud scuds across the sun. "Well, look who's here. Mr. Big Nose."

Kim said, "Jim Shay, I'd like you to meet—"

"Oh, we've already met," he said, his rat eyes gleaming, "although most of what I saw of him was his back. He don't respond to threats too well. Seems to me you can do a lot better than some chickenshit like this, Kim."

I didn't answer that. I know when someone is looking for a fight, and I chose not to plug into his silliness. Like Pablo, the guerrilla leader in *For Whom the Bell Tolls,* I do not provoke. He put his face close to mine, and the whiskey fumes almost knocked me off my chair. "I thought I saw that fancy faggot car of yours parked outside. What's with you? I mean, you come snooping around where you don't belong, I run you off, and son of a bitch if you don't come in here with my favorite girl and sit right at my table!"

"Your table?" I said.

"That's right, my table. My own special table. I'm a regular here, and I always sit at this table whenever I come in. And as you can plainly see, I'm in now." He turned to the bartender for support. "Am I right, Terry?"

The bartender said, "Take it easy, Jim."

"Come on, Terry," Shay snarled, "tell this guy. Am I a regular or what?"

Terry said, "Sit down and relax, okay, Jim?"

"Terry," I called over, "I'm tired of the clowns. Send in the acrobats."

I shouldn't have said it. I knew it as soon as the words were out, but I don't like being leaned on, and I don't suffer fools gladly.

The redhead's face went a few shades darker than the whiskey flush. "A big nose and a smart mouth. That's a bad combination."

"I'll try not to lose any sleep under the withering scorn of your disapproval," I said.

Kim said, "Jim, why don't you go sit down and let us finish our dinner?"

"You going to hide him behind your skirts? That's a good place for him."

All at once I grew bored with the game. "It must be a comfort being big enough to be obnoxious."

"You'll find out soon enough," he warned.

"Just what is your problem anyway?"

"My problem, asshole, is that you're sitting at my table!"

"And you're a regular."

"You're goddamn right," he said. "So why don't you just pick up all your crap and move it somewhere else?"

"Jim, go away," Kim said.

"I'm waiting for lover boy here to pick up and move."

I said quietly, "When we finish, you can have the table."

"Well, what if I want the table now?"

"Then," I said, "I guess you're out of luck."

Shay straightened up and took a deep breath, and his chest expanded to the size of a small office building. He smiled, his eyes as dead as black stones in a creek bed. "Well, you enjoy the rest of your dinner, then," he said. "And I'll see you outside later." He looked at my companion and said, "Nice seeing you again, Kim," and turned and walked out the door. His three buddies mumbled something among themselves and followed him out.

Kim said, "I'm sorry, really. I've known Jim a long time. He is a regular in here, and I come in a lot too because the

92

food is so good. He's been asking me out for the last two years. I keep saying no, and that just makes him more determined. We shouldn't have come here. I should have realized."

"I hate to burst your bubble, but Jim's tough-guy act has only a little to do with you. If that's all it was, he would have flexed his muscles and thumped his chest for a minute and then gone away. But I went around to Don Stack's well this afternoon and had a little run-in with Mr. Shay, and the only reason he didn't tear me apart then is because there was a padlocked gate between us."

She sipped her coffee thoughtfully. "It's all talk. He'll go somewhere else and get drunker and get over it."

I turned around in my chair, signaling the waitress for my bill. "Wouldn't it be nice to think so," I said.

"I'd like some more coffee." Her voice was anxious.

"Kim, I'm not going to spend the evening hiding in here."

"I still want more coffee," she said, and there was a steel belt under her soft words. I nodded, and when the waitress showed up with the check I put in the order.

"Don't be crazy! Jim is a brute. You don't have to get killed to prove yourself to me."

I smiled. "I have nothing to prove, Kim. I cross the street to avoid things like this. But there doesn't seem to be any convenient street available. So I figure I'll just go out there and try to talk my way clear."

We finished our coffee. I gave the waitress my credit card and she brought a slip for me to sign. She was in her late forties, a nice tired lady who'd seen this sort of thing before. "Jim is bad news," she said. "If you'd like to go out the back door, it's through the kitchen."

"That's okay," I said. "I came in through the front door and that's how I'm going out." But I added a dollar to her tip. I took the customer copy from the credit slip and dutifully tore up the carbons. I put my Visa card in my wallet, and then I took the mushroom-capped pepper shaker from its wire holder and began unscrewing the top.

93

"What are you doing?" Kim said.

"Just in case Shay doesn't feel like talking."

I emptied the pepper into my hand and dumped it into my left jacket pocket. Kim watched me with eyes even wider than usual. "Ready?" I stood up and held her chair for her and tried to pretend I wasn't scared silly.

It was close to nine o'clock and full dark now, the mist shimmering needlelike in the arc lights of the parking lot. I was disappointed but not surprised to see Jim Shay sitting on the fender of my car with one booted foot up on the bumper. His three companions weren't too far away, and they were passing a whiskey bottle among them in a paper bag. It was an educated guess on my part that Shay had consumed his share.

When we got to my car the big man uncoiled himself from my fender and loomed in front of me like a colossus. I knew if he ever got his hands on me he'd put me in the hospital. I said, "I think your table's ready." And then I added, "I'm sorry you had to wait so long." It killed me to say that. I rarely apologize, even when I know I should, but I really didn't feel like fighting and hoped it might defuse the situation. At least it would seem to Kim Ledbetter that I had tried.

"Well, that's real nice of you to say so. So why don't you get in your funny little gold car here and drive on back where you came from."

"That's my plan, as soon as you get out of the way."

He stepped aside with a graceful flourish. "That's a good idea," he said. "Maybe you aren't as dumb as you look."

I was putting teeth marks on my tongue biting my words back, but I didn't make any answer until he said, "And Kim's going to come back in and have a drink with me. At *my* table."

Neither of us said anything for a moment. Inside, Tony Bennett was singing "Just In Time," the sound struggling out through the closed windows. I'd taken out my car keys, but now I dropped them back into my pocket with regret. The guy was going to be a hardcase. I knew he would be;

hardcase was written all over him. Why is there always a hardcase to come swaggering along with too much booze in his belly, a bulge in his jeans, and his chest stuck out like a pouter pigeon, a guy who's seen too many movies but doesn't have the sense to realize that in those films the hardcase always loses? Hardcases make me tired.

"Not tonight," I said. The Kalahari Desert was on the inside of my mouth.

Kim was talking fast now, trying to save my ass. "I can't have a drink with you tonight, Jim," she was saying, "but why don't you call me tomorrow, and maybe we can—"

I took her elbow and moved her out of the way. I was wearying of the dancing. "Pound sand, Jim," I said.

That seemed to afford Shay a good bit of delight. An ugly grin split his face as if something vital to its structure had been removed, revealing gray snaggle teeth. His eyes were dulled from drink, small and cruel and fixed on my face. From his hip pocket he took a blue-and-white railroad handkerchief and wrapped it around the knuckles of his right hand with all the solemnity of an orthodox rabbi donning the phylacteries. This was evidently one of his rituals. He had all the moves down pat, all the bad moves. "You're history, asshole," he said.

He dropped his shoulders and assumed what he thought was a boxer's crouch, circling around me so that my back was almost against my car, which I supposed was my signal that the fistfight had officially begun. The way he was holding his hands told me he was wide open for a good left hook, but since his reach was several inches longer than mine it was doubtful I could get close enough to throw one. I stuck my left hand into my jacket pocket.

Shay's three pals had stepped far enough back to give us room, but they were making a lot of noise egging him on, boozy spectators having a high old time waiting for the cockfight to begin.

He moved in on me, so close that his massive bulk was all I could see, and pulled back his huge fist confidently; if he'd ever landed the punch it might have decapitated me. Before he could swing I took my hand out of my pocket and threw about six ounces of ground pepper into his eyes. There was no breeze to cause drift, and my aim was perfect. He screamed a curse, clawing at his face, and I stepped in and drove my right fist upward, just below his belt buckle. It was as hard as I've ever hit another human being in my life, and big as he was, it hurt him. He dropped his hands to cover the new pain and I roundhoused a left at his jaw. Some Neanderthal instinct made him pull his head back and out of the way, and because of that I hit him in the Adam's apple by mistake.

He made a hideous noise and lurched backward, his eyes dripping tears freely and threatening to pop out of his head, one hand at his throat and the other groping blindly into the space in front of him as if he hoped to somehow snatch a breath of air with his fingers and force it down his wind-pipe. Finally he tripped over an uneven spot on the surface of the parking lot and sat down hard on his tailbone, wheezing, struggling to breathe while he sneezed and coughed. There was a low muttering from his buddies, the sound the crowd makes when the cleanup hitter socks a three-run homer on the road, but no one came forward to help. That was against their code of machismo, I guess. It's better to let your friend get totaled than to make him admit he needed help.

I looked around to see whether Kim was all right. She had moved to the far side of my car, looking concerned but not frightened. I liked it that she didn't cry or faint. I don't know what I would have done if she had gone into hysterics. Probably nothing; I had other things to worry about.

With a loud grunt Jim Shay pulled himself upright and was heading toward me again, and his claque was cheering, calling for mayhem. He gurgled as he breathed, his head shaking from side to side, squeezing his eyes open and shut periodically to blink the pepper away. It was while he had them closed that I moved in quickly and hit him in the nose with a left jab. It wasn't much of a punch in terms of im-pact, but it did the job, snapping his head back and drawing blood. He grunted and swung blindly at me overhand, and I drove in under the swing and smashed my elbow into his rib cage. You could hear the bone crack down at the water's edge. He dropped to his knees in slow motion and bent double from the waist, choking and sneezing and in pain. He didn't look so big now.

Back inside Tony Bennett was taking it on home. Kim started around the car, but I froze her in her tracks with a look. Shay's pals weren't saying anything now, or moving. They were looking from me to him and back again, but there was no menace in it. Only a kind of wonder. This wasn't what they'd paid to see. I wasn't sticking to the script. I didn't imagine Jim Shay lost too many fights. I wasn't following their game plan, and they didn't know how to react.

And then incredibly he was pulling himself together and straightening up again in a series of spasmodic twitches, one portion of his body at a time, a puppet drawn upward by invisible strings, coming at me again, a nightmare out of a Frankenstein movie. His eyes were red-rimmed and his breath rattled in his injured throat, from which uttered a low, rasping hum that sounded like a chain saw. I was still backed up against the side of my car, so I quickly shifted my feet, working my way around to his left for maneuvering room. I shot out another jab that caught him high on the cheekbone and hurt my hand more than it did him. His cheek puffed up, spouting blood where my cameo ring had punctured the skin. One eye was half closed, both were streaming tears, but it didn't slow his forward progress any. He was like a wounded cape buffalo, his charge unstoppable, and I hit him in the face twice more before he clubbed me on the shoulder, numbing the entire left side of my body. It felt like a telephone pole had fallen on me. My knees went rubbery, but I managed to put the starch back into them before I hit the ground. I knew once I was down I was lost. Shay took advantage of the moment and wrapped his huge arms around my waist, squeezing all the air from my chest in a dizzying rush.

Nose to nose with him in a grotesque lover's embrace, I battered at his face with my fists, but it was like punching an oak tree, and with each impact his arms tightened around me. His breath was foul, the stubble of his beard scratchy against my cheek, and he shook me like an overstuffed pillow. My lungs were on fire, and there was a bright pain at the base of my spine. I knew if I didn't do something he was going to break my back.

I let my body go limp, and spread my arms wide, allowing him to shift his hands and get an even better grip around me. The pain was making me lightheaded, and I felt myself losing it. Then I cracked my open palms against his ears, and his scream shattered the night, as inside his head all the cymbal crashes from the 1812 Overture must have gone off at once. He dropped his arms from around my waist and raised them to his head, and I smashed at his injured ribs again, and when the pain bent him forward I grabbed a fistful of hair and jerked down. His face met the point of my knee, which was on its way up, sending a spear of pain from my kneecap to my hip and up through my side. He moaned, went slack, and toppled over sideways like a felled tree. Water ran from his eyes and blood from his mouth and nose, great shuddering breaths catching in his damaged windpipe. For a moment I was afraid he was going to die.

There was no sound in the parking lot outside Rusty's save the muffled beat of the jukebox within, the soft thrum of the surf, and Jim Shay's tortured breathing. He began to stir then, his huge body spasming. He rolled over onto his stomach. Still only half conscious, he attempted to get to his knees. I looked over at his three friends, who were white and pinch-faced with shock, and said in a constricted voice, "Make him stay down."

One of them came forward slowly, the others trailing behind him, silent witnesses to a near fatal accident. They knelt by their fallen comrade, murmuring words of comfort.

And I began to shake. I knew I had been lucky, as well as devious enough to anticipate the situation and give myself an edge from the beginning. One of these days my luck was going to run out. But looking at Jim Shay on the ground, his oil field pals hunkering over him like the seconds of a defeated duelist, I knew it hadn't been tonight.

I turned to Kim. "Get in the car," I said.

Nobody made as if to stop us, and pretty soon we were back on Vista Del Mar, heading south. I gripped the wheel hard to keep from trembling. Kim was looking at me, and it wasn't a rapturous look of adoration, either.

"That was awful. You could have killed him."

"See what happens," I said, "when you play with rough kids."

10

Sunday morning is my least favorite time of the week. There is usually no place I have to be, and in the last few years staying in bed of a Sunday has been no fun because I am generally by myself. I didn't feel like going to one of the pricey places in Venice or the marina where Sunday brunch is served. I would doubtless be the only one there dining solo, weekend brunch being the current fad for mornings after. I didn't care about pro football, which, from the sound of the television, was what seemed to be happening in my living room; it was too grim and chilly for any outdoor activities, and I couldn't go to church because I hadn't been in one for so long I had forgotten what you were supposed to do. I didn't even know the location of the nearest house of worship, Catholic or otherwise.

So I had some time to think about things, baby my sore ribs, and put an ice pack on my throbbing shoulder, where it sat like a pirate's parrot. It was only natural that what I thought about was the fight. And Kim.

Kim's Saturday good-night kiss was a lot cooler than the one the night before, and I preferred to think that she was generally upset by the incident. I couldn't believe she was angry with me. I'm sure she wouldn't have wanted me to let Jim Shay pound me into a patty. I suppose one might say I fought dirty, but when you think about it, it's pretty stupid not to.

Of course the stupidity begins at the same time the fight

does. I have never understood the thought processes of grown men who believe that a difference of opinion can best be settled by a punch in the mouth, but there are a lot of those grown men out there with their arms hanging limber and ready at their sides and the gleam of anticipated combat in their eyes, trying to recapture their glory days as schoolyard bullies, and I suppose my vocation brings me in contact with them more than I'd like. So once the decision to fight, or to defend yourself, has been made, it seems bubble-headed not to take any advantages you can. Jim Shay outweighed me considerably and spent his time hefting barrels of oil, while I huddle in my car to spy on wives who fool around. The pepper was my equalizer. It had been, therefore, a fair fight, and I had won it, despite the soreness of my ribs and the ache in my shoulder that felt like the beginnings of a toothache.

I staggered out into the kitchen past the Raiders and the Broncos and Marvel and made myself a pot of therapy, grinding the beans and using bottled water from the refrigerator. Marvel told me that he and the guys were planning on going to the mall and hanging out for the day. When knighthood was in flower one sat beneath the balcony of one's lady love and sang ballads with lyrics like hey-nonny-non the merry-o. In the sixties we did our courting at peace marches and love-ins. Ostriches and insects do peculiar mating dances. And modern adolescent boys hang around shopping malls and make rude kissing noises at young girls.

I went into the little storage room off the back porch that I call my den and dragged down several editions of the Pacific Bell White Pages from where they live atop a file cabinet. I started with the South Bay directory, then the airport area, then Santa Monica and Venice, and finally found the name I sought in the West Los Angeles book, on Wilshire Boulevard in Westwood. It had to be the right one. How many people could there be in Los Angeles named Rama Magdi Khali? I picked up the phone to dial and then decided against it. I'd drive up there and take the chance I'd catch him at home. If I didn't, little would be lost; I had nothing to do anyway.

The area of Wilshire Boulevard between Beverly Hills and Westwood Village is a high-rent district. The L.A. Country Club runs along one side of it for a stretch, and on this Sunday the bright Lacoste plumage of the elderly golfers was visible through the trees. The grass must have been wet, the ground mucky, and the greens very slow, but a little thing like weather would never deter a true hacker on a Sunday morning. After the country club the winding boulevard becomes a canyon between high-rise co-ops that are among the most expensive in the city. Why anyone would pay upward of a million dollars to live in a four-room apartment on a main artery invariably choked with automobile traffic and carbon monoxide fumes, several miles from the nearest supermarket or dry cleaner, is a puzzle. But if I spent all my time trying to figure out why the very rich do what they do, I wouldn't have any time for the important stuff.

I parked on a side street and walked back down to Wilshire. In the lobby of Khali's building was a sixtyish little man in a green-gray uniform and a smart doorman's cap. He was supposed to provide the security the tenants paid so dearly for, but he couldn't have defended the castle against a hyperactive seven-year-old. Most security guards are either retired cops or former salesmen of men's clothing at the May Company. This one looked like the latter. I told him who I wanted to see and he pushed some buttons on a console and picked up a white telephone and told someone I was here, then listened and frowned, and held out the receiver to me.

"He wants to talk to you," he said.

The male voice had a singsong lilt to it. "Yes?" it said.

"Mr. Khali. My name is Saxon. I'm investigating the murder of Peter D'Anjou, and I'd like to talk to you."

There was a pause. "All right," he said. "Come up."

I gave the phone back to the doorman, who directed me to the penthouse. As I walked into the elevator he was standing a bit taller, preening, having once again made certain that a crazed slasher was not being turned loose among the tenants.

This was only the second time I had been in one of these Wilshire Boulevard rabbit warrens, and both times I had visited the penthouse. As the elevator soared skyward I mused that perhaps the people who chose to live here were so status-conscious it had to be the penthouse or nothing, and so there were no other apartments on the lower floors at all, simply penthouses perched atop an empty monolith. The one I was headed for was twenty-five stories up.

The man who opened the door of penthouse B had a dusky dark brown face, half covered by a well-trimmed blue-black beard. He wore tan chinos and a blue sports shirt, and around his head was wrapped a white turban. A black hairnet peeped out from under the cloth in the front. He was about five foot seven and skinny enough to be the anorexia poster boy.

"I am Khali," he said. "Please come in." I walked by him into the large room and tried not to wrinkle up my nose. His body odor surrounded him like a force field.

"Sit down, please," he said, indicating a white sofa the length between home plate and the pitcher's mound. The windows made up two sides of the room, looking south over the city and west to the sea. On a clear day you could see Catalina. This was not a clear day, and one could hardly make out Santa Monica Pier some five miles away. Against one of the solid walls, just to my right, was a glass vivarium about six feet long. Next to that were a set of metallic hanging files, a rather odd decorating touch.

Khali sat in a chair opposite me, his back to the window. He said, "I was told you had already made an arrest in the unfortunate matter of Mr. D'Anjou." The clipped cadence of his speech was East Indian, and he said "de" instead of "the."

"I'm not with the police," I said, "I'm with an insurance company." The lie seemed serviceable enough to tell again.

He frowned and sat forward in his chair. "You said downstairs . . ."

"That I was investigating the D'Anjou killing. I never said I was official."

"Yes. Very resourceful," he said, his smile a rictus. "I would not have agreed to see you on a Sunday in that case." His black eyes were marble-hard and bright, almost hypnotically intense. If what Nanette had told me was true, that Peter D'Anjou had not liked him, I could see why. "I have no legal obligation to answer your questions."

"No, you don't, and I'll leave if you like. However, since I'm here, I'd appreciate it if we could talk a few minutes."

"I cannot think what information I might have that you would find useful."

"Maybe after we talk you'll know."

He sat quite still for a moment, then lifted his hands in acquiescence, exhaling rather pointedly. I took out my notebook and flipped through it until I reached the page I wanted.

"Peter D'Anjou was employed at Gamble Oil until about six months ago, is that right?"

"Approximately," he said. "I would have to look at my office records to give you the exact dates."

"That's all right. And he was terminated at that time?"
Khali nodded.

"Would you need to look at your records to tell me why?"

"It is confidential," he said. "I cannot in good conscience discuss the private business of my employer."

"Mr. Khali, I'm not sure that company confidentiality has any bearing here. It certainly isn't going to hurt Mr. D'Anjou's future job prospects."

He thought about that one for a while. Then he said, "You would have to speak to Mr. Gamble to ascertain the exact reason Peter left the firm."

"You mean you don't know?"

"As I understand it, there was a personality conflict between Mr. D'Anjou and Mr. Gamble."

"Was there a personality conflict between Mr. D'Anjou and yourself too, Mr. Khali?"

"Not at all," he lilted easily. Most of his sentences ended on an upward inflection. "Peter was an excellent engineer. His work left little to be desired."

"So he was let go by Mr. Gamble and not by you."

"Correct," he said.

"But you knew him quite well?"

"I would not say so."

"He worked directly under you, didn't he?"

"Correct again, although our relationship was business only. We did not socialize after office hours. We had little in common besides oil. Peter lived in such a way that is contrary to the tenets of my faith."

"You mean he drank alcohol?"

Khali gave me a cryptic half smile.

"So you weren't friends."

"A man has many acquaintances in his life. But few he can call his friends."

I wondered if that was an ancient Hindu homily. "What about enemies? Did D'Anjou have any at work?"

"Every man has his enemies in the workplace, his rivals, especially when he is highly placed and well regarded. But there was no one I know of who hated him enough to take his life."

"What about this conflict between D'Anjou and Mr. Gamble?"

"It was a private matter between the two men," Khali said. "I knew nothing of it. The order to terminate came from Mr. Gamble, and I followed that order."

"Without question?"

"Why should I question?"

"If D'Anjou was as good at his job as you said he was, you must have had some feeling about losing him from your department. Didn't you try to protest his firing? Or even ask why?"

Khali shrugged. "I am an employee, Mr. Saxon. I do as I

am told, when I am told. That is how I remain an employee."

He wasn't the first man to protest that he'd only been following orders. "But how did you feel about it? Personally?"

He remained impassive. Then he said, "I was sad to see him go. Personally."

"On what project was D'Anjou working at the time of his firing?"

"Please?"

"He must have been working on something in particular."

"That *is* a private matter, Mr. Saxon. You say you are investigating his death for insurance reasons. How am I to know you are not in the employ of a rival oil company bidding against Gamble on a particular lease?"

"I'm not, but let's let it go for the present."

"Any information of that nature would have to be cleared through Mr. Gamble himself." He stood up and wiped his hands on his pants. "I do not believe I can be of further assistance to you. And now I must beg you to leave. This is my day of rest."

When I stood up, the movement caused a disturbance in the glass vivarium at my elbow. I glanced down and recoiled reflexively. Raising its head to look at me was a snake, wavering on the stem of its backbone, its hideous little eyes riveted on me.

"Herpetology is my hobby," Khali said. "You like him?"

I stared through the glass at the serpent weaving hypnotically from side to side, its tongue darting in and out at me. I could see the tiny fangs on either side of its mouth, and the small pits at the side of the head. It flattened its neck into a hood, the shape of which reminded me of the wimple of Sister Concepta, the nun who used to teach me algebra. I said, "It's different, anyway."

"He is a cobra. They are native to my country. My home, my house, is in New Delhi, Mr. Saxon, but I work all over the world. I cannot carry my furniture and such

106

with me. So I keep him"—he indicated the tank—"as a reminder of my homeland."

"Aren't cobras poisonous?"

He nodded. "Do not be frightened. He poses no danger unless he is threatened or disturbed."

I shuddered. "I'm not frightened. But I'll be sure I don't ever disturb him." I've never had any great fear of snakes, but I don't think I'd like one in my living room, especially a venomous little sucker like an Asian cobra. The next time I visited Rama Magdi Khali I'd remember to bring my mongoose.

He escorted me to the door, and threw one arm around my shoulder. The smell of him almost made my eyes tear. "I have answered your questions as best I could, Mr. Saxon. Would you be so kind as to answer one of mine?"

"If I can."

"You are not with the insurance, I believe. Whom do you really represent in this matter?"

I winked at him, two conspirators suddenly in harmony. "That is confidential," I said.

11

On Monday morning I called Jo to tell her I'd be tied up for the next few hours, and drove to the hall of records in downtown Los Angeles. As I neared the Civic Center the traffic became an impossible gridlock, and by the time I found the subterranean garage I was looking for, my neck and shoulders were a solid block of bunched muscle, which didn't help the dull ache that had been put there when Jim Shay clubbed me on Saturday night.

The general public doesn't know how much supposedly privileged information is readily available to them. You don't have to have a private investigator's ticket to get a peek at the records on file with the city and the state. Voter registration, property titles, bankruptcies, fictitious business names, and the recordings of births, deaths, marriages, divorces, and felony convictions are all available for your perusal upon payment of a minuscule fee. If you're truly bored some rainy afternoon it might make an interesting diversion.

I pulled my reading glasses out of my pocket and set them on my nose. I am rarely seen in public with my glasses on. It's a vanity thing. Jo has suggested I get contact lenses, but frankly they're too much trouble; I've seen too many people down on their hands and knees in restaurants searching the carpeting. Fortunately I am able to see without augmentation. But if I'm going to do any heavy reading or hunt for numbers in the phone directory, the glasses are helpful. And for plowing through the near-microscopic print on the reams of paper in the hall of records, they are a necessity.

The first thing I looked up was Stack Oil, but there was no listing. Similarly I couldn't find Stack Petroleum, or Donald Stack anything. I decided to take another tack. I went to the real property section and looked up the owner-ship of the tract of land next to Gamble Oil's big facility on Vista Del Mar, and found it was on a twenty-one-year lease to Vista Petroleum, with a post office box in Inglewood. Donald Stack had named his company for the street on which his oil well was located, which suggested to me that he probably didn't have any other oil wells, or if he did, they were the property of another entity.

Back I went to the business files, where I discovered that Vista Petroleum was a public company whose majority ownership, sixty percent, as a matter of fact, was held by Donald Wilmer Stack. Marvel would have gotten a laugh out of Wilmer, I supposed. But there was nothing amusing about the other principal in Vista Petroleum; the ten percent of the remaining shares were in the name of one David Chandler Grayco, and that was a name I knew quite well.

David Grayco was a producer of motion pictures. He'd never had a blockbuster hit, a *Rocky* or a *Ghostbusters,* but over the last twenty years he'd produced some sixteen mo-tion pictures, independent releases that had been well fi-nanced, and almost all of them had turned a fair profit. Of course in these days of cable TV sales and videocassettes and foreign markets, it's hard to make a film that actually loses money, but Grayco was still considered to be one of the industry's minor whiz kids. He wasn't one of the giants like Ray Stark or David Begelman, but Grayco was well known enough to be able to book a table at Spago or the Beverly Canyon Room on a few hours' notice, and that was a be-all and end-all in the film industry. He drove a Rolls-Royce, lived in the hills that loomed over Sunset Boulevard in West Hollywood, and was generally perceived to be a success. No one was going to hold a benefit dinner for him, at any rate. Some producers hoard their money, put it back into their film projects, or spend it on overpriced art, overpriced homes, or overpriced women. David Grayco apparently invested his in wildcat oil. And, if the Hollywood jungle drums were to be believed, in some other rather shady enterprises, like pornographic films. No one had ever come up with proof, but in this town no one has to. A rumor is accepted as fact until proven false, and even then the suspicion hangs in the air like the acrid smell of smoke a week after a fire.

I wrote all the information down in my notebook and then ransomed my car, jumped on the Santa Monica Freeway, turned south on the San Diego, and got off at Inglewood. It was lunchtime, and I stopped about six blocks from the airport at a Chinese restaurant on Century Boulevard across from a place where nude girls danced on tabletops and spread their knees for dollar tips from tired businessmen who had an hour to kill between planes. I ordered shrimp egg foo yung, which seemed fairly safe, and after lunch I went to the phone book and found out where the Inglewood post office was located.

It took me about ten minutes to discover Donald Stack's home address. Another fact that most people don't know unless they happen to be policemen or a professional bill collector—or private investigator—is that a post-office-box holder doing business with the public *must* supply a physical street address on request. The nice lady wearing the U.S. Postal Service uniform that made her look like the head bull in a women's prison told me Donald Stack lived in Playa Del Rey about six blocks from the condo where Peter D'Anjou had died.

I spent another twenty minutes driving over there and finding the house. It was not a particularly imposing edifice, just a nice middle-class tract home on a quiet residential street up in the hills above the beach, done in the style I always think of as California Coastal, a spare 1950s modernism of bleached wood and glass favored by many people who live near the sea. I rang the doorbell, but there seemed

110

to be no one home except a dog, a small one, if his high-pitched yipping was any indication, barricaded in the back yard and madder than hell at the interruption of his daily routine. I looked at my watch. It was just past one o'clock in the afternoon, and it didn't seem unreasonable that the homeowner was not there. Most normal people were at work at that hour. Don Stack, however, was incommunicado at his workplace, so I was going to have to come back later in the evening.

I went back to the office. Hollywood Boulevard had returned to sleazy normalcy, and all the flotsam that lives and works and hustles in the neighborhood was back out on the street for the out-of-town visitors to see and ponder whatever happened to the glamour capital of the world.

I threw one leg over the edge of Jo's desk, straining my bruised ribs. "Jo, I wanted to thank you again for the other night. It was really special—for both of us. Marvel had a great time, and so did I."

"It was a pleasure having you," she said, handing me a stack of pink phone messages. "My God, that kid can put it away. I'd say you weren't feeding him, but knowing you I suppose you do something fancy and fattening every night. Your cholesterol count must be in the six figures." She shook her head. "Sometimes I feel sad about you."

"Is this going to be the why-don't-you-find-a-nice-girl-and-get-married speech?"

"You're so damn fussy, that's your trouble. With you if a woman doesn't look like Miss America you aren't interested."

"I could never marry a Miss America, Jo. Picture it: we're in bed and I ask her what she wants, and she tells me her big wish is for peace all over the world and to bake oatmeal cookies for those who are less fortunate."

"Look, there are plenty of very nice women out there—"

"You aren't going to fix me up again, are you? The last friend of yours I went out with had thighs like a giant redwood."

111

"I wouldn't submit one of my girlfriends to your crap," she said, "so don't worry."

"Whew! That's out of the way, thank God. Want to do a little work?"

She rolled her eyes at the heavens, or at where the heavens would be were there not an acoustical tile ceiling and a fluorescent light in the way.

"See if you can discover where David Grayco has his office and find out if he's in and if he'll see me today."

"David Grayco? The producer? Fat chance. Do you think he's just sitting around waiting for your call?"

"Tell him it has to do with Vista Petroleum," I said. "That ought to get some kind of rise out of him."

It did. Five minutes later Jo was back saying Grayco would see me at Paramount Studios at four o'clock.

The Paramount lot is a landmark, especially the old De Mille Gate on Marathon Street just off Melrose Avenue, in a rather seedy neighborhood. It is the only major film studio left in Hollywood proper since Columbia moved their operations out to Burbank. There's a lot of movie history floating around in the ozone at Paramount along with the dust from the old soundstages. Perhaps it's not quite as potent as over at Warner Brothers, where the ghosts of Bogart and Cagney and Errol Flynn and Bette Davis hold sway, or at what's left of MGM in Culver City, where Gable and Tracy and Judy Garland and Lionel Barrymore might be right around the corner of the next soundstage. But Paramount was the studio of Hope and Crosby and Barbara Stanwyck and Alan Ladd and the young William Holden, and in later years Captain Kirk and Mr. Spock and their spacebound crew hung out there, and to a guy like me who loves the movies' golden era, it's always fun to visit.

The keeper of the gates directed me to a building on executive row where David Grayco kept a suite of offices. Every building on the lot has a different type of exterior that can be used as scenic window dressing for a film. It's commonplace to come in one morning and find a sign proclaiming the writers building to be a hospital and advising that only doctors may park there, and the next morning to discover it's been magically transformed into the Mason County Courthouse. One day there are trees on the sidewalks, the next day they are gone.

Grayco's office building, which he shared with two other producers, resembled a residential street that might have been anywhere in Europe; Amsterdam, perhaps, or Zurich. I was sure I'd seen it a dozen times on *Mission: Impossible*. It's no wonder the people involved in the making of films sometimes lose touch with reality.

Once inside, a dumpy middle-aged secretary who had probably been at the studio since the Adolph Zukor years gave me the kind of look reserved for garden slugs but supplied me with a cup of coffee strong enough to stand a pencil in upright. She disappeared into some inner sanctum to announce my arrival. Not surprisingly the only reading material on the table were copies of *Variety* and the *Hollywood Reporter,* neither of which I read because they are ninety percent press agent hype. I scanned a couple of movie reviews and then checked the obituary page to see if I had erred in getting up that morning. The only listings were for a film cutter at Universal, a vamp of the silent era, and an old-time radio announcer, so I figured I was safe. I don't know what the secretary did in the interior corridors of power besides tell David Grayco I was waiting, but I had read all the obits in both papers and finished the coffee by the time she came out to get me.

Grayco's private office was pleasantly elegant without being ostentatious, although it was at least three times as big as it needed to be. It was more like a large living room with a big glass desk over in one corner, its top pristine and uncluttered, as befitting a man too important to do anything as mundane as work. Expensive reproductions of Braque and Cézanne hung on the walls behind glass, and what was undoubtedly a genuine Persian rug stretched across the wide expanse of floor. Grayco was not at his desk but lounging on a sofa against one wall, a tumbler of what seemed to be vodka in his hand. Billy Ledbetter would not have approved. He was in his middle forties, tall and slim with sandy brown hair, a winter sunlamp tan, and blue eyes just squinty enough to let the casual observer know he played a lot of tennis. He wore a black suede zippered jacket and brushed cotton pants, and the ankle between his cuffs and his Gucci tasseled loafers was bare. Really cool movie guys don't ever wear socks. He was elegant-looking and well put together, but there was something slightly shoddy about him, like an antique gold watch the provenance of which is suspect.

Next to him on the sofa was a stunning-looking dark-haired woman, whom I recognized from a few minor movies of ten years ago and from pictures in the society pages as Grayco's long-time lady love, a semicelebrity actress named Jaclyn Johnson, who had, upon her arrival in the movie capital in the seventies, engaged in several well-publicized affairs with some of the most famous actors and executives in the business. Somehow the movie press always got wind of their names. Her life between the sheets had given her a good deal of notoriety and even a brief time—the zenith of any career and the unspoken dream of millions—when Johnny Carson did nightly jokes about her promiscuity. But the wide green eyes and pouty mouth that gave her the appearance of a depraved little girl had never brought her the major stardom she had craved, and so, past thirty-five and with no prospects of making a career breakthrough, she had opted for moving in with Grayco and being part of the Tinseltown social scene as one of the "fun" cohabiting couples. Between his films and her reputation, David and Jaclyn were firmly ensconced in that elite company often referred to as "the Beautiful People."

That's what the world's gossip press calls the stars and the socialites, the rich and famous, the used-to-be jet-setters, the people who let the Sunday supplement magazines come into their homes and take pictures of their living rooms. The ones who only go to the right parties and the right restaurants to be seen by other BPs and remarked upon, who put their heads together and make kissing sounds in the air by way of greeting, who don't need reservations at Primi or Le Dome or 72 Market Street. The husbands make mega-million-dollar distribution deals while their wives are home fucking their exercise coaches. The wives play tennis and head up fund-raising drives for arcane charities, while the husbands get blow jobs from starlets under the desk in the office. They drink too much blush wine and do too much coke and have sex orgies where nobody knows whose ass anyone is grabbing and no one really cares, and the world waits breathlessly to see at what "A-list" party they show up next and what they wear when they do. The women have their own special designers, favorite caterers, and pet performance artists who live in downtown lofts and deal crack; the men have each cultivated a real working cowboy or a hunting guide or a fishing boat captain whom they keep around to convince themselves that they are truly men's men. Those are the Beautiful People.

Let me tell you about the real beautiful people. The little Italian lady who runs a small restaurant and makes her own sausage and pasta fresh every day so she can control the quality. The neighborhood mechanic who takes an extra hour to work on your car without charging you for it because he doesn't want it to leave his shop until it's purring like a calico cat and running perfectly. The little old tailor from Poland who works magic with his fingers when you put on a few extra pounds and have to have your expensive suit let out but don't want anyone to know. The schoolteacher who's more interested in making your kid a decent human being than in teaching long division. Those are the real beautiful people, and don't let some Jello-head society columnist tell you any different.

But I had to deal with these particular Beautiful People at the moment, and the look on Grayco's face didn't make me feel all warm and tingly from the welcome.

"You've got a hell of a nerve coming in here, Saxon," he said by way of greeting. He had a reputation in the business of being pugnacious and difficult, and I suppose he felt honor-bound to live up to it. "I don't know what you hoped to gain by mentioning Vista Petroleum to my secretary, and I don't know what you want, but I was so taken by your colossal gall that I agreed to let you come over here so I could tell you off."

"It's nice meeting you, too," I said. "Both of you."

Jaclyn Johnson acknowledged me with an amused nod.

"You know," Grayco went on, "I've had actors approach me in the damnedest ways. They've thrown pictures and résumés over my fence at home; they've braced me on the street, in public restaurants, even while I was stopped at a red light. But this is the first time one ever claimed to be a private detective in order to get an appointment with me. You've been around this fucking town long enough to know this kind of showboat shit won't get you anything but a bad rap as a sicko."

I laughed. "Is that why you think I'm here?"

"Why else?" He looked at Jaclyn and smiled that very special smile lovers use to exclude everyone else in the room from their own private little understanding.

I took out the photostat of my PI license and handed it to him, and since no one had invited me to sit down I seized the opportunity to do so while he was looking at it. The whisper of a smile teased the corner of Jaclyn Johnson's mouth. She was wearing a knee-length skirt, and she uncrossed her legs and then recrossed them for my benefit, noticing me noticing. They were very good legs.

"Son of a bitch, you *are* a detective! I only know your work as an actor. You're not bad, either; you have good presence. Of course, I see you as a second lead, not the star—I'm sure you see yourself that way too. Well, what's this supposed to mean, anyway?" Grayco said, shoving the photostat back at me. The charm with which he navigated the shark-infested Hollywood waters seemed to have deserted him.

"It means I'm not here about a part in a movie," I said. "I'm looking into the death of a man named Peter D'Anjou."

116

"So? I never heard of him. What is he, an actor? He should have changed his name. Ethnic names are no good for a leading man, although I don't suppose you'll ever convince Al Pacino or Omar Sharif of that."

"Peter D'Anjou was a petroleum engineer who did some freelance consulting for Donald Stack."

Grayco's blue eyes turned to slits. "I still never heard of him."

"Aren't you one of the principal stockholders in Mr. Stack's company?"

Jaclyn dimpled and said, "I have about three thousand shares of AT&T, Mr. Saxon, but I don't know any of their repairmen."

I smiled back at her. Sleeping with telephone repairmen wouldn't have advanced her career any, which is why she probably didn't know any.

"Who told you I hold Vista stock?" Grayco demanded.

"It's not important," I said.

"It is to me."

"Well, it's a matter of public record. That's why they call them publicly owned companies."

"Thanks for the lesson in economics," he said. He shook his head and spoke more to Jaclyn than to me. "There's no privacy anymore. It's a sorry fucking thing to know you can't even take a pee without half the population of the English-speaking world knowing about it."

"Look, Mr. Grayco," I said, finally becoming annoyed, "it wasn't something your press agent planted in the trade papers. Nobody cares what stocks you own *or* when you pee. I've been looking in vain for Donald Stack and I found you were the other principal in Vista Petroleum and here I am. It's not that hard to figure out."

Grayco paused—I guess it took him a while to come to terms with the idea that no one cared about his bladder. Then he said, "I still haven't a clue as to why you want to talk to me."

I said, "I'd just like some background on Vista Petroleum and Don Stack, that's all."

He shrugged and waved a hand airily at me. "Vista owns one oil well down in El Tercero which at the moment is yielding a whole lot of muddy water and not much else. Don is the head honcho, and when he bought that lease he needed some start-up money, so I invested in him. End of story."

"Wait a minute," I said. "You say that well isn't producing?"

He smiled strangely. "Nope. Not a drop."

"I understood it pumped about five hundred barrels a day."

"That was at the beginning," he said. "Now, nothing."

"You don't seem very upset about it."

"I got my money out," he said with a smugness I couldn't quite fathom. "And then some. You win a few, you lose a few."

"And you didn't know Peter D'Anjou was working for Stack?"

"How the hell should I know who's working for him? When I produce a picture I don't know the names of the crew either. It's an investment, for Christ's sake, not a way of life."

"Is that a pattern, Mr. Grayco? You invest in things but don't really want to know where the money comes from?"

His sneer turned dangerous all of a sudden. "If you're implying what I think you're implying, I'll have you in court so fast the breeze will muss up your pretty hair. And you'll be using that license of yours as wallpaper."

I wasn't impressed by the threat, but I changed my tone anyway. I wasn't finished asking questions. "I'm not implying anything," I said.

"You've been around too long to believe a bunch of vicious rumors started by people green with jealousy. The bigger you are, the bigger a target you become. I'm frankly sick of it, and so are my lawyers."

I turned to Jaclyn, trying hard to look at her face and not her knees. "How about you, Ms. Johnson? Ever hear the name?"

She batted her phony lashes at me. "Which name is that?"

"Peter D'Anjou."

She wet her lip gloss. "Sounds French."

She was as subtle as an avalanche. "I suppose."

She shook her head, never taking her eyes off me. "I don't recall it."

"Are you a Vista stockholder, too?"

She shook her head. "All *my* investments are blue chip."

"Look, I think I saw something about this on the news," Grayco said. "Didn't they arrest his girlfriend or something?"

"Yes," Jaclyn Johnson said, "and she was married, too." Her eyes widened in mock shock. I wasn't sure if she was putting me on, or Grayco, or the whole world.

"Mr. Grayco, you said that Vista Petroleum just owned the one well. Were they doing any other exploration? I mean, did Stack have plans to drill anywhere else?"

"We talked about that before I gave him the money. His intention was to eventually buy other leases but for the moment he was going to concentrate on Vista Number One, because he said it was a sure money-maker."

"That lease was originally owned by Gamble Oil, wasn't it?" I said.

"I'm not sure of that, but I think so."

"And they gave up the lease because the well had run dry."

Jaclyn purred, "That sounds like a line from a country western song."

"But yet, when Don Stack bought the lease, the well began producing again. How do you explain that?"

"I don't," he said. "I'm in the picture business, not the oil business. You want to talk box office grosses in Detroit over the holidays? You want to talk distribution deals, negative pickups, how much a hit song on a soundtrack can goose up the admissions? I'm your guy. But you want to talk the technicalities of getting oil out of the ground, I'm a vestal virgin. I bought stock in Vista Petroleum the way I

119

buy stock in a lot of things—because I have faith in the company and in its management."

"And I guess that faith was repaid with profit."

"That's the American way."

"You mind telling me how much profit?"

He put his glass on the table with a loud clunk and stood up. "You're double D right I mind! You've got the guts of a burglar coming in here and asking personal questions like that. I'm doing you a goddamn favor just talking to you."

"The police won't put it on a favor basis."

"The police won't be coming around, and if they do, they won't do doodley-squat, and you know it. I never met this French guy, I didn't know who he was working for or why, I never even heard his name until he got himself snuffed and made the eleven o'clock news. And if the local *ton ton macoute* think they can come in here and poke around in my financial records, my lawyers will make rat shit out of them. And speaking of my lawyers, I'm going to instruct them that if you ever come near me again, or even call me on the phone, they are to institute proceedings against you for harassment and invasion of privacy." He looked at me as though I'd come in the door on the bottom of somebody's shoe. "It's no fucking wonder your acting career is in the crapper," he said.

12

By the time I arrived back at the office, Jo had already gone for the day, but she'd left a stack of pink phone messages in the middle of my desk. The only one that interested me was from Billy Ledbetter. I poured myself a Johnnie Walker Black Label before I called him back. That's not my preferred Scotch, but my brand, Laphroaig, is not to everyone's taste, and the office bottle is for company. After my meeting with David Grayco and Jaclyn Johnson, however, I needed a relaxer.

Finally, after the Black Label kicked in, I called the Ledbetters. Kim answered the phone.

"Oh, hi," she said. "Hang on a sec, I'll get Billy."

She sounded friendly enough but was a bit abrupt. That bothered me. Billy was his usual garrulous self on the phone, and he told me Jason Gamble had agreed to see me the next morning at ten. "It's easier getting hold of the pope," Billy said, "but I managed it. Old Jesse used to answer his own phone, but these young people today don't feel important unless there's nine secretaries screening their calls."

"Thanks, Billy."

He said craftily, "I understand you had a little set-to with Jim Shay the other night."

"Kim tell you that?"

"Kim and about four other people. The jungle drums work full time in our business."

"Is Kim angry with me?"

"You'll have to ask her that," he said. "Why don't you come over tonight?"

"Are you sure she wants me to?"

"I want you to, damn it!"

"I have to go home and feed my son first."

"That's all right," he said, "there's some Glenmorangie here with your name on it."

"Okay," I said. "And Billy, I really appreciate your help with Gamble."

"Hell, I'm happy to do it. Gives me something to do besides sit here watching the waves and wishing I was out someplace getting my hands dirty. See you about nine?"

"With bells on," I said.

I drove home to Venice wearily. The sky was tarnished silver plate, and I could almost taste metallic rain in the air, hanging over the basin like an unspoken threat. Since it was now four days past Thanksgiving, tinsel and shiny paper festooned the store windows, and the billboards featured Santa Claus and colored bows and merry glittering wreaths. The city was strapping on its holiday clothes, and like an old drag queen wearing too much makeup, it wasn't fooling anybody. I stopped at the butcher's and bought two nice steaks, a hollow attempt to get into a festive mood.

When I got home I marinated the meat for a few minutes while I chatted with Marvel about his school day. I felt really proud of the kid. He said he had a history exam to cram for, and we discussed the Founding Fathers for a while as I baked a few potatoes and popped the steaks under the broiler, the weather being too uncertain to risk outdoor charcoal broiling, and when the phone rang I didn't want to answer it. But the curiosity that got me into the investigating business in the first place won't allow a ringing phone to go unanswered, and so I picked it up after the fourth ring.

"George Amptman here," he said. "What's going on? I haven't heard from you in two days."

"I'm working on it, Mr. Amptman," I said.

"For what I'm paying you that's not a very satisfactory answer."

"It's going to have to do."

"In my business we pay a man money, we expect results."

"In my business," I said, "I weed out all the clients that lean on me when I'm doing the best job I can. You can always tell me to forget it. There are other investigators."

"Saxon, it seems that every time we talk, you get defensive and threaten to quit. Are you always this prickly?"

"Usually I'm a pussycat, Mr. Amptman." I glanced at my watch and then at the door of the broiler. The steaks were too expensive to burn, especially for a jerk like this. "But frankly, you piss me off when you talk to me like one of your serfs. And in the future I wish you'd confine your calls to my office during working hours unless there's an emergency. This is my home, I have a family, and I don't like bringing my business where I live."

"Perhaps not, but I think I'm entitled to a progress report."

"When there's any solid progress, you'll get one. But I'm not going to come running to you every time I scratch my ass. That's the way I work, and you can live with it or not."

He was silent for a moment, then I heard him sigh. Through the phone it sounded like a Kansas twister. "Very well," he said. "What are you going to do next?"

"Eat my dinner," I said.

I guess I put the receiver down none too gently, because Marvel was grinning at me.

"Was that the nigger man?" he said. "Every time you talk to him, your eyes get all Chinese." And he did a passable imitation of the way I narrow my eyes when I'm angry. It made me laugh, even though I knew that my inability to keep my inner feelings off my face had, over the years, cost me a small fortune.

"That's not me," I said, "that's Charles Bronson. Now

you want to do Jimmy Stewart, or are you going to set the table?"

He chuckled off to the kitchen. He knows how to push my buttons. I followed him in, turned the steaks, and did a sauce of butter, garlic, and crumbled Roquefort cheese to slather on them and managed to scrape together some salad fixings from the leftovers in the fridge. It's downright foolhardy to leave anything edible where Marvel can find it, because it has a way of disappearing, often in a matter of seconds.

After dinner Marvel repaired to his room with Alexander Hamilton, Ben Franklin, and Miles Davis, not necessarily in that order of importance, and I rinsed off the dinner dishes, stacked them in the sink, and took a quick shower before going out.

It was only eight thirty by the time I got down to the South Bay, so before hitting the oceanfront highway to Billy and Kim's place, I decided to use my time effectively. I drove up into the hills of Playa Del Rey to where Donald Stack lived. I really didn't expect him to be home, but it wasn't too far out of my way and I was becoming curious about him. I was beginning to think he was a mythical creature, like Bigfoot or the Tooth Fairy.

There were no lights on in the house, although a single sixty-watt bulb glowed beside the front door, and the dog was still barking. I thought about getting out and looking around, but it was dark out, there was obviously no one home, and if any of Stack's next-door neighbors kept guns in the house, I didn't want them mistaking me for a burglar and getting nervous and overeager and thinking they were Rambo. I drove up to the end of the narrow street, made a U-turn, and started back down to Vista Del Mar, when I was momentarily blinded by the high beams of a large white car that swung onto the street and came toward me. I slowed, pulled over to the curb, and watched while the car, a Lincoln Continental, rolled to a stop in Stack's driveway. A man got out on the driver's side and ran around to open the door for the passenger. I saw her legs come out of the car first. Whatever else might follow would have to be an anticlimax.

The Lincoln's door slammed with that comfortable, luxurious-sounding *snick* you only hear in an expensive car. The two people went to the front door of the house and the man began fumbling with his keys. I swung out of my car and called out, "Mr. Stack?"

He stopped his key jingling and they both looked over at me. The woman's upper half didn't nearly live up to the promise of her legs. She had a wide, tough mouth that seemed drawn back toward her ears, and her hair was a helmet of dyed gold rendered stiff with hair spray. Donald Stack was a size forty-two portly, with a fast-disappearing hairline and a muscular neck. In his mid forties, he wore a tan sports jacket over a chocolate shirt open to reveal his hairy chest, but I could imagine him in work denims and a hard hat. He put his right hand into his jacket pocket like Jack Kennedy used to.

"I'm Don Stack. What is it?" he said.

I walked into the glow cast by his porch light. The little dog in the back yard was going berserk.

"Who are you?" Stack's eyes moved from my face to my gray hair, and he shifted his body a bit to show me more profile. Then he said, "You're Saxon."

I already knew that.

"I heard all about you. You were poking around my well on Saturday, weren't you? And then you messed up my driller. Hard to believe a guy like you could take Jim Shay." He took me in from head to toe the way a barfly might scrutinize a pretty woman on the adjoining stool. I guess I didn't pass his physical. "Shay says you fight dirty."

"Wouldn't you?" I said.

He laughed at that, then handed the woman the keys. "Go on in, honey, fix yourself a drink. I'll be right in."

The woman gave me a wounded look, turned the key in the lock, and went inside, disappointment at the exclusion hardening her mouth even more. The front yard sprang to life as the lights went on behind the living room drapes.

"So what's the deal, Saxon? You gonna throw pepper in my eyes and sucker-punch me too?"

"I wasn't planning on it."

"A good thing," he said, and took his hand out of his pocket. There was a little nickel-plated .32 in it, but he wasn't pointing it in my direction, simply showing it to me. "I'm not as dumb as Shay is."

"You're dumber, if you go waving that thing at people."

"The oil business can get rough," he said, only he pronounced it "bidness." There was a lot of Texas in his speech, not the mushy hill-country accent of Lyndon Johnson but the harsher, flatter sounds of the lowlands. "This is my pocket insurance policy. What do you want?"

"I've been trying to talk to you for the last couple of days, but you're a tough man to track down. So I came up here to see if you were a homebody."

"Where'd you get this address?"

"I'm a detective, remember?"

"Is this some sort of a shakedown? It won't work, boy. If you think you can bounce me around you have stepped in shit."

"You have a suspicious mind, Mr. Stack. I just want to talk, and it won't cost you a dime."

He hefted the toy pistol in his palm and then slipped it back into his pocket. I guess he thought I wasn't much of a threat. "Why don't you people just leave me alone?" he said.

"What people?"

"Forget it. Look, I don't want to talk now. I've got something going. You know." He inclined his head toward the house with a conspiratorial just-guys smile, hoping I'd back off so he could go inside and get laid.

"I know," I said. "What about tomorrow?"

"Late afternoon is okay."

"Four o'clock?"

"Come by the shack at the well."

"With Shay there? No, thanks."

"I'll see to it he behaves himself, if that's what's worrying you."

"It's not worrying me, but it's a consideration."

"Forget it," he said. "Jim does what I tell him to."

"Then you must have told him to start something with me the other night."

In the semidark I could see his chest expand as he took a breath. He let it out. "I'm beginning to want to talk to you as much as you want to talk to me. Four o'clock tomorrow at the well." He looked at me for a long moment and then turned and went inside. I didn't try to move toward him; he'd shown me his insurance policy. I got back in my car, drove down the street to where I could see the house, and waited. After about ten minutes the light went off in the living room and another one went on upstairs in what I assumed to be a bedroom. I was getting damn sick of sitting in my car in the damp dark while everyone else was inside making the beast with two backs.

I cruised quietly to the bottom of the hill, turned left, and headed down the coast on Vista Del Mar. The wet, cold ocean mist spattered against my windshield, and finally I had to get the wipers going. It wasn't exactly rain, it was just wet air. I drove past Stack's Vista Number One where I saw a light burning in the doghouse up on the side of the hill, then past the sprawling prisonlike grounds of Gamble Oil, and finally to the Ledbetter place, which looked warm and inviting, like a hostel in the Alps.

I labored up the hill. It was no wonder Billy didn't leave the house much; at his age, too many trips up that grade might cause serious complications. He came out on the porch to greet me, the yellow light silhouetting him from behind. "I'm glad to see you," he said. "I was about to start without you."

It was cozy inside, with a fire crackling and the lamps turned low, and the Glenmorangie was warm too. Kim wasn't there, apparently.

"Young Jason," Billy said, "is anxious to talk with you. He's pretty shaken up over what happened to D'Anjou."

"Gamble was the one who fired him in the first place."

"I s'pose he was, but the man's dead now. All bets are off." He took a bite of his drink as if it was important to him. "You ever think about dying?"

"The subject comes up every so often."

He wiggled his scrawny butt deeper into the cushions of his chair. "It's not fair," he said. "A young man like that especially, but at any age it's not fair. There's always something more that you want to do, that one last big one you want to finish. And then there's one more after that."

"I guess you just have to be grateful for the time you're given, Billy."

"Oh, hell, I've had a good run at it, and I'd be happy even if all I'd had were my mistakes. I guess when you get to my age you start thinking about one more."

"One more what?"

"Gusher, in my case. But one more anything would do. One more deal, one more drink, one more beautiful woman. We humans are greedy little bastards, if you look at it that way."

"Some more than others."

"That's true. Especially in oil. You take Jason Gamble, for instance. He's got it all—big company, big profits, a good reputation in the industry and invites to the White House every so often. But it still grabs him in the ass every time he passes a Texaco station and realizes the oil they're selling isn't his."

"It's the nature of the beast," I said. "There's no such thing as enough, for any of us. The trick is to be happy with not quite enough. Otherwise you just make yourself crazy."

"There's a lot of crazies out there. Is that what makes 'em that way?"

"It's as good an explanation as any." I thought it was time for a change of subject. "Billy, what do you know about this Donald Stack?"

"Not much from firsthand experience. His background is in sales, though."

"Oil sales?"

"Yep. He was with several of the majors before he decided to wildcat." He shook his head. "A salesman can sell anything—suits of clothing, tenpenny nails, life insurance. But it takes an oilman to produce oil."

"You don't approve of Stack?"

"Hell, it's not for me to approve or dis."

"But you don't like him?"

"I'm not sure I'd trust him. He's a sharper."

"How do you mean, Billy?"

He went to get us another round before he answered. When he'd settled back down, he said, "The locating and producing of oil is not an exact science, no matter what technocrap these egghead kids come up with in their schools. It's always a risk. And it's a capital-intensive industry, too, so there's always people around on the fringes looking to make a quick buck without really getting dirt and crude under their nails. Now, this Don Stack, he's about as much of an oilman as my aunt Fanny, but all of a sudden he buys up this watered-out lease, starts drilling, and hits paydirt. Next thing you know he's on the big sprocket."

I laughed. "Translation, please?"

"He's a big shot, joins the Petroleum Club, starts acting like he's J. Paul Getty himself, with one lousy well. There was some kind of lawsuit with Gamble Oil, but it was all kept pretty damn quiet and no one knows what happened, except that the word went out it's costing Jason Gamble a bundle."

"When was this lawsuit?"

"About nine or ten months ago, I think."

"And who sued whom?"

"Stack sued Gamble Oil—he seems to be a litigious little bastard—but the case never got to court."

"And you don't know what the suit was about?"

129

"Like I said, it never went public. Jason didn't let it get that far."

"An out-of-court settlement?"

"Nobody knows for sure. But Jason seemed to think that Stack had dug a deviated hole."

I shook my head again, and Billy said, "Sorry, I keep forgetting I'm talking to a civilian. All wells are off the vertical to one degree or another. But some of the shafts are so deviated that the actual bottom hole can be about two thousand feet away from the surface location. And Jason seemed to think that Stack's hole slanted right into Gamble property."

"Then Gamble sued Stack?"

"Nope. The other way around. Why, I don't know." He slurped at his drink. "Say, look here, what's all this got to do with this D'Anjou boy's murder?"

"I don't know, Billy. Maybe nothing. But it's worth looking into."

He set his glass down on the coffee table. "We're talking about a lot of money here, son. You stick your nose in where it shouldn't be, you might get it cut off."

"I've got a pretty tough nose," I said.

"You showed that with Jim Shay the other night."

"You think Shay was told to come after me?"

"I don't know. He's a big, mean mother, and it could be he was just jealous about Kim. But I wouldn't put twenty bucks on it. You just watch that nose."

I heard a car's engine outside, then it cut off and the car door opened and closed. Billy Ledbetter was twinkling at me when I glanced over at him. "Looks to be about my bedtime," he said.

Kim came in the front door, bundled up against the chill in a quilted jacket, her nose slightly red from the cold. People from Minnesota would laugh at it, but a few years in Southern California and the blood thins, making us extremely sensitive to temperatures below fifty-five degrees, and to dampness of any kind. Kim seemed surprised to see me, and not too happy about it.

"We've been talking oil," Billy said. "Come join us."

She stared at me. "I was invited," I said.

"I don't know. It's kind of late."

"Horse pucky!" Billy said. "Sit down, girl."

Kim shrugged out of her jacket. She was wearing blue jeans, serviceable Wranglers, topped by a faded University of Oklahoma sweatshirt. She sat down on the sofa with me—at the far end.

"How was the movie?" Billy asked.

"It was all right. Nothing to write home about. Well," she said with a kind of false heartiness, "have you had a nice visit?" It was the kind of remark I would expect from a nurse in a British old-age home.

"I've learned a lot," I said. "But then I've found all my dealings with this family to be enjoyable and informative."

Kim shot me a look which could have started a new Ice Age. Billy caught it and made a big show of coughing. "Well, me for a nice warm bed," he said, pulling his old bones out of his chair. "No need for you to run home on my account. Stay and talk to Kim for a while."

I stood up too and we shook hands. He put his face close to mine and said, "Mind your nose, now," and with a dry chuckle disappeared into the back of the house.

Kim was trying to memorize the fire when I sat back down, and the silence was long enough to drive a convoy through. I took another pull on my drink. "Are you mad at me?"

"No," she said.

"Are you glad with me?"

She laughed in spite of herself. Then she sobered and said, "I don't expect you to understand."

"Try me."

She curled her legs under her. "What happened the other night upset me a lot."

"I can see where it would. But it wasn't my fault."

"Maybe not," she said. "But I've spent a lot of time around oil roughnecks, and I hate it. It's like the whole evo-

131

lution of the human species gets thrown out the window. There's got to be a better way to settle an argument."

"I agree with you," I said. "I don't like to fight. But there's no avoiding hardcases, Kim. They're everywhere. If any good came out of Saturday night, it's that Shay might think twice before he tries to muscle the next guy. And if it's any consolation, I don't think you had anything to do with Shay's coming after me. You were just a convenient excuse. I met him where he works that afternoon, and he would have torn me apart then if he could have gotten to me."

"Why?"

"That's what interests me. It has something to do with Donald Stack, I think. They're trying to hide something at that well, and they don't like the idea of my asking questions. Mail carriers get chased by dogs, construction workers fall off beams, and private detectives sometimes get punched. Occupational hazard." I moved closer to her on the sofa. "He called the play, I didn't. I planned to walk along the beach after dinner with my arm around you, stopping every so often and look into those incredible china blue eyes and kiss you. Part of my anger with Shay was that he screwed that up."

She smiled faintly. "China blue?"

"Like the blue on a delft plate."

The smile brightened. "It wasn't a bad plan," she said. "It could still work."

13

The next morning at ten o'clock I was back at the main gate of Gamble Oil trying to convince the guard I wasn't a Soviet spy or a flasher or there to steal a Xerox machine. When I finally got through all the checkpoints and had been issued a badge assuring everyone who saw me that I was somehow safe, I found myself up on executive row again, this time looking for a door marked OFFICE OF THE PRESIDENT. It wasn't hard to find, located as it was at the end of the corridor behind a double door made of sterner stuff than the others on the floor. I could almost hear the heavenly chorus as I opened it and stepped into the waiting room, sinking ankle deep into the rust-colored plush of the carpeting.

The woman behind the glass reception desk was in her late thirties, attractive, slim and efficient, wearing aviator glasses and a light gray power suit. In the movie or television business she would have been twenty-two, fluffed blond hair surrounding a head full of air and breasts like the prow of a minesweeper. This one could be the company president herself. That's the way she moved, anyway. I sensed an underlying femininity that was strangely exciting coming across the big desk. She put out her hand for me to shake. It was soft and warm, with slim tapering fingers, but the handshake was firm and no nonsense.

"You must be Mr. Saxon," she said. "I'm Agatha Rusk, Mr. Gamble's assistant."

"It's nice to meet you," I said.

"He's expecting you. Won't you have a seat?"

I sat in one of the big leather chairs opposite her desk and tried to remember if I'd ever met anyone before whose name was Agatha. She offered me coffee or tea, which I declined, and then excused herself and disappeared behind another door. I glanced around the waiting room. It was full of framed awards and browning photographs of old oil wells and old oilmen. The one that caught my attention was almost directly behind my head; I had to turn all the way around to look at the shot of the powerfully built white-haired man in a three-piece suit, circa 1950. With him was a younger and more vigorous-looking Billy Ledbetter. I imagined the white-haired gentleman was Jason Gamble's father, Jesse. The two men were grinning for the camera, their arms encircling each other's shoulders, and each was holding a champagne glass in such a way that it was obvious neither of them drank champagne. It reminded me of a photograph of Branch Rickey and Walter O'Malley that hangs in the Dodgers front office.

Agatha Rusk came back out, leaving the door open, and asked if I wouldn't come in. I would.

Jason Gamble rose from behind his massive desk to greet me. He was a big man, taller than I and heavier, with short curly sand-colored hair beginning to gray. Billy Ledbetter had referred to him as "young Jason," once again proving that everything is relative. Jason Gamble looked a bit like his father in the photograph, without the aura of power and authority. His handshake was hearty and friendly. "Come in, Mr. Saxon, I'm glad to meet you. You know Mr. Tomita, I believe?"

I glanced to my right at the little Japanese standing in front of one of the two visitors chairs, and he bowed stiffly to me. Next to Jason Gamble he looked like a half grown child. I bowed back, then took the chair Gamble was indicating.

"Can I get you something? Coffee? Or a drink?"

134

"It's a little late for coffee and too early for anything else, thanks, Mr. Gamble. I know you're busy."

"Hell, that's all right," Gamble said as he took his seat behind the desk again. "Billy Ledbetter thinks the sun rises and sets on you. He and my father go back more years than either of us care to remember. You want to talk about Pete D'Anjou."

"That's right."

"Well, anything that I can do to help, count me in. I was sickened by what happened. Peter was a good man, and a friend."

"You were close, then?"

"He was like a son—check me on that; a younger brother."

"But Mr. Tomita tells me that six months ago he was let go at your request."

Gamble shrugged. "Those things happen," he said, "but in no way does it reflect on my personal regard for him. This is a business, after all, not a country club."

"D'Anjou was bad for business, then?"

"As I told you," Mr. Tomita put in, "that is a matter of confidentiality to the company."

"I was hoping to have that confidentiality waived under the circumstances. That's why I asked to see you, Mr. Gamble."

"I'm not sure I understand what you want," Gamble said.

"Let's start with the reason for D'Anjou's dismissal."

"Well," he said, and rubbed his hand roughly over his eyes and nose. "Let's see." He cocked his head, thinking. I wasn't sure if he was trying to come up with just the right phrase, or just the right story. "This is a tough, competitive industry, Mr. Saxon, and it requires the sort of commitment that entails a certain amount of sacrifice, if you know what I mean."

"What kind of sacrifice?"

"It's more than a nine-to-five job. The wells pump twenty-four hours a day, and that's about what the hours

135

are on the job. It's tough to keep a step ahead of the wolves and maintain a social life. You can hunt for oil or you can hunt for pussy, but you can't do both."

This seemed to amuse Mr. Tomita, who giggled like a junior high school girl caught looking at a *Playgirl* centerfold.

"But he was employed here for, what, eleven years?"

"Right," Gamble said, "and for ten of them he was a model employee. But when he hit his middle thirties I guess he started worrying that time was running out in the female department."

I certainly didn't want to hear that time runs out in the female department in the middle thirties.

"We had several conversations about it," Jason Gamble went on. He glanced at Tomita. "Personal conversations, Kenji; I didn't see any point in bringing you into it. I didn't want anything going into his personnel jacket until I'd exhausted all the options."

"Was there any woman in particular?" I asked.

"Anything that moved," Gamble said. "That was the problem. You can have a career and a relationship. You just can't make getting laid your career. I cut him as much slack as I could, because he was a friend. Then I had to say goodbye."

"I suppose you know he went to work for Don Stack after leaving Gamble Oil."

Gamble tried to look noncommittal. It didn't work. "I could only be glad for Peter that he hooked on somewhere else local. I had no problem with that."

"Even though Stack had filed a lawsuit against you?"

The innocent look fell away like Salome's veils. "One thing had nothing to do with another."

"Would you mind telling me what the lawsuit was about?"

"Yes, I would," Gamble said, putting his palms flat on his desk. "There are some things about this company that stay within the four walls, Peter D'Anjou notwithstanding. And you ask some damn funny questions for an insurance investigator."

I'd almost forgotten the lie I told Tomita to get into Gamble Oil in the first place. "Okay," I said.

"Okay?"

"Okay. You said you were glad D'Anjou found something local. Are local jobs hard to come by?"

"Well, they're the most desirable ones, so they get snapped up the quickest. There's lots of oil jobs around if you want to go live somewhere fun like Jakarta or Dubai or Aleppo where you taste sand in your morning coffee, have to tiptoe everywhere so as not to offend local and religious customs, and never see a woman anywhere who isn't wearing a veil."

"Had D'Anjou worked abroad?"

"Sure. That's where we start all our people. They have to earn the right to come back home."

"And where did D'Anjou get his wings?"

"India and Pakistan," Gamble said.

"Did he make any enemies over there?"

Gamble snorted. "If he did, they waited a hell of a long time to do anything about it. Peter had been back in the states for eight years."

"Did he know Mr. Khali in India?"

Tomita's sparse eyebrows went up. "You know Mr. Khali?"

"I had the pleasure of speaking with him on Sunday evening. You'll be happy to know he was very supportive of your company's confidentiality."

"What did he tell you?" Tomita asked.

"Not much. That's why I'm here."

Gamble said, "As far as I know the two men never met before Khali came to work for me here. At least, neither of them ever said anything about it."

"And what about stateside enemies?"

"He had no company enemies. There were those he got along with better than others, like anybody else, but no real

137

enemies." Gamble sat back in his chair; with its high back it looked like a pope's throne. "Mr. Saxon, you're overlooking something that's as plain as a pimple on your nose. The police have made an arrest and the district attorney's going for an indictment. I figure the scenario went something like this: Pete was screwing this woman and maybe got tired of her, and she doesn't take rejection well. It certainly jibes with what I've been telling you, doesn't it?"

"It certainly does, Mr. Gamble. Perhaps a little too neatly."

"What do you mean by that?"

I said, "Have you ever passed on a lease that turned out to be worth a small fortune?"

"Every company has done that," he said with some rue.

"I wonder why," I said, "when it must have been as plain as a pimple on your nose."

It was just past eleven when the security guards let me out of Gamble Oil, and I couldn't say I'd learned a hell of a lot, although sometimes when you think you've got nothing, later it turns out to be something. It was frustrating, too, to think I was just a few yards from Vista Petroleum and Donald Stack but that I had to wait another five hours to see him. So I checked in with Jo at the office, who told me I had messages to call George Amptman and Joe DiMattia, neither of whom I felt like talking to. I drove back downtown and once more went into the hall of records.

Gamble might have forgotten more about the oil industry than most people will ever know, having been born to it, but he didn't know much about information gathering. Every lawsuit filed in the state is listed in the civil index, a public document that anyone can look at to their heart's content. It would have saved me some trouble if he'd told me about it himself, but I somehow preferred the official version to that of anyone who was involved with the suit. An interested party's rendering of a story can put Ted Turner and his colorization ghouls to shame.

Bill had told me Stack's suit against Gamble had occurred

about nine months before, so I began with February first and started working forward from there. Some of the cases I thumbed through were small-potatoes stuff, grist more suited for the mill of *The People's Court;* some of them were for more substantial amounts. But the lawsuit filed by Vista Petroleum against Gamble Oil in March was a whopper: Vista was asking damages of fifty million dollars.

I took off my jacket and hung it over the back of the chair, put on my glasses, and began to read.

Two years earlier, Donald Stack had bought up an oil lease originally belonging to Gamble. It had quit producing oil about twelve years before, and Gamble had sold off the lease to a corporation called Pacifica Properties, before Vista Oil stepped in and took over from Pacifica. Vista drilled a new well, hit a big pocket of oil, and had begun pumping an average of five hundred barrels a day. Apparently Vista's neighbor, Gamble Oil, had suspected Stack of slant-hole drilling under the property boundaries into the Gamble fields and had demanded the right to inspect. Vista had been happy to acquiesce. Gamble drilled their own inspection shaft, only to find that Vista's hole was nowhere near their property. After the inspection, Vista One had dried up, yielding only water and mud, and they claimed that Gamble's newly drilled shaft had interfered with their production and caused them problems. The fifty million represented ten years' possible production, plus punitive damages. Some three months later, after a court date had been assigned, the suit had been withdrawn.

I wanted to know why.

I copied all the necessary information into my notebook, including the name of Stack's attorney, Harold Heubner. It wasn't quite one o'clock, so I headed back to the office.

When I arrived Jo was looking a little strained. "You have a visitor," she sang, glancing over her shoulder at my door.

"In my private office?" I said. "The sanctum sanctorum?" I went on past her to find Lieutenant Joe DiMattia sitting in my chair, watching a soap opera on my little black and white TV. Aurora was telling Keith that she wanted a divorce so she could marry Brent, who was little Bobby's natural father.

"Don't you return phone messages anymore, dickhead?"

"Patience, Joe, patience. You just called this morning."

His brown eyes glittered. "You don't mind my taking your chair?"

"Mi casa es su casa," I said. "What's on your mind, Joe?"

"It's come to my attention," he said, "that you're messing around my case."

"What case is that?"

"Don't fuck with me, Saxon, 'cause I'm mean as shit."

"Oh," I said, "you must mean the D'Anjou murder."

He settled back and laced his fingers over his bulging paunch. DiMattia wears suits that went out of style in 1958, and today's little number was a grayish-brown double-breasted you'd buy in a thrift shop for a theme costume party. His necktie resembled the one Barton MacLane wore in *The Maltese Falcon.* "That's very good," he said. "Talk to me before I tear your nose off for the fun of it."

"I was under the impression that it wasn't an open case anymore," I said. "You arrested Nanette Amptman; the district attorney is pressing for an indictment. You're out of it."

"I'm out of it until concerned citizens call up and bitch that you're running up their arm," he said. "You know how I hate talking to assholes, don't you? So I'm back in it again, because of you. And I want some fucking answers—*now.*"

"What concerned citizen might you be referring to, Joe?"

"One with enough clout to give me a migraine."

"David Grayco, perhaps?"

"Then you admit it?" The only thing missing from the sentence was the "A-*ha!*"

I said, "I'm trying to get Nanette off the hook, that's all. It doesn't compute, Joe, and you know it, and if the DA wasn't such a guts-and-glory guy, he'd know it too."

He sighed audibly, a note beginning at the top of the scale

and sliding downward like a pigeon dying on the wing. "Why can't these goddamn people leave me alone?"

"The man loves his wife."

His glower almost took my head off. "She's a hooer," he said. I hadn't heard it pronounced that way since I was a kid on the West Side of Chicago.

"If we sent everyone to the gas chamber whose morals didn't meet your exacting standards, Joe, Los Angeles would be a small inconsequential village."

He savored the fantasy for a moment. Then he said, "You're a hooer too. You'll take anybody's money, no matter how dirty. Even to get a killer off."

"If I find out she is a killer I'll be the first one to cheerlead for the prosecution. But if she's not, she deserves every bit of my effort."

"And you don't care if the department comes off looking like dogshit."

"I don't follow."

"We've got a closed case, Saxon. You bust it open again it's going to make me look like a monkey."

"And that's worth sending up an innocent woman?"

"Innocent?"

"There's a lot of stuff going down here, Joe, all having to do with Gamble Oil and Vista Petroleum."

"What stuff?"

"I don't know what stuff," I said somewhat lamely.

"Would you know if I took you back to Culver City and bounced you off the walls for a few hours?"

"I don't have anything concrete."

"You don't have anything period, asshole. You're just mind-fucking these poor people and letting the meter run."

"I'm sure Mr. Amptman would be touched by your concern."

"I'm a public servant."

"And I'm the public," I said. "So you're fired."

He heaved himself out of my chair, and for a moment I thought he was going to hit me. Joe DiMattia dreamed of hitting me; it was a career goal for him, like socking thirty home runs in a season or winning the Cy Young Award. Then he said, "Just give me a reason—a breath of a reason—to lift your ticket. I need an excuse to throw a party."

He lumbered out into the reception room, leaving the door open. He stopped at Jo's desk and looked at her sadly, shaking his head. I thought he was going to give her the what's-a-nice-girl-like-you-doing-in-a-place-like-this speech. Instead he just said, "You ought to be ashamed of yourself. Your looks and brains, you could get a job anywhere." He didn't wait for her answer but walked out, and the atmosphere in the office lost its heavy density. DiMattia could brighten any room by leaving it.

I went out to Jo's desk. "Come on," I said, "put the phone on automatic pilot and I'll buy you lunch."

"You don't have to," she said. "He doesn't bother me half as much as he does you. He's just like that."

"I know I don't have to, I want to. I just don't feel like eating alone."

She switched the answering machine on and started putting on her coat. "Well," she said, "if it's an errand of mercy . . ."

We drove east on Hollywood Boulevard to a storefront Thai restaurant near Wilcox. Two transvestite hookers manned their posts on the corner. Both wore miniskirts, sky-high heels, puffy wigs, and looked about as much like women as Mike Tyson.

Jo ordered a Thai iced tea with lots of honey and cream, and I had an Amarit beer, and while we waited for our mee krob and pork and shrimp mince, I filled her in on the Amptman case.

She nodded, the intelligence snapping behind her quick dark eyes, and after I finished she said, "It doesn't sound like you have very much at all."

"I know," I said, "and that's the hell of it. It's entirely possible that Stack and Gamble are just chewing on one another and it has nothing to do with D'Anjou. And that leaves Mrs. Amptman twisting in the wind."

Jo sipped tea through her straw. "You don't like either of the Amptmans very much, do you?"

"They're hard to like. Especially him."

"But you don't believe she's guilty."

I took a deep breath and blew it out through compressed lips. "She just seemed too damn happy that night on her way to her lover. She didn't look like someone with murder on her mind."

Jo smiled. "That's as flimsy as generic toilet paper."

"I know," I said. "But I'm stuck with it."

"And you're going to Stack's this afternoon?"

"At four o'clock. I want to know why the tight security at an oil well that isn't producing. I want to know why he runs his business like it was the CIA. I want to know whether that goon tried to rearrange me on his own Saturday night or whether it was Stack's idea. And I want to know what Peter D'Anjou was working on for Stack when he was killed."

"And you think you can just walk in there and ask him?"

"Sure," I said. "Whether he'll answer me is another story."

We went back to the office after lunch, and I repaired to my inner room to call Donald Stack's attorney of record in the lawsuit he'd filed against Gamble.

"Mr. Heubner," I said after I'd introduced myself and told him what I was working on, "I'd like to know about that lawsuit."

"I'm afraid that's none of your business," he said. "And as a private investigator, you should know better than to ask."

"But the suit was suddenly dropped."

He said, "It was settled out of court."

"You can't discuss the settlement?"

"Can't and won't. You'll have to ask Mr. Stack or Mr. Gamble, I'm afraid."

"I just may do that."

"I might warn you, Mr. Saxon, that stirring up a lot of bad feelings and upsetting the applecart may be actionable."

"And I might remind you that withholding evidence in a murder case is a lot more serious than a parking ticket."

"Are you threatening me?"

"We seem to be threatening each other, which is a plentiful waste of time. So I'll just hang up, Mr. Heubner, before we descend to the level of my dad can lick your dad."

Lawyers, I thought. Mark Twain called them pettifogging bad lawyers, and Shakespeare suggested killing them all. Great writers, both of them.

Jo buzzed me. "More company. You're very popular today," she said.

Jaclyn Johnson came into my office wearing a fuzzy pink sweater and tight pink silk slacks through which her bikini panties were as visible as if she'd worn no slacks at all. She extended her hand to me; I think I was supposed to kiss it, but I didn't. I shook it instead.

"This is a pleasant surprise, Ms. Johnson."

"I like surprises, don't you?" She sat down on the leather couch against the wall and patted the cushion beside her. I wasn't much in the mood for game playing, but she had something to say and I didn't want to antagonize her, so I sat where she wanted me to.

"I got a kick out of the way you stood up to David at the studio yesterday," she said, the silk pants whispering as she crossed her legs. "Not many people do, you know. I'm afraid it rather shook him up. He's not used to it."

"Remind me to apologize."

She stuck out her lower lip in a grotesque Shirley Temple parody. "That'd spoil it."

I leaned against the back of the sofa and waited, trying to look at my watch discreetly. Whatever Jaclyn Johnson had to say, I hoped she'd do it quickly so I could get over to Vista Petroleum for my four o'clock meeting. But she didn't seem in any hurry; she was having too much fun playing the vamp, although she was pretty obvious about it. It wasn't surprising that her acting career had foundered.

"David didn't seem to want to talk to you very much," she said. "Seems a shame, your wasting the trip."

"Nothing is ever wasted. We learn from our mistakes."

"The trick," she purred, "is not to make any. Your big mistake was not pushing harder. David's a cream puff whenever anyone leans on him."

"And what should I have pushed him about?"

"How about Stack's suing Gamble for fifty million bucks?"

"Sorry," I said, "but I know all about that."

She looked disappointed. "You know they settled out of court?"

"Yes, but I don't know the terms."

She brightened. "Goody. I know something you don't."

"Are you going to tell me what it is, or do you like knowing secrets?"

"No," she said, her lower lip extended like Chevalier's. "I'll tell you if you're a good boy."

"The best," I said.

"I think I knew that already. Well, there's this law," she said, "that if in the course of an inspection of a well you cause that well to dry up or stop producing, then you are liable for what the well would have generated before you interfered. Did you know that?"

"News to me."

"Well, Jason Gamble knew it, and to avoid a costly trial he couldn't win anyway, he settled out of court with Stack."

"For how much?" I said.

"Vista Number One was pumping five hundred barrels a day. At eighteen dollars a barrel, which is more or less the going rate, it would have grossed nine thousand daily."

"Yes?"

"Times ten years. That's what Gamble is paying for: Vista One's lost oil production for ten years."

"My God," I said. "That's—"

"I'll save you the arithmetic. It's thirty-two million dollars. And change."

I didn't say anything. I didn't have the breath for it— thirty-two millions bucks took it away.

Jaclyn Johnson sat back, arching her back, very pleased with herself. "Now you can see why David isn't screaming about his investment."

"And Gamble is paying . . . ?"

"Once a year, three million something."

"But wouldn't Stack have to prove that the Gamble inspection caused the well to stop?"

She shrugged. "Five hundred barrels a day before the inspection, nothing two days after. It doesn't seem like there's anything to prove."

I sat there with a lot of ideas playing bumper cars in my head. Where would someone stop when thirty-two million bucks was on the line? Certainly not at murder. But what did Peter D'Anjou have to do with anything? Gamble had fired him three months after the suit was filed. There didn't seem to be any connection, but for my money it was too damn pat.

"Now aren't you glad I came?" Jaclyn said.

"More than I can tell you. My question is, why?"

"Why what?"

"Why come and tell me all this? Did Grayco send you?"

She threw back her head and laughed. "You're really kind of sweet, you know that? Dumb, but sweet." She reached over and put a red-nailed hand on the side of my face and stroked it slowly. "I came because I want to fuck you."

Jaclyn Johnson was one surprise after another. "You always take that long to get to the point?"

"Let's not joke around," she said. "I like being David Grayco's live-in. It opens doors for me, to a world I wanted to make but never could, and the pay is terrific. But there are things in this world besides a new Porsche every year." She took a pack of Virginia Slims from her purse and handed me an expensive gold lighter. Just an old-fashioned girl.

"I've always approached sex the same way men do," she said when I'd lit her cigarette. She smoked it as though the cameras were turning. "I see a guy I want, I do something about it. People make jokes about me, and the papers have a good time painting me as a modern Whore of Babylon, but I don't care. I'm more interested in what feels good. I feed my hedonism when and where I want to. And right now I want you."

"Why?"

"Well, you're good-looking, but so are a lot of other people. I told you I admire the way you spit in David's eye. Let's just say I like your style, and I'm wondering if it's just as good when you're horizontal."

"Did you want some references?"

"Don't kid yourself. If I wanted some, I'd get them. But I prefer my own instincts. They haven't failed me yet." She blew a cloud of smoke in my face. "Well?"

"Ms. Johnson," I began, and she interrupted me.

"If we're going to screw, don't you think you could call me Jaclyn?"

"If we were going to, I would."

The disbelief in her eyes was almost comical. "Are you turning me down?"

"I'm flattered you like my style," I said. "But I really don't much like yours. You make me feel like the prize package at a slave auction."

A rasp caught in her throat. "Nobody turns me down, son of a bitch!"

"I thought you liked surprises," I said.

"What do you want? Romance? Candlelight dinners and walks on the beach at night?"

"It would be nice," I said.

"You're talking about lovemaking, Saxon. Not fucking."

"It's not that I don't find you attractive. I don't like the deal, that's all."

"Is there someone else?"

"No. Just me."

"Christ, you're a child! You know what I'm offering you? There are ten million men that beat off every night fantasizing about me."

"I know," I said. "But I don't like feeling like a slab of beef. It would destroy the few illusions about myself I've got left. Thanks for the offer. And the information. I appreciate that."

I stood up and held out my hand to her. She took it, pulled herself upright, and then pressed my hand against her left breast. "What if I said I don't accept rejection well? Suppose I told you I was going to make getting into your pants my hobby?"

I smiled at her. "Then I'd suggest you go to the nearest hobby shop and get some electric trains instead. You can turn *them* on any time you want to."

Anger flared in her eyes like the sulphur on a lit match and died just as quickly. She dropped my hand and went to the door. "You're an interesting man," she said. "I'll be in touch."

And then there was nothing left of her in the room but the essence of her perfume, and a great deal of residual heat.

I looked out the window. A light drizzle was making little beaded pinpricks on the glass. It was time to leave if I didn't want to be late for my meeting with Donald Stack— at an oil well that was grossing him more than three million dollars a year by *not* producing any oil.

14

It took me almost an hour to drive about fifteen miles across town. Each afternoon in L.A. the homeward-bound workers rush westward lemminglike to the sea and create a traffic horror not even the sunniest disposition can withstand. Some commuters take advantage of the time to plug Berlitz language lessons into their car tape decks and learn Spanish or French; others more affluent speak on their cellular telephones. Most just sit and fume and clutch the steering wheel, experiencing an unreasoning glee whenever they are able to move more than ten miles per hour and promising themselves, often aloud, that they will be leaving Los Angeles any day now and moving someplace where the air is clean, the autos minimal, and the life-style wholesome and decent. The trouble is, there's not much else to recommend Zook, Kansas, and so the population of the Los Angeles basin continues to grow.

Sepulveda Boulevard was a parking lot, so I twisted in and out of traffic on streets like Rose and Culver until I finally reached Playa Del Rey and turned south on Vista Del Mar toward El Tercero. On summer weekends Vista Del Mar was as crowded as any main artery in town, but on this wet afternoon there wasn't much of a problem. The drizzle that had started in Hollywood had gotten serious about it and turned into a full-fledged rain.

I parked outside the gate at Vista Number One and slipped on the canvas raincoat I always keep in the back seat of my car between October and March. The ground under-foot had not yet turned to mud, but it was wet enough to suck at the soles of my shoes as I approached the fence and pushed the call button. I looked up at the doghouse as a figure appeared in the doorway and started down the hill. It was Jim Shay. When he got about thirty yards from me I could see the ugly bruises and swellings on his face, and I hoped that Donald Stack had given him a heart-to-heart talking-to. I put up the collar of my coat, but it wasn't only the rain that was giving me a chill.

We glared at one another in mute hatred through the chain link like two pit bulls in adjoining cages. Finally he said, "You got lucky Saturday night, pal. Don't count on it twice." There was sand in his voice that hadn't been there before, and I hoped I hadn't permanently damaged his vocal cords. He was a goon, but he wasn't *that* bad.

I said, "Let's bury the hatchet, Shay, what do you say?" But he didn't answer me. He just kept staring. Finally I said, "Are you going to let me in or what?"

He took a key from his pocket and opened the padlock as if it was his own idea. The gate swung outward, fast, and I decided to be charitable and believe he hadn't tried to bash me with it as it opened. He followed me up the hill, close enough behind to make me nervous. I wasn't armed, and even if I had been, you can't shoot a man for taking a swing at you, even if that swing is likely to shorten your spine by several inches if it connects.

When we reached the doghouse at the top of the hill and I opened the door, Shay suddenly disappeared out of sight around the corner. I don't know where he was heading, but I hadn't seen any other structures on the premises. Perhaps like a faithful hound he was going to huddle against the side of the building under the eaves, out of the rain.

Inside the doghouse was one long room, with several card tables and mismatched chairs along one wall, a few combat-veteran recliners, and a TV set that had probably seen *Leave it to Beaver* before it was in reruns. Against a far wall was an army cot, made up neatly, and another corner was walled off with some sort of flimsy partitioning material; I assumed that was the john. Just inside the door was a pipe-metal coatrack.

Opposite the door was Stack's desk, gray metal, functional, cluttered with papers arranged in no discernible order. Behind it and to the right was a locked steel filing cabinet, and next to it an off-model copying machine, probably the only item in the room that had been manufactured after 1958. Stack stood up behind his desk when I came in but didn't offer to shake hands.

"You found us, I see." It seemed a singularly stupid thing to say, since we both knew I'd been to Vista Number One before. "Take off your wet slicker, why don't you?"

My raincoat didn't remotely resemble a slicker, but I took it off anyway and followed Stack over to one of the card tables, where we both sat in metal folding chairs and put our elbows on the dusty table along with a bottle of Canadian Club and two smudged glasses. Stack poured a few fingers for each of us, no ice, no mixer, and we drank without a toast.

"I'm trying to get a fix on you, son," Don Stack said, "but I'm having some trouble. I don't know why you're poking around me. We ever cross trails before?"

"No, not unless you count the other night."

He shook his head and snorted. "I can't even get laid without you camping on my doorstep. That little lady was kind of upset, I can tell you, and it took me half a bottle of vodka to get her feeling relaxed enough to get friendly again. Why are you riding my fences?"

I pushed one of my business cards at him. He read it and put it in his shirt pocket. "This don't tell me much."

"All right," I said. "An employee of yours, Peter D'Anjou, was murdered a couple of days ago."

"Well, now, let's get right to the bottom line here so we don't start out down in the big hole. Pete was not, in the strictest sense of the word, my employee. I had contracted with him to do some work on a part-time basis. They call them consultants now. But he wasn't on my regular

151

payroll, I didn't take out withholding tax, he had no benefits here. He just did some special work for me. It happens all the time in the oil bidness."

I looked at Stack curiously, not understanding why the subtle difference was so important to him. "Either way, he's just as dead."

Stack spread the blunt fingers of both hands on the table. "Am I a suspect?"

"I never said you were. You're D'Anjou's last employer, part time and freelance or not. It seems logical to talk to you."

"And who is your client?" he said.

"Someone who's interested in who really killed him."

"That's evasive, isn't it? You want answers but you won't give them."

I thought about that and it sounded fair. I told him, "I'm working for the husband of the woman who's been accused."

"Amptman?" he said.

"You know George Amptman?"

"Hell, yes, I bought this property off him."

My mouth dropped open. I can't imagine how foolish I must have looked. Until that moment it had never occurred to me that there was any connection between Amptman and Peter D'Anjou other than the fact they were both sleeping with Nanette. I said, "George Amptman is Pacifica Properties?"

"Pacifica Properties, Amptman Developments, South Bay Land, Seaward Developments—they're all Amptman. Him and a bunch of other guys, sure. George buys and sells a lot of land down here." His smile was pure Cheshire Cat. He said, "She's quite a little gal. Of course, she'd have to be for old Pete to do the deed with her."

"Do you think we could drop this good-old-boy shit and just talk to each other, Mr. Stack?"

The smile on his lips didn't go away, but the one in his eyes snapped off like the bathroom light. "I don't have to say squat to you, Saxon. You're a regular old buttinski,

152

aren't you? First you come poking around my oil well so my driller has to run you off, and then you beat him so bad he won't be able to talk right for a month. You dig up all sorts of personal crap about me, and then you go and hassle my investors and make me look bad—damn near insinuate I have something to do with the murder of a guy I just barely knew. You hide in the bushes at my home and frighten my guests. And now you come in here and tell me to drop the good-old-boy shit? I oughta have you hung up on that hook outside and left in the rain."

"If you do, you need to get better muscle than Jim Shay."

"I'll do it myself," he said.

"Right, I forgot your little pocket insurance." I stood up slowly and stretched my back. "You're on target when you say you don't have to talk to me, Mr. Stack. So I'll just discuss the matter with Lieutenant DiMattia of the police, and then you and he and Mr. Heubner can have a nice chat together."

He frowned. "How do you know about Heubner?"

"I'm a regular buttinski, remember? Here's the deal. A man's dead, and he didn't wrap a scarf around his neck by himself. Either talk to me or talk to the law. You aren't being accused of anything, so unless you did kill D'Anjou it doesn't cost you anything to cooperate with me."

He looked at me thoughtfully, leaning back as well as he could in the hard, cold folding chair. "Sit down," he said.

I sat down.

"I've done some shitty things in my life, Saxon, but murder was never one of them, and I take a dim view of any accusations along those lines. I'm a Christian, and I believe in the sanctity of human life." He took a pack of Marlboros from his shirt pocket and offered it to me; I shook my head. He lit a cigarette and took a few puffs. "Go ahead with your questions."

"Thanks," I said. "When did Peter D'Anjou start working for you?"

"About three weeks after they cut him loose at Gamble.

Pete had a great reputation, and as soon as I heard he was on the beach I went after him."

"How did you hear? Grapevine?"

"As a matter of fact, Pete called me. We had known each other slightly over the years. We weren't ever close; I'm a competitor of Gamble's, so we never got to be buddies. Jason Gamble and I have gone round and round a time or two. But I guess Pete wanted to hook on someplace local so he wouldn't have to uproot and go overseas. I was glad to get him, and I never held his working for Gamble against him."

"But you didn't hire him full time?"

"I'm a small operation here. This well is all there is. So I put him to work on a consultancy basis."

"Consulting about what?"

He looked around the room as if the answer were hanging on one of the walls. "There are some leases over on the marina peninsula that I'm thinking about buying. I wanted him to research them, whether or not they'd be a good place to dig."

"Are those leases currently owned by George Amptman?"

He laughed. "I said George controlled a lot of property, not *all* of it. No, these leases were held by Unocal at one time but never developed."

"And what did D'Anjou find out about those leases?"

Stack put a finger in his ear and did some digging of his own, examining the findings on the end of his finger before flicking them away. "You know," he said, "you could be working for some other oil people trying to find out my bidness. This crap about Pete could be a cloud of dust."

"It could be."

"So I reserve the right not to answer certain sensitive questions."

"All right," I said. "Let me put it another way. Were you pleased with D'Anjou's work?"

"Not particularly. He was dragging his feet, and we had words about that. But he knew the technical end, so for a time I let it ride." He shook his head as though deeply disappointed with himself. "I might as well have thrown the money down a mud pit."

"You mean he died before he finished it."

"Right. Of course, he did a well history on Number One for us too."

"What's that?"

"Just what it sounds like—a written record of the drilling, completion, and operation of this well before we bought it, and since. I needed it for the lawsuit."

"With Gamble?"

"You know all about that, I suppose."

I nodded. "Unless you'd like to tell me more."

He tipped his chair back against the wall, the two front legs about three inches off the ground. "It was a case of a big guy trying to push a little guy around," he said, unwittingly bringing to mind Jim Shay and myself. "Jason Gamble was insisting that we had slanted a hole up under the fence, pumping out oil that belonged to him. He got a court order to drill an inspection hole of his own. Well, he found out he was wrong, that we were tapped into oil reserves under our own lease, but somehow the hole they dug did something funny to our well, and the next thing we knew, we were pumping five hundred barrels a day of seawater."

"And so you sued him?"

"We're talking about a lot of money."

"And he settled out of court?"

Stack smiled at the memory. "That's right," he said.

"So in effect, you're getting a lot of money for *not* producing oil."

"I'd be getting it one way or the other."

"I wonder, then," I said, "why the tight security? The secret phone number, the locks and the barbed wire?"

"A poor thing but mine own," he said. "I can't afford Gamble's private army, so I do what I can."

"Not good enough, Mr. Stack. I came here on Saturday in a nonhostile way, but Jim Shay threatened me with physical violence if I didn't leave. Later that evening he tried to

155

follow through, and it was only my good luck and his bad that kept him from putting me in the hospital. Are you saying he acted on his own? That you didn't have him rough me up?"

"I'm telling you I protect what's mine any way I can. Jim is loyal to me—that's what I pay him for. But I didn't send him after you. I fight my own battles. What was between you and Jim was between you and Jim."

I didn't believe him. "What did all this have to do with D'Anjou?"

"Nothing. Like I said, the only thing he did was to write the well history, but that was after Gamble drilled their hole and we'd gone to court."

I took a small taste of my drink—I dislike rye and bourbon as much as I enjoy Scotch and Armagnac—and said, "Do you know why Gamble Oil fired D'Anjou?"

"Never thought to ask. I like to make up my own mind about a man without someone doing it for me."

"Gamble said it was because of D'Anjou's womanizing."

He threw back his head and laughed. "If that were cause for dismissal half the people in this town would be on the unemployment line. Myself included. And you, too, if I hear rightly."

"What do you mean by that?"

He cocked his head in what I'm sure he thought was an elfin manner. "Aren't you porking Billy Ledbetter's little granddaughter?"

I said, "That's no way to talk about a lady," and threw the remainder of my drink in his face. It completely startled him, and he teetered sideways on the rear legs of the folding chair and almost went over, waving his arms wildly at the last minute to regain his balance. He brought the chair forward, the two front legs thunking hard against the floor.

"I don't believe you did that," he said, wiping his face.

"You'd better get your believer working, then." I waited to see if he was going to do anything about it, then grabbed my coat and shrugged into it. "Stack, if you've got an idea

156

about waving that cap pistol at me, forget it, or you'll have to have it removed surgically."

I stepped out of the doghouse. The rain was cold and hard, puddling in the dirt, as close to winter as we ever get in Los Angeles. At least back in Chicago it was an honest winter, dumping snow and bringing Arctic air and winds that cut through the heaviest clothing, and not masquerading behind transplanted palm trees, pastel-shaded buildings, and the painted face of a whore.

15

The lavish bird-of-paradise bushes and jacaranda trees in front of the Amptman house looked like an impenetrable tropical forest in the rain, their leaves and branches dripping. I was dripping myself from my walk down the hill from Stack's doghouse to my car. My hair was wetly plastered to my head and several shades darker than normal. Both the Amptman automobiles were in the carport and there were lights on inside. I pushed the doorbell and heard chimes deep inside the house. After a few moments the door opened and Nanette Amptman stood there with a drink in her hand. She was wearing white lounging pajamas, and her blond hair was pulled back with a red ribbon.

"Mr. Saxon. We weren't expecting—"

"I have to talk to you and your husband," I said. "Do you have a few minutes?"

"We were just going to sit down to dinner."

"It's important."

Amptman appeared behind her, sans jacket but wearing a tie and a beige shirt. "In future it would be better if you called first. This is our home," he said, and the irony wasn't lost on me.

"Gee, I'm sorry," I said. "Why don't I just go away and come back a week from Thursday?"

"Oh, for God's sake, come in," he said, making me feel as welcome as an outbreak of cholera. We went into the picture-book living room after I took off my wet coat and hung it on a rack near the door.

"I have some questions," I said, "and I have to warn you they won't be pleasant."

"Our dealings have been unpleasant from the start," Amptman said.

"All right, I'm not a nice human being. But I haven't run into very many since the day you walked into my office, so I'm entitled. Mr. Amptman, you sold Don Stack the property on which he built Vista Number One."

"Are you asking me or telling me?"

"Did you know Peter D'Anjou was working for Stack when he died?"

Amptman's normal pasty color went a bit gray at the mention of his wife's lover. He moved to the portable bar and built a drink. It was a stiff one. "I didn't know it until a few days ago," he said.

"Who told you?"

He swirled the bourbon around in his glass, staring at it as though an answer might be floating there. "It isn't germane."

"I'll decide what's germane."

"Your insolence is—"

"Donald Stack told us," Nanette interrupted. Her husband gave her a look that could have vaporized a panzer tank.

"You and Stack are friends?"

"We're business acquaintances," Amptman told me. "That doesn't presuppose friendship."

"This won't look very good to the police, Mr. Amptman."

"Why the hell not?"

"Because they might just 'presuppose' that you knew Peter D'Anjou, that you knew of his—relationship with your wife."

Nanette said quickly, "I told you I met Pete at Reuben's."

"That's what you told me."

"Are you calling my wife a liar?"

159

"I leave the name calling to you, Mr. Amptman. I'm just asking questions. That's what you pay me for."

"That can be remedied."

I stood up, as sick of George Amptman as I'd ever been of another human being. "I think that's a good idea," I said. "I'll send you a statement."

"Wait!" Nanette said. Then she turned to her husband. "George, you can't just let him walk out of here."

"He's an insolent bastard!"

"But he's trying to help me."

"I'll hire someone else to help you."

She stood up and went to him. Now we were all standing. "He'll go to the police. He'll tell them you knew Peter."

"I never met Peter," he hissed, his lip curling with loathing he could barely contain. "Peter was your friend."

"Good night, folks," I said, and started for the door. I heard Nanette's heels clicking on the linoleum after me.

She touched my arm. "Mr. Saxon, don't go."

"I think I've just been fired."

"Saxon, God damn it, hold up!" Amptman said in a voice accustomed to command. I turned to see him lumbering after us, his drink sloshing around the edges of the glass.

"Mr. Amptman," I said, "you've got a lot of money and you're used to people brownnosing you. But I've flipped people off who could buy you with their pocket change. You're not rich enough to bully me, and you sure as shit aren't big enough. So either you cooperate with me fully and start telling me the truth or you can hire a whole regiment of private detectives who don't mind a little ass-kissing now and then. I assure you it's immaterial to me either way."

"Goddamn," he said, taking a long pull from what was left of his drink, "but you get on my nerves. Now come on back inside and let's talk."

"We can talk here," I said. Mary Mary, quite contrary. He shook his head. "I told you the truth. I never met

D'Anjou, never heard of him until . . . the other night. I couldn't have killed him. I was in Dallas."

"Convenient alibi."

"Well, if I knew about him already and I was going to kill him, why in hell would I have hired you? It doesn't make sense."

"It makes a lot of sense, because you could say that very thing to the police. It wouldn't buy you much credibility though, but you could try."

He was weaving on his feet, and I was afraid he would faint. He put one hand against the wall to steady himself. "You've got to believe me."

"The grand jury convenes on Friday, Mr. Saxon," Nanette said, "and I'll be publicly accused of murder. You can't just walk out on us."

"All right," I said. "Then be straight with me, both of you. You negotiated the sale of Vista Number One to Donald Stack, Mr. Amptman. When was that?"

"Two years ago," he said.

I took my coat from the rack but didn't put it on. Peter D'Anjou had still been with Gamble when the property was sold, lending a certain verisimilitude to what Amptman was saying. "And you dealt with Stack directly?"

"No," he said. "With his lieutenant."

"Jim Shay?"

"I don't know who that is. Stack's chief of operations was an East Indian—I don't remember his name. Skinny guy with a turban, stank to high heaven. I couldn't bear to be in a closed room with him."

The thing forming in the pit of my stomach felt a lot like a warm brick. "Rama Khali?"

"Something like that," Amptman said.

"He works for Gamble Oil."

"Maybe he does now, but then he was with Don Stack."

"Are you sure?"

"Certainly I'm sure. What the hell do you think?"

161

I shrugged into my damp coat. "I don't know, Mr. Amptman," I said. "I don't know what I think."

I stopped at a bar down on Highland Avenue, which was wall to wall with people ten years younger than I, all trying desperately to adjust their attitudes after a long day at the computer terminal bartering stocks. Some of them still had on their work togs, the men their gray suits and red ties and the women their tailored ensembles that would have made them look just like curvy men had it not been for the one bow to femininity: skirts slit almost to the hip and showing a long sexy expanse of stockinged leg. The rest of the customers were garbed in the sort of casual wear that trumpeted to the world that they were sand people. I fought the crush of humanity to get up to the bar, where I asked for single malt Scotch and the bartender didn't know what I was talking about. I settled for a Cutty on the rocks and carried it back to the hallway where they hid the rest rooms and waited for a twenty-five-year-old adolescent to get off the pay phone.

"Look," he was saying urgently into the receiver, "these two dollies are ready to play. I told them all about you and they're ready, but you gotta bring some blow." He leered at me. "You can pick the one you want, all right? It makes no nevermind to me, they're both hotter than shit, but they're cokeheads and they want to do blow and I'm fresh out. . . . Can do? . . . Well, do your best for me, compadre. Call me here before nine, all right? . . . Outstanding." He hung up, grinned at me again, and went back out to the main room where he was swallowed up in the crowd. As I put two dimes into the phone I saw him step between two young women at the bar, throwing a proprietary arm around each of them. They were both wearing scoop-necked blouses and those tight cotton pants that resemble long underwear. They looked like depraved, vacant-eyed puppets.

I dialed Gamble Oil and asked for Rama Magdi Khali, but it was after six and the woman on the switchboard told me he'd left for the day at about five o'clock. I called his house and listened to the ringing. As the phone company suggests, I gave it ten rings before hanging up. I felt as though I wanted to call someone else, but there was a woman in a gray suit with one of those slit skirts waiting to use the phone and pointedly tapping her foot. I'm easily intimidated. I picked my drink up from the shelf beneath the phone and went back out into the bar.

"Hey, compadre," my friend from the phone said as I passed. "Come on over here and meet Staci and Beth. This is—what did you say your name was again?"

"Holden Caulfield."

"What a great name," Beth said. I think she was Beth.

"Outstanding," the guy agreed. He removed his arms from the girls' shoulders and moved closer to me than I normally allow strangers to get, but there were too many people standing around for me to move away. His breath smelled of gin and his cheeks of Halston after-shave balm. "You haven't got any blow, have you, compadre?"

"I left it in my other suit."

"Curses," he said, and went back to Staci and Beth.

I finished my drink and went back out into the wetness. Highland Avenue was about a block and a half from the beach on the crest of a fairly steep hill. The water was gushing down the side streets in oily rivers to the sand, and it took a certain amount of grace and balance to cross the street without being swept into the sea by the ankle-deep current. I got into my car, grateful to be sheltered from the elements, and headed north for Los Angeles and Wilshire Boulevard. The rain roared on my convertible top, and by the time I got to Westwood and had found a place to park about two blocks from Khali's apartment, I had a stiff neck and a Saint Patrick's Day Parade of a headache behind my eyes.

The doorman in the lobby of Khali's high rise was a new one I hadn't seen before. He was tall and slim and about ten years too young for the job. He had the ruddy complexion of a drinker. I told him I was with the Department of Water

163

and Power and that there had been a report of a major leak in the tank on the roof and I wanted to investigate.

"It's kind of late," he said.

"You're damn right," I said. "And if that water continues running it's going to build up and the whole roof is going to go."

"I can't let you upstairs without an authorization," he said. He took his job seriously. Doormen usually do.

"That's fine with me. I was supposed to go home at six o'clock. But if the roof caves in, you're going to have a bunch of unhappy tenants in your penthouse apartments."

He folded his arms across his chest to show me how intractable he could be. I took out my notebook and a pen. "Could I have your name?"

"What for?"

"Just in case any trouble comes down later, I want your name on record so my ass is covered." I looked at his badge. It said H. JIMSON. "Okay, Mr. Jimson," I said, and flicked the button on my ballpoint.

"Well," Jimson said, practicality winning out over duty, "I guess it would be all right if it's an emergency. I mean, I wouldn't want anyone getting flooded out or anything."

"Now you're being sensible," I said, and walked across the lobby to the elevator.

When I got to Khali's apartment I rang the buzzer. I figured that if I'd been formally announced he wouldn't have let me upstairs; this way the worst he could do was look through the fish-eye peephole and refuse to open the door, and I'd make such a noisy fuss in the hallway he'd have to change his mind. I rang again. After a few seconds I pressed my ear to the door, but I couldn't hear anything. I took out a set of slim metal strips that I sometimes carry, illegally, and inserted one into the lock. It didn't work, so I tried another one. On the third effort I heard some tumblers click. I was glad there were only two penthouses on the floor, as I wasn't anxious for foot traffic. I kept working for about five minutes and finally got the lock to give and opened the door.

The drapes were wide open in the living room, although the rain had beaded up on the window and the inside had fogged up, pretty much obscuring the million-dollar view. There were two lights on, a floor lamp near an easy chair by the window and a high-intensity desk lamp that sat atop the filing cabinets. A brown suit jacket and a green tie had been carelessly tossed onto the sofa. The four drawers of the filing cabinets were open, looking for all the world as if they'd been jimmied, and the files and papers were strewn around on the floor or had been half lifted out of the drawers and left sticking up.

Rama Khali smelled even worse than usual. A long knife with a curved ivory-inlaid handle was protruding out of the back of his neck, having been jammed upward into his brain. The impact had caused him to fall forward into the vivarium, knocking it from the table to the floor and smashing the glass. He lay on his side in the wreckage, and what the jagged edges had done to his face, chest, and hands is best left undescribed. The blood all over the carpet was still glistening wetly. It was now just past seven. If Khali had left Gamble Oil at five, factoring in the rush hour traffic, he couldn't have been home for more than a few minutes before he'd been killed.

I walked over to the body without touching it—not that I wanted to. His left cheek was impaled on a sharp shard of glass that hadn't separated from the vivarium's frame, and his eyes were staring in blind horror at nothing in particular. I stepped around the puddles of blood and the mounds of gravel and sand that had spilled onto the carpet from the shattered tank and looked at the explosion of papers in and around the file cabinets. I leaned over to examine the few documents I could read, but I wasn't going to pick anything up. Most of them had to do with petroleum, and to a nonexpert like me they would mean little. It didn't take much of an expert, though, to figure out what had happened to Khali, or why. Someone had been looking for something, something they wanted very badly to find. Badly enough to kill.

Since I didn't know what they'd been after, I couldn't tell if they'd found it. It's hard to look for something that isn't there. I studied the headings on the folders: the fattest one was labeled GAMBLE. Then there was JAKARTA #1. JAKARTA #4. AUTO. PERSONAL RECEIPTS. MEDICAL. INVOICES. Khali had evidently been fairly meticulous about his record keeping, but there was nothing unusual in that.

I looked over at the body again. He was wearing the pants to the brown suit, heavy brown cordovan shoes with a swirl of eyelets on the toes, and a white dress shirt open at the neck. The sleeves of the shirt were rolled up, and I noticed that on his right wrist there were two little puncture marks, jagged around the edges, about two inches apart. The hand was blackened and swollen. My first thought was a silly one—vampires only exist in the movies.

And then I broke out in a sticky, cold sweat and a wave of icy fear shook me right down to my shoes: Khali's pet cobra had to be somewhere in the apartment, and I had no idea where.

When I turned to move for the door, I found him.

He was coiled in the middle of the room and had raised himself up so that his head was about thirty inches off the floor, quivering slightly as he nailed me with his gaze. He weaved back and forth on his elongated backbone, his hood enlarged and flattened, and he never took his eyes off me for a second. I returned the favor. I have never been so frightened in my life.

I have said I'm not phobic about snakes. I raised garter snakes when I was a kid in Chicago, and a young lady of past acquaintance had owned a pet boa constrictor named Harvey—after an ex-husband—with whom I'd had a working relationship. Harvey, a nine-footer, had apparently decided early on that I wasn't a mouse or rat and had actually developed a fondness for me. He would curl around my arm and shoulder with his face inches from mine, looking into my eyes with a rather loony expression on his face, his tongue darting in and out like a William F. Buckley impersonator. Snakes are not slimy to the touch, but dry and smooth and rather pleasant.

But garter snakes and boas are nonvenomous and not very aggressive. From what I know about Asian cobras, they do not strike like rattlesnakes, but chomp down and hold on, grinding their jaws while the poison flows from their short fangs into the puncture wounds. Untreated, an average-size man will live for about ninety agonizing minutes before the poison reaches his heart and stills it for good. And even if he is lucky enough to get immediate medical attention, the effects of reptile poisoning are as unpleasant as one might imagine, quite often causing permanent physical or mental impairment. From what I could ascertain, Khali had been lucky—the knife in his neck had killed him before the snake venom had gone to work.

The thing was about seven feet away from me, too far for him to get to me in one lunge, I thought—or hoped. But if I wanted to reach the door of the penthouse—and I wanted to as much as I've ever wanted anything—I would have to move directly into the snake's sphere of influence. And I wasn't even going to think about doing that. However, the smashed vivarium and the body of Rama Magdi Khali were right behind me so I couldn't very well retreat, either. The cobra and I were at loggerheads.

He continued to look at me with a kind of reproachful wariness, his head a lollipop at the end of his long body, quivering indignantly at the upset in his routine. I just stood there, sweat pouring down my face and my sides, a primal fear sucking the saliva from my mouth. My testicles were residing somewhere in the vicinity of my Adam's apple. I have been scared before, but this was my first genuine taste of terror. There's a difference.

It must have taken me at least two minutes to raise my hand to my throat. When it finally got there it was out of control from shaking, and I had to grab the collar of my raincoat and hold it tightly to keep the hand still. Slowly, more slowly than I had thought possible, I unbuttoned the top button. The snake's raisin eyes were mesmerizing, and his little tongue tested the air. As I undid the second button I almost imagined he was smiling at me, his ugly head swaying back and forth as if disembodied from the rest of him. I understood why the small animals that are a cobra's prey simply freeze in place and wait to be killed.

Khali had told me the snake was harmless unless disturbed. Of course he was already upset, having been rudely awakened and dumped out onto the floor by Khali's falling body, but every iota of concentration and will I possessed was going to keep me from disturbing him further. I tried to undo the third button of my raincoat. My hands were sweating so badly my fingers slipped off the smooth buttons, and my throat was so constricted I couldn't have yelled if I wanted to.

The smell of death was familiar, acrid and foul. I've run across more dead bodies than I care to remember. But there was a strange odor in this room that sickened me even more, because it was the smell of my own fear. My clothes were drenched, and perspiration was running from my forehead into my eyes, but I didn't dare wipe it away. I had established a rhythm with the buttons, one the cobra had grown accustomed to, and he rocked to that rhythm in a grotesque attitude dance.

The raincoat was completely unbuttoned now, but I was terrified to put my next move into operation. I had to, I kept telling myself, I couldn't just stand here face to face with a venomous snake all night. Eventually he would grow bored with the game and kill me. As if I were defusing a bomb, I put both hands on the lapels of the raincoat and moved it off my shoulders in a slow-motion imitation of an ecdysiast. It must have taken me another five minutes to carefully ease it off my arms, until it hung from my right hand, trailing beside me on the floor. I glanced down at my left hand. The fingers were stiff from tension, and I flexed them very slowly. My back ached. I hadn't moved my body from the hips down in more than ten minutes, and my sore ribs from Jim Shay's bear hug were beginning to stiffen up. And still the snake stared at me with his nasty eyes, his head a flower blossoming on the stem of his neck, his tongue flickering at me in an obscene parody of lust.

I slowly brought the raincoat up in front of my body, holding it by the lapels with both hands and spreading it wide. The stiff material crackled slightly. I inched a step forward and the cobra jerked its head, suddenly more watchful, and I almost lost control of my bladder. My clothes were so wet it wouldn't have made much difference. I took another step, and the snake began weaving even more, his head like an upside-down pendulum moving a foot in either direction. I wished that when I'd visited my first bullfight in Tijuana the year before I had paid more attention to the way the matador works his cape, swirling it in front of him and to the side to distract the bull. One more step and I would be within the snake's striking distance—and he within mine.

The tension in the room, mine and the snake's, was palpable. With that final step the creature jerked his head back as if in surprise, and then shot it forward at the only thing that was moving, the heavy coat, and I took a leap and fell on top of him, smothering him with the wet, stiff canvas. Beneath the fabric I could feel him thrashing against my body. I hadn't realized how strong snakes are; it was as if I were riding an unseen bucking horse. In a panic, I glanced around on the floor next to me and saw a large sliver of glass from the vivarium, about fourteen inches long, with a sharp point. With my weight still pressing down on the snake, I picked it up and plunged the point again and again into the raincoat, feeling the reptile convulsing beneath me. The edge of the glass dug deeply into my palm, but I didn't even feel it, so distracted was I by the terrible screaming.

It wasn't until much later that I realized the screams had been mine.

16

Before taking my statement, Lieutenant Joe DiMattia had kindly allowed me to go to the emergency room of Saint Anthony's Hospital, where they took twelve stitches in my hand. After talking to Joe about Rama Magdi Khali and what I knew of him, his history, and his possible connection to Peter D'Anjou, I went home, where I had three Laphroaigs, neat, and tried to avoid Marvel's questions. I'd called him from police HQ and told him to order a pizza delivered, which was no small triumph for him in the first place, and when I got home and told him what had happened, he was pretty jazzed about the snake. Most kids are fascinated with snakes and lizards and dinosaurs, and Marvel wanted to hear that part of the story again and again. I didn't even want to think about it.

Conrad's Lord Jim and Hemingway's Francis Macomber had each known a single moment of fear that blighted their lives forever. Shakespeare said, "Cowards die many times before their death." It isn't easy living with the knowledge of your own capacity for terror. No fancy tricks of lighting when you go in to shave in the morning can quite disguise it, or make you feel anything but a coward, no matter how justified your fear. And no amount of Scotch could make me forget how I'd lost my cool and my reason, and eventually my pride, there in a room with a dead man and a live cobra.

It was one of those times where a long walk alone might

be therapeutic, but in the downpour it would have been impractical. So I watched television for a while and couldn't have told you five minutes later what I'd seen. I was too wired to read. I called Jo and Marsh but got their answering machine, remembering then that Jo had said they were going to catch a movie. I paced the house, smoked a few cigarettes, and stared out the window at the rain falling in the canal.

I felt someone behind me, watching. I turned around. "You spooked, huh?" Marvel said.

"To the max."

He shook his head. "It's all over now, you know?"

I nodded. "That's not the problem."

He half sat, half leaned on the windowsill and took a pull from his ever present can of Pepsi. "You raggin' on you'self 'cause you lost it?"

It amazed me that he could read me so well. He always could, from the moment he'd relaxed enough to feel safe in my house. My own biological child couldn't have been more attuned to my feelings. I looked up at him, at the soft brown eyes, so full of wonder and inquisitiveness and mischief and, at times like this, compassion. For a sixteen-year-old, Marvel had a lot of that. But of course, Marvel had been through a lot of things that most kids his age never even dream about, so he was blessed with insight beyond his years. I said, "Something like that."

"You think you the only one ever get scared? God damn! I be scared half my life, man. Ain't nothin' to hang your head on. What? You think you too good? You think it be okay for everybody but you? Shee-it! You jus' a ordinary person, man. Jus' 'cause you got that license, you don't got to be no hero! You got no VIP ticket say you better'n everyone else. *Anybody* look at a snake that way get spooked! He be a fool not to."

I didn't say anything.

Marvel said, "You didn' do nothin' wrong, you unnerstan'? Mos' dudes jump out the window 'fore they mess aroun' no snake. You fought that sucker an' kill it! Don'

171

matter you scared while you do it! You *do* it, an' it's all in the past now."

I wished it was all in the past. I wished it had happened a hundred years ago and was nothing more than a vague memory. But I could still see the snake, still feel it thrashing beneath the raincoat. And I could still taste my own fear, bitter as bile.

Marvel sighed. "Well, if you gonna be feelin' bad about you'self, you do it alone. I'm gonna crash." He sat there looking at me for a half minute, then he uncoiled his lanky frame and went into his bedroom.

He was right, of course. As scared as I had been, I'd acquitted myself rather well, under the circumstances. I still wished I could have dispatched that cobra with the stoicism of an old-time movie hero, but real life doesn't work that way, which is why they stopped making those corny movies. I stood there for a while watching the storm roil the waters of the canal, and then I went and knocked on his bedroom door.

"Yo," he said, and I went in. He was in bed, the covers up to his chin. He usually sleeps with a small desk lamp on, probably because he has his own nightmares to deal with, his own demons under the bed.

"I'm going out for a while, I think."

"In this weather?"

"Yeah. I'm antsy, I guess. You be okay?"

"What if I ain't? You gonna hire me a baby-sitter?"

"I might."

"Make it Lisa Bonet, awri'?"

I leaned against the doorjamb. "Sometimes I think you're smarter than I am."

"Tha's a given," he said.

I got my Raiders jacket out of the closet and put it on. My raincoat was in bloody shreds at the police station, and I never wanted to look at it again anyway. I headed for the door and tripped over a pair of Marvel's shoes and almost broke my neck. I picked them up, marched back into his room, and threw the sneakers at him one at a time. "And if you don't start picking your shoes up I'm going to hang your ass on the wall," I yelled.

I backed the car out into the alleyway and turned the wipers on high, which did only minimal damage to the sheet of water on the windscreen. I rolled over the bridges that spanned the Linnie and Howland canals to Venice Boulevard and turned east, heading for Lincoln. Visibility was lousy. At Lincoln I hung a right down past the marina, and swung over on Culver Boulevard to Playa Del Rey, and that made me think about Peter D'Anjou, and that made me think about Rama Magdi Khali. I had to believe their deaths were connected, and that Nanette Amptman had nothing to do with either killing. Whoever had murdered Khali was looking for something in his files; I could only speculate on whether he—or she—had found it.

I knew from the blackened punctures on Khali's wrist that the snake had bitten him when he crashed through the vivarium, and I wondered if the killer had escaped that fate. Probably so: as I have noted, cobras bite and hang on, which would give anyone with a lick of sense time to get out of there while Khali's pet was finishing him off. Would that I'd had the luxury.

It was past one o'clock in the morning, and the streets were empty. Los Angeles is not a late night town at the best of times, and in the rain it was eerily quiet. I turned down Vista Del Mar, my stitched and bandaged hand throbbing like an automatic drum machine. To my right the surf boiled, the waves smashing like cracks of a bullwhip, more graycaps than white, churning up bottom mud. The beach looks grim and depressing in the rain, one more instance of California dreaming unmasked. And Pacific beaches are not like those on the other side of the continent. Somehow the Atlantic *should* be storm-tossed and gray, the sands lonely and deserted, just right to walk on at night and feel the aloneness more keenly. But the beaches of California are supposed to be for fun—sixteen-year-olds in dental floss bikinis, bronzed surfers in thermal wet suits, family picnics and wienie roasts and Marlon Brando riding his horse along the surf.

Not in a November midnight, brother.

I passed the Ledbetter place. Only the porch light gleamed yellow in the darkness, barely visible through the rain streaking daggerlike on the diagonal. What did I expect at this hour? I wasn't sure, but it suddenly dawned on me that I had driven down this way because I wanted to see Kim, needed to feel her arms around me. The little drama I'd played out in Khali's apartment had left me shaky. But I couldn't very well climb the hill and knock on the door in the middle of the night and say "Hold me."

Could I?

I drove by Vista Number One, the well pumping quietly. A light burned behind the window in the doghouse, testimony to the vigilance of Donald Stack's crew. I passed the huge prisonlike compound of Gamble Oil. There were lights on in the guard shack and at all the well sites, but only the lobby of the headquarters building showed any sign of life. I seemed to be one of the few people awake in the world.

Through the rear window of my car, plastic to accommodate the raising and lowering of the rag top, I saw the headlights of another car about half a mile behind me, making diamond sparkles through the rain. I was almost glad someone else was out and about in this weather. It made me feel less alone.

Past Gamble Oil there's virtually nothing on the landward side of Vista Del Mar until you reach Mimosa Beach, with its fern bars and restaurants with nautical themes and rabbit-warren apartment buildings. A sewage disposal plant hunkers ominously on a hill about half a mile inland, and the rest is barren hillocks, sand and saw grass. In a state that relentlessly overdevelops any land within hailing distance of the ocean into condos and industrial parks and manmade yacht basins, it's a peculiar stretch of roadway.

The headlights in my mirror got bigger, closer, right behind me, and the driver swung out to the left to pass. I slowed down to let him; if the damn fool wanted to drive that fast on a night like this, it was his funeral, not mine. When he drew even with me I saw it was a big dark car, the kind that fuel-conscious consumers have turned into dinosaurs. Then he swerved sharply to the right and deliberately smashed his fender into my door. There was that terrible crunch of metal that you hear even before you feel the impact, harsh as fingernails on a blackboard. The jolt snapped my head back against the safety-mandated headrest and sent my Le Baron into a wild skid, tires sliding on the wet oil-slick roadway beneath me. He rammed me again, and my little convertible, a thousand pounds lighter than his big sedan, fishtailed, went out of control, and made a complete three-sixty-degree skid. I wrestled the wheel, thinking all the time that if I saw this in a movie I wouldn't believe it. The shoreline real estate rushed past my eyes like a speeded-up travelogue. I was heading for one of the squat concrete stanchions that support the railing separating the roadway from the levee of sand, and my foot flailed wildly for the brake pedal, which didn't seem to be there anymore. I hauled on the steering wheel with all my weight, enough to alter the trajectory of the car, and instead of hitting the stanchion I managed to miss it and crashed through the barrier on the right side of the road. The car bucked down a bumpy hill, hitting the ground only occasionally, and finally rammed its nose into the wet sand and saw grass of the beach. My upper body jerked forward and my forehead banged the steering wheel hard, and all at once the muddy, roiling waves of unconsciousness came at me and over me and I sank into them until I hit bottom.

17

Coming out of unconsciousness is not like awakening from a sound sleep, but rather like floating out of a black-bean-soup fog into the sunshine. There was no sunshine here, just a frigid darkness wet enough to swim in. My face was pressed against the steering wheel, and there was an ache behind my eyes that seemed to bore all the way through to the brainpan. I sat up to discover that my back hurt, though whether the crash had caused it or simply aggravated Jim Shay's work, I didn't know. And if I ever found the guy who'd driven the blunt wedge into my forehead I was going to speak to him about it.

I pushed down the door handle, but the door stuck until I gave it a bump with my shoulder, which set off a tap-dancing chorus line in my head. The door popped open and I squeezed out of the car, steadying myself against the roof until the waves of dizziness receded. When I had ascertained that I wasn't dead and that most of my body was still in working order, I surveyed the damage. The right front fender and bumper were completely mangled. The grille was crushed in, at least the visible part of it that wasn't buried in the sand, which probably meant my radiator was gone, too. The door on the driver's side had a couple of dings that could have been put there by a charging rhino. And even a mechanical moron like me could see that the front axle was broken. There was no way I was going to drive the car out of there. I'd have to call AAA for a tow truck to haul me out.

I looked at my watch. It was 1:20 in the morning. I don't know how long I'd been in dreamsville, but with the inclement weather causing a paucity of traffic on Vista Del Mar, I'd have a hell of a long wait if I were to depend on a passing Samaritan for a ride. Besides, the guy who had run me off the road onto the beach might come back to finish the job, and I didn't want to be standing on the highway with my thumb out like a hippie in a time warp. I zipped my Raiders jacket up to my neck, an exercise in futility since it wasn't waterproof anyway, and climbed up the hill to the roadway, sinking into the sand up to the calf with every step. I suppose to an onlooker I would have presented a pretty funny picture. I didn't feel funny. First attacked by a cobra and then bumped off the highway with intent to kill. It had been one bitch kitty of an evening.

I got up onto the asphalt of the roadway and looked around, as if I could see anything through the whipping water. I could have headed south, which would mean I'd wind up in Mimosa Beach at about two A.M. looking for a pay phone. Or I might go north to Ledbetter's, where I knew I'd get a warm blanket, a drink, and a hug. The two were practically equidistant. It was one of the few easy decisions I've ever had to make. I began walking toward Kim Ledbetter. The thought of seeing welcome in those china blue eyes prodded me on as the rain lashed my face. I hadn't gone ninety feet before I was soaked through.

Let me give you the real skinny on walking in the rain. It's damn depressing. It's debilitating. It's wet, it's cold, and it's frightening, especially when the ground beneath you turns to a treacherous, slip-sliding river of mud. Walking in the rain is something to be undertaken only when unavoidable, when you're out of gas, out of carfare, and out of options. It's what the military calls a "field expedient." It isn't wonderful and magical. What it is, is the pits. Especially when your head feels like someone's poured battery

177

acid in your ears. Especially when you're half in shock. Especially when you have to skulk in the shadows and stay out of sight because someone, you don't know who, has just tried to kill you.

Like hot dogs at the ballpark and sex orgies and arty European films shot in grainy black and white, walking in the rain is vastly overrated. You don't turn your face to the skies and let the raindrops plash sensuously on your tongue. You don't wriggle and giggle when the water gets into your collar and runs in icy freshets down your back. You don't laugh with childish delight, you don't cavort in the puddles, you don't dance and skip. And you certainly don't sing.

It took me the better part of an hour to reach the Ledbetter place. During that time only one car passed me going in either direction, and I hopped down off the road onto the sand at its approach, squatting down behind the berm below pavement level while it roared past me. Now I know how the fox feels with the hounds yipping after it.

The rain was monotonous; it never got any heavier, it never abated, it just continued falling in icy sheets. The wind from the ocean kicked up a bit and made the big drops that hit my face sting like the flick of a metal-tipped shoelace. Climbing up the steep incline to Billy and Kim's place in my condition was not a whole lot different than scaling the Himalayas; all I lacked was a Sherpa guide. The hill had never seemed so steep before, the pathway never so long, and the mud sucked one of my shoes off. I had to bend down and retrieve it and put it back on. Bending, with the kind of headache I had, was a particularly exquisite agony.

When I got to the door I realized Billy had come out on the steps to meet me each time I'd been there, and I didn't know if there was a doorbell. I looked around for one in the yellow glow of the porch light, and then gave it up as a fool's chase and hammered on the panels with the knuckles of my good hand. Every knock sent vibrations through my head and shooting pains all the way down my backbone, and I leaned against the wall and stared at my muddy shoes until the giddiness went away.

A light went on in the back of the house, followed a few seconds later by another in the living room, and I heard the locks and chains of modern urban wariness being unfastened on the other side of the door. It opened, and Billy Ledbetter stood in the doorway pointing a nickel-plated .32 at me, Kim hovering behind him. Both were in their bathrobes. When he saw who his visitor was, Billy lowered the gun. He looked at the bump on my forehead, my torn clothes, and my general pitiful physical condition.

"Jesus Christ," he said. I guess he had me mixed up with somebody else.

After I phoned Marvel to tell him I'd been delayed, I got a hot shower and the expected blanket and drink. The hug was not forthcoming, but it's hard to hug someone when they're lying flat on their back on your sofa. Kim did stroke my face gently and apply a cold compress to my bruised forehead, and that was almost as good as a hug. I looked up at her with gratitude and said, "Hello, prettiness."

"Shh, don't talk," she said, putting a finger to my lips.

I kissed it. "I have to talk," I said. "That's the only way I know I'm not dead."

And then I told them what had happened to me—not just the accident, but discovering Khali's body and the encounter with the snake. Kim was horrified, overwhelmed with concern, and any temptation to embellish the snake part ebbed as I realized no hyperbole was needed. The reality was horrendous enough, and I still hadn't come to terms with my own feelings about it.

"So you think," Billy said, "that this Indian guy getting killed is hooked up to young D'Anjou's murder?"

"I'm sure of it," I said.

He nodded thoughtfully. He was having a pretty good

time with my case. My unexpected visit had provided him with an excuse to pour some drinks, and I doubted if Kim usually allowed him to tipple at two A.M. Besides, I could tell that the intrigue and the chance to play detective were giving him a high.

"Seems to me," he said, "that the victims had two things in common: they both had worked for Jason Gamble and they both had worked for Don Stack."

"But Khali left Stack and went to Gamble long before D'Anjou left Gamble and went to Stack," Kim said. "If that means anything."

"It might," I said. I felt silly making Sherlockian pronouncements while wrapped in a blanket.

"What about Stack buying the property through Amptman?" Billy leaned forward in his chair. "That seems like a coincidence, doesn't it?"

"I suppose so. But Amptman was in Texas when D'Anjou was killed."

"He could've hired somebody."

"He could have," I admitted, "but why kill Khali too?"

"Was his wife sleeping with both of them?" Kim asked.

"If you'd ever gotten downwind of Khali you wouldn't have to ask. And being under threat of indictment for D'Anjou's murder it's unlikely she'd have slipped out and committed another one tonight. No, I still think she was a convenient fall girl."

"Well, then, who ran you off the road?" Billy said.

I sat up, my ribs shrieking protest. "I'll find out."

When I felt somewhat better, I got dressed again. Kim had run my soaked clothing through the washer and dryer; there wasn't much she could do about my shoes. She also put a clean dry bandage on my hand, which hurt like hell. We called the police to report the accident, but they had already found my car and traced the registration back to the company I'd leased it from. They were glad to hear from me, angry I hadn't called earlier, and somewhat smug when they told me the car had already been towed to a police impound lot. That meant a lot of running around, signing papers, getting repair estimates, talking to insurance companies, and I had no inclination to spend my next month doing that. Nanette Amptman's freedom was more important than a bunged-up car.

As for the driver who had run me off the road in the first place, when Sergeant Sandoval of the El Tercero PD, a handsome youngish man with a Viva Zapata mustache and lines of fatigue etched at the corners of his mouth, showed up at the Ledbetters' some ninety minutes later, he shrugged and promised that the department would look into it but he wasn't holding out much hope of "nailing the perp." I didn't bother telling him that this might or might not have to do with two murders, because I had no proof of that; neither Playa Del Rey nor Westwood was his jurisdiction anyway. He did say that it was obvious from the car's condition that I had been hit from the side, saving me from the insinuations of a claims adjuster with the same kind of investigator's license as mine trying to prove I'd been drunk and had driven off onto the beach on my own, and saving the insurance company the price of a brand-new Le Baron convertible.

By the time Sandoval had taken enough notes to write his own novel and gone home, the rain had stopped except for intermittent bursts, there were smudges of light in the eastern sky behind the house, and I had switched from Scotch to coffee. My forehead had turned an amusing shade of purple, which clashed with my green eyes, but the timpani between my ears had fallen silent unless I tried to make any sudden moves, which I was loath to do. The all-night session had finally gotten to Billy and he made his farewells at about the same time Sandoval did, so Kim and I sat quietly on the sofa and held each other and watched the morning take the baton from the night in the perpetual relay.

Finally she said, "I'd better drive you home."

"I can call a cab," I said.

"Are you kidding? Let me run in and throw something on."

She was gone only a few minutes. She came back out wearing a green jogging suit and holding her car keys in her hand.

"Is that the outfit you were wearing the first time I saw you?" I said.

"What a guy! You're supposed to remember things like that. It's romantic."

"Well, is it?"

"No," she said, "that one was red. I have five. Running is the only thing that gets my blood going. Or it was until you came along. This has been more excitement than we've had around here in a long time."

"Is that good or bad?"

"I don't know," she said seriously, sitting down on the sofa again. "I don't believe in violence."

"That's like not believing in the ocean. It exists, whether you like it or not."

"Well," she said, "I still don't like it. But then sometimes I don't like the ocean. During a storm, when it gets angry and smashes things." She looked at me for a minute. "But I do like you. Ever since you snagged that first kiss. I like the way you kiss, and I like having you around. So that almost makes up for it."

"Almost?"

"I could go out with another engineer or something every night of the week. But they're all so *bor*-ing. You're a kick."

"A kick," I said. I started feeling jerky, repeating everything she said.

"Let's not spoil things by defining them, okay?" And she laid a kiss on me that faded out the echoes of what I'd gone through in the last twelve hours. As soon as I started getting involved in the kiss, she pulled away. "Come on. I'm taking you home."

We stood up. Easier for her than me. "Where's that gun of Billy's?"

"Why?"

I said, "Whoever forced me onto the beach knew what they were doing. If they try it again I want to be prepared."

Kim laughed, but her eyes didn't. "Who'd do anything like that in the middle of the morning rush hour? And who knows you're here, anyway?"

"Who knew I'd be on Vista Del Mar last night? Nobody. I didn't know myself until I got in the car and started driving. I was followed. From my house."

"You're paranoid."

"I hope so. But until we're sure . . ." I held out my bandaged hand. She looked at me with concern, then went into the back of the house. She returned a moment later holding Billy's little .32 like it was something foul a dog had left on the carpet. I took it and jammed it into the pocket of my jacket. "Home, James," I said.

Oil bidness gears up early in the morning, so even though it was just past seven, Vista Del Mar was choked with cars. It took us about forty-five minutes to make the twenty-minute drive up to Venice. Kim was properly impressed with my little bungalow at the edge of the canal, and cooed excitedly over the ducks paddling by and quacking good morning, and I thought it only fair to invite her in for coffee.

I unlocked the door and tripped over a pair of sneakers.

"Hey," Marvel said when I introduced him to Kim.

"Hey, Marvel," she said back.

He evinced a good bit of filial concern over the Technicolor bruise on my forehead, and was as polite to Kim as he had to be while he ate his breakfast, which in the perverse way of his age group meant, I suppose, that he approved of her. She wandered around the living room looking at the paintings I'd collected over the years, mostly Southwestern artists like Charles Stewart and Mario Larrinaga, which had looked a lot better in my modern apartment in Pacific Palisades than they did here in an aging canalside cottage in Venice. She checked out the bookshelves, which held lots of classic American fiction, many contemporary mysteries, and nonfiction mostly about movies and true crime. I put on a pot of coffee and went in to change into a pair of jeans and a sweater. I put Billy Ledbetter's gun in the top drawer of the dresser. When I emerged, Kim and Marvel were deep in a heated discussion of the Los Angeles Lakers. She was saying that in a few years James Worthy was going to be the superstar of superstars, and Marvel argued that there would never be another Magic Johnson. I had little to contribute to that particular debate, so I remained quiet until he left for school, and then Kim and I sat at the dining room table and I drank coffee while she had orange juice.

"Why do you do this?" she said.

"What?"

"Put yourself in jeopardy. You've got a great kid there, and he needs a father. What if something happens to you?"

"What if I fall in the canal and drown some night when I'm taking out the garbage? I can't live in a plastic bubble."

"But you could concentrate on your acting career. You have lots of options."

I thought about that for a minute before I answered. "It may surprise you, Kim, but God help me, I love what I do. And if I can prove Nanette Amptman is innocent of murder, I'll have made a difference."

"Isn't that really ego?"

"Sure it's ego. But I'm not playing God, I'm just helping out while he's busy elsewhere." The kitchen clock said it was after eight. "And if I'm going to help him today I have to grab some sack time."

"You're kidding," she said.

"Why?"

She put down her mug, her blue eyes big and steady. "This is the first time we've ever really been alone together without my grandfather snoring in the next room. Are you really sending me home?"

I stood up and put out my good hand to her. She took it and rose from the chair. The top of her head came to just under my chin. I took a strand of her long brown hair in

184

my hand and kissed the end of it. "I said I wanted to get to bed. I don't remember mentioning anything about going alone."

She reached up and put her arms around my neck. "You've had a rough night. Are you sure you're in the mood?"

"Get serious," I said.

18

One of the nice things about making love to a woman who is into health and fitness is that she doesn't insist on having a cigarette afterward. Of course, that's just *one* of the nice things. I used to be a heavy smoker myself, and I still smoke when I'm under stress, but I've always thought the postcoital cigarette was one of those loathsome habits people indulge in because they feel it's expected of them, like TV newscasters reading the stories to one another instead of to the viewer, or baseball players scratching their testicles and spitting. And the bedroom smells like tobacco smoke for days afterward. *So what!!*

No such problems with Kim, though. She was a cuddler, not a smoker, and after our lovemaking she nestled in that warm space between my shoulder and my neck, her long hair all over the place, and we laughed as we tried to get it behind her head and out of the way.

"Don't worry about it," I said. "I love long hair."

"Most men do. Why is that?"

"I can't speak for most men, but I like the way it looks spread across the pillow."

"Coming right up," she said, and sat up a bit so her hair fanned out across the pillow and my arm. She looked like a model in a shampoo ad, and her hair smelled clean and fresh, without any hairspray or flowery fragrance to disguise it. I rubbed my face against it, working up the length

186

of it to her cheek. It was a very nice cheek, baby soft against my lips. She said, "Well, I guess we have a situation here."

"What do you mean?"

"Once to bed isn't exactly a relationship. And I'd hate to think it was a one-morning stand. So it's a situation."

"Do you always put labels on things?"

"Hey, I'm an engineer. I've got that type of mind. Labels bother you?"

"Sometimes. Not this time."

She raised herself on one elbow. "Labels peel off. I'm not putting a brand on you, if that's what you're worried about."

"I'm not worried. I'm happy. And this is no one-morning stand, if you don't want it to be."

"Good," she said, and lay back down. "One day at a time, with no unreasonable expectations on either side. You can run things if you want, I don't mind. At work I head up a department of four other people, all men, and I get pretty tired of being tough and capable all day."

"I don't want to run things, or be run. I'd like it if it works for both of us. If it isn't, then what's the point?"

"You mean you're not going to tell me to change my hair style or wear a different kind of clothes or to stop running every morning because it makes my legs too muscular?"

"I want to be your lover, not your father. I've got a kid already," I said, "and I don't even run him."

The silence was luxurious for a few minutes. "Hey," she said, "why don't you and Marvel come over for dinner on Saturday? I'll cook something special."

"Only if you let me help."

She screwed her face up, thinking about it. "Why not? We run an equal-opportunity kitchen here."

"And Marvel can help with the dishes."

She kissed me and made herself a little more comfortable on my arm. "Well," she said, "I guess we've got a situation, all right."

Kim left at eleven o'clock, and while I whipped up an omelette of linguica sausage, sliced almonds, and jack cheese for my lunch, I called the office to fill Jo in on the previous night's events. When I heard myself reciting them in order—finding Khali's body, killing a cobra, getting run off the highway, walking through a rainstorm—it sounded pretty melodramatic. Next week, *East Lynne*.

"What do you want me to do?" she said, concern in every syllable. Jo worries when I do dangerous things, or more accurately when dangerous things are done to me. It's part of why our personal and business relationships work so well. As an unmarried male whose family, what there is of it, is half a continent away, there aren't too many people who make a fuss over me when I stub my toe. Jo is my surrogate mother-sister in more ways than one; she makes me think that at least someone out there cares when I don't wear my galoshes.

"The first thing is," I said, "to find out when and where the Rama Khali funeral service is being held. The second thing is, try to make a cocktail date for me this afternoon with Jaclyn Johnson."

"I told you when I started this job, if you're going to run around with bimbos, you make your own dates."

"It's not that kind of a date."

"Thank God for small favors."

"But it might be okay to let her think it is."

I hung up and called the nearest auto rental agency, and within fifteen minutes they had picked me up in a Chevy Cavalier, whisked me back to their office to sign the papers, and sent me on my way. I figured that under the circumstances I ought to buy the extra insurance.

The first place I drove the Chevy was to Amptman Developments.

The woman at the desk was in her early thirties, with a pretty little face and chubby cheeks. Her hair looked as though it had been cut around the edges of an upended salad bowl in front and was blond on top; low along the back of her long neck it had been almost buzz-cut and was a dark brown. When she turned away from me the back of her head resembled a mushroom on a stalk, or an erect penis. I always marvel that in an age where people are not bound by fashion trends and can look any way they choose, so many people choose to look the way they do. This woman's hairstyle was at least ten years too old for her. She regarded me with a deep and profound disapproval when I told her I didn't have an appointment, but she disappeared into Amptman's office and reemerged a bit later to tell me that Amptman would see me for ten minutes.

"Damn it, you shouldn't have come to my place of business!" Amptman said, standing behind his desk. His office resembled that of a county administrator's, all functional with few flourishes or furbelows, in keeping with his own dishwater-dull image. "The whole point of hiring you instead of someone local was to keep this thing as private as possible."

"You bitch when I don't report in and bitch when I do. You don't want me at your home, but you get mad when I come to your office. Working for you full time must really be grins."

"There's a time and a place . . ." he began.

"Sure. But it's okay for you to bust into my home whenever you feel like it. Mr. Amptman, I almost died last night. Twice. And I am truly sick of you. Now sit down and shut up."

He sat down but he didn't shut up. One out of two wasn't bad. "I'm not used to being spoken to that way, Saxon. Not by an employee." The way he mouthed that last word it might have been *leper* or *pederast* or *traitor*.

"I don't care what you're used to," I said. "And don't threaten to fire me again or I may let you, which will not only make me a nonemployee but will leave you and your lovely wife at the source of Shit Creek."

He slumped in his chair, his mouth set like a petulant child's. "Get on with it, then."

"All right. First off, do you own a big dark car?"

"You know very well what cars I own."

"Then the answer is no?"

"The answer is no."

"Fine. Where was your wife last evening between five and eight, let's say?"

"She was home with me."

"Can you prove that?"

"I don't care for your implication."

"I don't care whether you do or not. Answer me."

"Yes, I can prove it. We had dinner guests."

"Who are they? We may need them as witnesses."

"To what?"

I told him about Rama Khali. When I'd finished he was very quiet for a moment. Then he rubbed his eyes under his glasses. "Did you think Nanette had done that, too?"

"No," I said. "And that's the good news. Because I think D'Anjou's killing and Khali's are related. And if Nanette didn't kill Khali she probably didn't kill D'Anjou."

"I wonder how the district attorney will see it," he said sadly.

"Maybe it won't ever get to the district attorney. How about the names of your dinner guests?"

"I'd rather not involve them."

"They came to dinner when their hostess has a murder indictment dangling over her head—I'd say they're already involved. Names, please."

He fiddled with a brass letter opener. I think he wanted to use it on me. "Donald Stack," he said.

If looks could kill there would have been a high requiem mass for George Amptman in the morning.

"I told you we did business together on occasion. I don't see anything wrong—"

"Nobody sees anything wrong with anything," I said. "But two people are dead and someone tried to make me the charm. And if I have to throw Donald Stack to the sharks to save your wife from spending her life in prison, don't be surprised to find yourself going over the side along with him."

He thought about getting nasty again, I could tell by the look in his eye, but I guess he just didn't have the stomach for it anymore. He stood up and went to look out the window. His office was several blocks of highrises away from the ocean, but he seemed to be staring across a vast expanse of space anyway. "How do we get ourselves in these boxes?" he mused. "How is it some people always say and do the wrong thing?" He turned and looked at me. "Take me, for instance. Everything I say to you gets you angry. I don't mean for it to. I'm—we, Nanette and I—are actually very grateful to you. For what you're doing. I wanted you to know that. Whatever happens."

"Whatever happens?"

He took a deep breath. "Real estate is a highly speculative business, Mr. Saxon, and so before we involve ourselves we always have to plan for the worst-case scenario. So when I say whatever happens, I mean that the thought has crossed my mind that Nanette may indeed be guilty of killing that—engineer." I knew what it must have cost him to say that. George Amptman didn't like to spend anything except money; his emotions were rationed out grudgingly, like a miser's pennies.

"And what will you do, if that's true?"

A tear rolled down his cheek from behind his glasses. "That's the hell of it," he said. "I haven't the vaguest idea."

The Sunset Strip occupies an unincorporated section of Los Angeles County and is not officially part of the city at all, even though it's right in the middle of things; it's the result of one of those labyrinthine political triple deals that happened so long ago no one remembers it anymore. The Strip was pretty hot stuff in the forties and fifties when Bogart got into fistfights over stuffed pandas at Ciro's; in the sixties it was taken over by the scraggly-haired members of the counterculture, who would engage in whatever protest was current, sell their bodies to passing motorists, hitchhike, and peddle marijuana on the street. In the past twenty years a few marginal film companies have set up offices there, and there are some discos and overpriced clubs and eateries for the spike-haired set, but mostly the Strip has drifted into quiet, seedy anonymity, a neighborhood in search of its character.

High on a cliff overlooking more mundane parts of the city sits Le Cirque, one of the few restaurants left on the Strip that caters to the deal makers and ballbreakers of the film crowd. Their view site does them little good, since neither the dining room nor the bar has windows, but at any hour of the day or evening Le Cirque is filled with middle-aged people wearing trendy clothes that make them look silly, eating meals that cost too much, and talking too loudly about how much money they make. At cocktail hour, sad young secretaries who have spent a week's salary on an outfit drop in for a drink, hoping to find either a career in the movies or the rich man of their dreams, and sleazy pretty boys with Italian or Arabic names and gold neck chains prowl the lounge like carrion dogs after the lonely wives of neglectful executives. Around Le Cirque's noisy round bar many dreams are made and shattered, often in the same evening.

When I walked in, the Italian maître d' wrung my hand as though I were an old friend on the off chance I might be someone important and ushered me into the lounge. Jaclyn Johnson was perched on a stool at the bar, facing the door, so that she could see everyone who came in and they could see her. For the occasion she had chosen a miniskirt—always dangerous when you're going to be sitting on a high barstool—and a peach-colored silk blouse through which I could see the outlines of an undergarment no bigger than a handkerchief. And Jaclyn Johnson had passed that stage long ago. She was drinking champagne out of a crystal flute.

"Fabrizio, bring another glass for Mr. Saxon," she told the bartender. It must have been her version of hello.

"I'd rather have Scotch. I'm not much of a champagne drinker," I said. "It makes me sleepy."

"Well, we can't have that." When Fabrizio brought the

glass she amended the order. "Anything you want," she said. "It's on David's tab." That seemed to amuse her.

I climbed up onto the stool next to hers. "I appreciate your meeting me."

Her eyes danced. "I figured you'd change your mind. It's curiosity more than lust, I know. Like cocaine. People just want to experience what everyone else is talking about."

"I hate to burst bubbles, but I've never tried cocaine."

She shrugged. "Everyone to his own vices."

Fabrizio set my drink down with a flourish, and I took a sip of it. For a place so high-priced, Le Cirque served a lousy brand of bar Scotch. "Jaclyn, tell me about Vista Petroleum."

"Oh, Jesus, you make my ass ache!" She drained her flute and set it down with a clunk on the marble bar. Fabrizio fell all over himself running to refill it.

"I thought we were friends," I said.

"I don't want to be friends. You don't fuck your friends."

I raised my own glass in a toast to her. "To a single-minded lady."

"If you were as single-minded about sex as you are about your damn case, Warren Beatty would have to leave town."

"Have you had Warren Beatty, too?"

"Ask me no questions," she said cryptically.

"Just one."

She sighed deeply, and her breasts did a fertility dance under her blouse. "Vista Petroleum?"

"Vista Petroleum."

"Why ask me? I'm not David's business partner, for Christ's sake, I'm his trick! I hire and fire the household help, I send out the Christmas cards, I go to parties with him and drive him home when he drinks too much, and on rare occasions when he's not too drunk or stoned or preoccupied with trying to make a three-picture deal at Universal, he lifts my nightie. I don't know anything about his investments unless I can wear them." Absently she put her hand to her throat and touched the emerald pendant that hung in her cleavage. Emeralds sure know how to live.

"I don't know how I can help you," she said.

"Look, your friend David Grayco is a cautious man. He doesn't throw money around on maybes. From what I hear he's more into sure things."

"*You* wouldn't know a sure thing if it bit you on the ass," she said. "Which, come to think of it, might be worth a try."

It was difficult trying to question someone whose only thought seemed to be my ravishment. I said, "I'm just interested in why a man like Grayco would put money into something as speculative as an oil well. Especially when the well had watered out years before."

"From what I remember," she said, "Stack told David it *was* a sure thing. As a matter of fact, the contract they signed was a money-back guarantee. David wouldn't have invested otherwise."

"How in hell can you guarantee a watered-out oil well is a sure thing?"

"*I* can't, but apparently Don Stack can, because David is happier than a pig in shit with the checks he gets every month." She swiveled around on her stool so her back was to the bar, I suppose on the off chance that Fabrizio was a lip-reader. "Give me a break, okay, Saxon? Forget about this oil well business and talk to *me*. You really interest me—mainly because you're the only man I've ever met who treats me like I was an underweight boy."

"That's sure not how I think of you."

"Is it because of David?"

"That wouldn't stop me."

She put her index finger on my lips and traced their outline. "Maybe you're threatened by aggressive women. Maybe you like them submissive. Are you into S and M?"

"No," I said, "but if I were I'd be S, because I'm sure as hell not M. Jaclyn, I appreciate your taking the time to talk to me. You've been a big help."

She sat back and regarded me with distaste, her mouth turning hard and nasty. "You *don't* like aggressive women, do you?"

194

"I love aggressive women," I said. "I just don't like the ones who keep score."

I climbed down from the stool and went out through the front door, getting a second handshake from the aging continental at the door. In the parking lot, the Arab kid who fetched my car put his hand out too. Friendly place, Le Cirque.

The gamblers—the Broadway types with no visible means of support who run their business out of their hats and make the phone company rich, understand sure things. That means the fix is in. The horse has been doped, the power forward has been paid off, or the star pitcher has a torn rotator cuff that even his manager doesn't know about. Sure things don't come along very often. That's why it made me wonder about David Grayco and Donald Stack. And Stack's former connection with the late Rama Magdi Khali.

The sky over the ocean was the color of a Confederate uniform as the day prepared to retire. Billy Ledbetter shoved his hands deep into the pockets of his hooded sweatshirt as we walked along the damp beach across the road from his house. With the hood up he looked like a grizzled gnome. "There's been times," he said, "when I've felt a gusher in the toes of my feet. Other times I felt 'em when they weren't there. Either way, I don't think I could convince anyone outside the business to dump a bunch of money in because of my toes. Oil wells don't work that way."

I looked ahead of us about four hundred feet where Marvel was jogging, his sneakers kicking up the wet sand behind him like a quarter horse. "Then how could Don Stack make a written guarantee to Grayco that he'd get his money back?"

The crinkles around Billy's eyes deepened when he smiled. His face looked like a contour map of Idaho. "He must've known something nobody else does. I bet if you find out what, you've got an answer to your problem." He turned his head toward the surf as a wave made a particularly loud slap against the shore. "How can you be so certain any of this is tied in to those killings?"

"I can't. But if it has to do with Vista Number One, I want to know about it."

"What makes you think it does?"

"Shay. He didn't even know what I wanted when I went over there the first time, he just wanted me the hell out. And I can't believe that our little set-to later was because of Kim."

He carefully didn't look at me. "She's worth fighting for, boy."

"I know it."

"I know you do."

"It just seemed too convenient, him showing up where we were that evening. I think he was on the clock for Vista Petroleum."

Marvel turned and jogged back toward us. "You gonna run," he panted at me, "or you just gonna dog it?"

Billy waved a hand at me and I pushed off, surprising Marvel and leaving him flat-footed. As I pulled away from him, I heard his upward-inflected "Man . . . !"

My triumph was short-lived. It took him less than a hundred yards to overtake me, and when I was spent and winded he was just getting started.

Kim and I collaborated on dinner. She served a lovely brie with warm French bread and whipped up a salad, and I grilled chicken breasts on the barbecue with two different kinds of mustard and baked some corn ears wrapped in foil. It was more than pleasant to be bustling around the kitchen with her, bumping into one another a trifle more often than absolutely necessary. I had brought some John Courage beer from home, and it complemented everything neatly for Billy and me. Kim stuck to her Perrier and Marvel, to no one's surprise, drank Pepsi.

The subject of sure things came up again with coffee and the New York–style rum cheesecake I'd picked up on the way.

"There's always hot oil," Kim said. "But that's against the law."

Her grandfather said, "I suppose you never heard of anyone breaking laws before?"

"Tha's right," Marvel said. "Jus' say no."

"Fill me in, everyone. What's hot oil?"

"A fast one some of the old wildcatters used to pull years ago," Billy said. "They'd drill a well that turned out to be useless, then buy some oil from somewhere else, dump it into the hole at night, and pump it out again in the morning. It impressed the hell out of any potential investors. It worked, too." He shook his head. "I haven't heard of a hot oil prosecution in thirty years, though."

I took a bite of my cheesecake. I'm not big on sweets; I could go forever without ever tasting chocolate again. But wave a slab of New York cheesecake under my nose and all bets are off. I said, "Vista Number One was producing for months before the Gamble people drilled their inspection shaft."

"Besides," Kim said, "you don't buy large quantities of crude the way you pick up a six-pack from the supermarket. There are records, sales receipts, shipping manifestos, computerized records. In this day and age no one could ever get away with it."

"How about a nice after-dinner something?" Billy said.

We had several. And Marvel had two more pieces of cheesecake. He asked for a third, but I stepped in to play heavy/father and said no.

Marvel sat in the car, the stereo blasting jazz while Kim and I kissed good night in the driveway. It took us a while—through Dizzy Gillespie's "Night in Tunisia," Oscar Peterson's "Something's Coming," and the Manhattan Transfer doing "Jeannine."

I finally slid behind the steering wheel and turned the volume down. Marvel shook his head sadly, forever put upon. "When you gonna git your own wheels back?" he said. The rental car didn't have a tape deck, and he chafed at the injustice of it all.

"Probably never," I said. "It's pretty much of a disaster. I'll bet the insurance company totals it out."

"Gonna buy a new one?"

I pulled out of the Ledbetter driveway and onto Vista Del Mar, heading for home. "That car was leased for me by a client, Marvel; the insurance money will go to the leasing company, not me. I'll have to come up with enough cash to buy another car. It probably won't be a new one."

"Shee-it," he said. "All the time money."

"Try living without it."

"You oughta git you a scam runnin' that hot oil shit," he said. "Sound like a good one t' me." He slumped down in the seat and put his sneakered feet up on the dash. Marvel contributes little to the conversation when we're in group situations, but he listens carefully and rarely misses a trick.

And then I slammed the heel of my hand onto my bruised forehead, because I couldn't say the same for myself.

19

"I hated to let you go last night," Kim said. Her voice on the phone sounded pleasantly throaty.

"I hated to leave. But that's what happens when you have kids." I cradled the phone between my chin and my shoulder and poured another cup of coffee. "I need a favor."

"And I thought this was an obscene phone call."

"I prefer my obscenities in person. Kim, do you have access to your company's shipping records?"

"Not directly. I suppose I could call someone."

"I want to find out if Texaco delivered any crude oil to Vista Number One any time between eighteen and thirty months ago."

There was a silence on the other end of the line. Then she said, "You're kidding, right?"

"It's a long shot, I admit."

"Texaco isn't the only oil company in town."

"I know. I'm going to call all the others."

But first I called Joe DiMattia.

"Did you talk to the doorman at Khali's building?" I said. "Did he mention that Khali had any visitors?"

"The only thing he remembered was your lousy impersonation of a DWP inspector. Don't you know that's illegal?"

"Call a cop. I've got something for you, Joe. Before Khali went to work for Gamble Petroleum he worked for

Donald Stack. And after Peter D'Anjou left Gamble *he* worked for Stack. Does that suggest anything to you?"

"Have you talked to Stack?"

"Not for a while. Not since Khali was killed. He doesn't like me much—"

"A man of taste," DiMattia observed.

"—and he's got enough security over there to keep out a battalion of invaders from Mars. So maybe you ought to chat with him."

I heard him breathing heavily through his flattened nose. Finally he said, "Okay, Saxon. Thanks. Keep in touch," and hung up. And I sat and stared at the wall for a long time. Joe DiMattia thanking me was enough of a departure from the norm to set me off balance. I wasn't sure if I could handle it. Damn him, anyway, for spoiling our perfect adversary relationship.

I spent the rest of my morning calling the shipping departments of Shell and Mobil and Standard Oil and all the other oil companies from Santa Barbara southward.

"Why in hell would we deliver crude oil to an oil well?" the man at Mobil asked. His name was Ed Billts, and his phone demeanor told me I was the capper to a generally lousy morning.

"Would that be unusual?"

"Damn right."

"So if you had, you'd remember it?"

"I think so," he said defensively.

"Does that mean you aren't going to look it up for me?" Billts changed his tone to sly and wheedling. "What's in it for me?"

"What do you drink?"

"Black Jack."

"Okay. Two bottles of Jack Daniel's will be delivered to your office before you go home today."

"Fine. When they get here I'll look it up for you."

"Look it up for me now and the two bottles might have a couple of babies."

"Okay, ace, hang on." I hate being called "ace," but I

couldn't say anything about it because he put me on hold, and as I listened to Barry Manilow modulate upward on the radio station that was plugged into their phone system I wondered if the whole world was corrupt. When the pope appears on his balcony at the Vatican to bless the multitudes, does he collect vigorish?

Ed Billts came back on the line. "You're SOL, pal," he told me. Shit Outta Luck. "No records of any deliveries to Vista for the past three years."

I crossed Mobil off my list. It was one of the last names on the yellow pad. "Okay, thanks."

"You're not gonna forget about those four soldiers?"

I sighed. "I'll give them their marching orders soon as I hang up."

I called a liquor store in Torrance and ordered the delivery and charged it on my credit card—I don't know how people manage to get through the day without one.

Kim called me back to tell me Texaco had no record of delivery to Vista either.

"That just about tears it, then," I said, snapping my pencil in two with my thumb. "It seemed like a good idea at the time. I've called every oil company in California, and even a few in Mexico."

"Even Gamble?"

I laughed. "Why in hell would Gamble Oil . . . ?" I stopped laughing. "Son of a bitch!" I said.

When Agatha Rusk ushered me into Jason Gamble's office at five o'clock that afternoon, I found him wearing a dark suit, a white shirt, and a sober gray tie. He had just come back from the funeral of Rama Magdi Khali and his somber look matched the occasion.

"This is not a convenient time, Mr. Saxon."

"It never is," I said, "but it's necessary."

"Damn it!" he said. "My friends are dropping like flies. It's beginning to make me nervous."

"I can understand that."

201

"Then you can also understand I'm not much in the mood for socializing."

"This isn't a social call," I said. "Mr. Gamble, I'd like you to call your shipping department and find out whether they shipped any crude oil to Vista Number One in the last two years."

"I can assure you that is highly unlikely."

"Can you, Mr. Gamble? Assure me?"

He lowered himself into his big throne chair, staring at me. "Are you saying what I think you're saying?"

"I'm just asking a question."

"About hot oil?"

"It's a possibility, isn't it?"

"One I thought of, believe me." He made a sour face. "I thought of just about everything, including voodoo. But there's no way Stack could get away with that in the computer age. And if he could, the last place he'd likely get his oil is here."

"What will it cost to check it out?"

"I'd laugh if it wasn't so damn grotesque."

"Laugh after you make that call."

He pushed a button on his phone console and Agatha Rusk appeared in the doorway. Today she was wearing a deep burgundy suit with shoes that almost matched in color. She was a very good-looking woman; the large aviator glasses added to the appeal.

"Ag, could we rustle up a drink for Mr. Saxon?"

She turned to me and smiled coolly, professionally. "Certainly," she said. "You have a preference?"

I wondered if she and Jason Gamble had anything going. Maybe I just have a dirty mind. "Scotch, please, if you have it."

"I think so," she said, secure in the knowledge that even if I'd asked for a piña colada she'd have the fixings. "Rocks?"

I nodded as Gamble picked up his phone and tapped out a few numbers.

"Go ahead into the rec room and relax," Gamble said, "this'll take a few minutes."

I followed Agatha out across the reception area and into another room in the suite. It was casually furnished with leather sofas and easy chairs, complete with a refrigerator, a microwave oven, and a small bar. She knew her way around in there, and moved efficiently if a bit too sensuously. Hips like that were not created to be encased in business suits.

She tonged some ice cubes from a thermal bucket and poured expertly and efficiently from a bottle of Dewar's.

"Join me?" I said.

She shook her head. "I'm still working, Mr. Saxon."

"Sure, sorry. How long have you been with Gamble Oil?"

"Eleven years," she said. "It's the only job I've ever had since college."

"Business degree?"

"Geology." She handed me my drink. "Cheers."

I took a sip. "Miss Rusk, did you know Peter D'Anjou?"

Something happened behind those oversize lenses and she turned her face away quickly. "Yes," she said, and although there was nothing near her mouth, her voice sounded muffled.

"Tell me about him."

"Why ask me?"

"I figured as Mr. Gamble's secretary you'd know just about everyone around here."

"I do, but I don't know anyone well."

She was squeezing the words out in a way that was not like her, at least, from what I had seen. It made me want to push. "So you didn't know Peter D'Anjou well, then?"

"Not terribly well, no."

"How well?"

She spun around to face me. "That's not your concern," she said, and I could see her eyes were tearing.

"I'm sorry, Miss Rusk, I just thought—"

"You didn't think at all, Mr. Saxon." She was pacing in front of me, now, her long fingers curled into fists at her sides. "Is that why you came here today? Because you'd poked around and found out about Peter and me, and now you want to pump me for information? That's pretty low." She fumbled in the pocket of her jacket and took out a Kleenex, into which she blew her nose in such an efficient way as to let me know the blowing of it was simply to clear the nasal passages and was not to be construed as the admission of weakness or the exposure of any chinks in Agatha Rusk's formidable emotional armor.

"I swear I didn't know," I said. "I was just asking a general question. I'm really sorry."

She waved me away and turned her back, leaning both hands on the bar and taking a few deep breaths to compose herself. "It doesn't matter anymore, I suppose. I was seeing Peter for two years and then it was over. Those things happen to people sometimes. All the time. But when you've been close to someone, physically and emotionally close, and then they . . . get *killed,* it's—sometimes difficult to deal with."

I took another pull of my drink, feeling as small as a cockroach in a corner. "I don't mean to hurt you, Miss Rusk—Agatha. But I'm trying to find out who killed him."

"Why not ask Her?" she said.

"I don't think she did it."

She turned back to me, her expression somewhere between anger and grief. "Thanks a lot," she said. "Is that supposed to make me feel better?"

"I'm sorry, but my job isn't to make you feel better. Agatha, why did he leave Gamble Oil?"

"That's enough, Saxon!" Jason Gamble spoke from the doorway, biting the words off. "What the hell's going on here?"

"D'Anjou is dead and now Khali is dead, and it's about time I started getting some answers."

"Then don't harass the people in my office. Ask me."

"Consider yourself asked."

Gamble went over and put an avuncular arm around Agatha Rusk, who stood with her chin out, her back rigid. He spoke to her, but he was staring at me without warmth. "Go on home, Ag," he said. "The day's over."

"I'll be all right."

"Be all right at home, then."

Her body relaxed just a bit, and she said, "I'm sorry, Jason."

"It's a tough time for all of us," he said, giving me a heavy look. "I'll deal with Mr. Saxon."

Her glare as she passed by me would have withered an oak tree. Neither Gamble nor I moved until she had taken her purse from her desk in the next room and her coat from the rack and left, closing the outer door behind her.

"You're an insensitive son of a bitch," he said. "The only reason I don't kick your ass is because you're a friend of Billy Ledbetter's. Finish your drink and then you're out of here."

It's amazing how we mellow as we get older. For one brief shining moment I considered inviting him to try and kick my ass, but I decided it would be unproductive. Instead I said, "You don't seem to understand, Mr. Gamble. Two people have been murdered, one an employee of yours and one a former employee. The cops are going to be around sooner or later—"

"Sooner," he said, "they were here yesterday."

"And what did you tell them?"

"The same thing I told you. I don't know what's going on and I'm not happy about it."

"You can be more help than that."

"Just tell me how," he said. His anger was flattening out to simple annoyance.

"First of all you can tell me the real reason you fired Peter D'Anjou."

He screwed up his mouth as though he were chewing taffy, a deep furrow appearing between his eyebrows. I said, "Was it because of Miss Rusk?"

"Hell, no," he said. "I didn't like it, of course. Office

romances are unhealthy. But in this day and age people spend more time at their jobs than they used to, and it's hard to avoid. I just bit the bullet and waited for it to run its course—and it did."

"Then why was D'Anjou let go?"

He looked away. "I told you."

"I know, but I don't believe you. You said you fired D'Anjou because he was screwing everything that moved. Now I find out he had a long relationship with Agatha Rusk before he got fired. What's the real story?"

He went to the bar and poured himself a bourbon with no ice, and bit down a good portion of it before he refilled his glass. Then he crossed the room and half fell onto one of the sofas. "Sit down," he said.

I sat across from him in a big leather club chair. He studied his drink as if it were alphabet soup spelling out pat, easy answers. "What I'm going to tell you had better be kept confidential," he said. "Because if a single word of it gets out, it could cause me all sorts of legal problems, to say nothing of embarrassment. If that happens, I'm going to sue you and then I'm going to have you cut up in pieces and fed to the crows. You understand?"

I nodded. "Level with me and you have my word. Why did you fire D'Anjou?"

He swallowed some bourbon and exhaled loudly. "I didn't," he said.

"You mean he quit?"

"I mean that Pete D'Anjou was on my payroll up until the day he died."

I blinked, then stared at him for a moment.

"What's all this business about 'termination,' then?"

He made himself slightly more comfortable on the sofa. "You have to understand the oil industry. For all the money it generates, it's really pretty small. Not just on a local scale, but internationally as well. Everyone knows everyone else, and everyone else's business. Donald Stack's lawsuit against this company was common knowledge, and it was pretty damn embarrassing to me, to say nothing of expensive."

"What's all this have to do with D'Anjou?"

"That's where it gets sticky. I knew—I still know—that somehow or other Don Stack has snookered me royally. I mean, we owned that well at one time, and I've been around enough to know when a hole is watered out! There's no way in hell it could have started producing five hundred barrels a day again. That's why I sold it off to Pacifica. But I couldn't prove it, and until I could I was stuck with Stack's lawsuit."

"You settled out of court, though?"

"Oh, I could have let it drag on another three years and wound up paying another million or so in attorney's fees. But I decided to do it a different way."

"What way?"

"Espionage." He drank the rest of his drink to cover his embarrassment. "Sounds hokey, doesn't it? Like a Ludlum novel. But I needed someone on the inside at Vista, someone who would have access to their records and files, and I chose the guy closest to me."

"Are you telling me Peter D'Anjou was spying for you?"

He nodded. "We staged a very noisy breakup here, me yelling accusations, him yelling at me to mind my own fucking business. Everyone in the industry heard about it. Hell, everyone in the building could hear us yelling. Nobody but Pete and me knew it was all an act. We made up that bullshit story about Pete chasing too many women as a cover. Unfortunately it wrecked things between Pete and Agatha. Or it was the last straw, anyway—the relationship was already pretty well over. But Pete never did have any trouble in the female department, and I guess he hooked up with this Amptman woman shortly after that. About the same time he went to Don Stack and begged for a part-time consultancy with him."

"He did legitimate work for Vista, didn't he?"

"Oh, sure; a day's work for a day's pay. Pete was that kind of guy. But Pete never left my payroll, either. My personal payroll. And I promised him a substantial bonus if he could get anything on Stack about Vista Number One."

"How substantial?"

Gamble said, "If Pete could have found out the real story behind Vista Number One, it would have saved me thirty-two million dollars. I thought that ten percent was the least I could do."

I sat back in my chair, visions of a three-million-dollar-plus payday dancing in my head like sugarplums. No wonder D'Anjou had told Nanette Amptman that he was expecting to come into some big money very soon.

Which meant that he had been pretty close to getting the goods on Vista Petroleum when he was killed.

I said, "And nobody knew about this?"

"Nobody. I may be crazy, Saxon, but I'm not dumb. There's not two people in this whole world I'd trust when it comes to money like that. Pete was one of them, God damn it. Like I told you, we were very close." He sniffled, trying to make it sound like a macho snort. He got up, took my glass from me, and refreshed both my drink and his at the bar. "Now you know why this has to remain just between us."

I nodded, taking the glass.

"Because somehow or other, I'm going to find out the truth about Vista Number One, and then Don Stack's ass belongs to me."

"Mr. Gamble, did you make that phone call for me? To your shipping department?"

"Oh," he said, still standing, "I almost forgot. Yes, I did. There's no record of a delivery to Vista. Besides, anything so unusual would need to be authorized by either Tomita or Khali or myself. I didn't do it, and I'm sure the other two would have checked with me first."

"Didn't Khali work for Stack before coming here?"

"So what? I told you, petroleum is a small world. If I didn't hire people who once worked for my competitors I'd have a bunch of pimply twenty-year-olds with the ink still wet on their sheepskins." He sat down on the sofa again, and the air hissed out of the leather cushion. "Besides, Rama's dead, too."

"I know," I said.

He drained most of his drink in a single swallow. These oil folk really know how to put it away. "I want you to stay away from Aggie," he said. "She's had a bad time of it because of Peter. We all have, but her especially. There's a time for sorrow, I know that. But now it's time to go on."

"Easy for you to say," I said. "You aren't facing a murder rap."

"But I'm running a multinational company," he said, "and I'm grieving for two friends, and I'm about sick of talking to you. So if you'll excuse me . . ."

"Can I make a quick phone call first?"

He waved at the telephone on the wall next to the bar. "Help yourself," he said. "And then go away." He got up and went out through the reception area to his own office. I carried my drink over to the bar and dialed Joe DiMattia.

"What have you got?" he said. No hello, no pleasantries. Just hello.

I told him what I'd just learned from Jason Gamble, and for a moment he didn't say anything. I assumed he was writing it all down. Then, "All right."

"Tit for tat, Joe. What have you got for me?"

"I don't have to give you shit. You know that."

Annoying as DiMattia could be sometimes, that made me feel better. I'm always more comfortable on familiar ground. "Give me a break, Joe. I'm trying to be a good guy."

"You? Might as well try to be a Chinese acrobat," he said. I waited, knowing anything I might say would provoke another insult at best, and at worst he'd hang up. Finally he said, "I went to see Stack today. That's a big man he was hanging around, the one with the raspy voice."

I had to smile at that one.

"If you're trying to make him for the killings, you're out of luck," he said. "When D'Anjou got put in the pond, Stack was in a business meeting with three other guys in Long Beach. And he was having dinner at the Petroleum Club on Sunday night when the Indian gook bought it."

"What about the big guy? Shay."

"He's alibied up the wazoo. He hangs out in a bar down by the beach—he was there both times. Besides, a guy like that doesn't strangle you with a scarf. He sits on you till your lungs collapse. So we're back to square one."

"Maybe not, Joe."

"Whattaya mean by that? You holding something out on me?"

"I'll let you know," I said, and hung up.

When I went out into the reception room I could see Gamble behind his desk in his private office. He looked up and called out, "I mean it about staying away from Agatha Rusk. Bury the dead, Saxon."

I went to the open doorway. "Mr. Gamble, could it be that you and Agatha Rusk are more than business acquaintances?"

The whiskey flush on his face turned a few shades darker, and he dropped his eyes. "Not yet," he said bitterly.

20

I made my way down the deserted corridors of Gamble Oil, past the portals of executive row. There was something very sad about Khali's nameplate on his door, about knowing it would be taken down soon. No matter what happens the world keeps spinning; new executives are hired, new loves are found, new nameplates replace old ones. A day or two of solemn looks and sorrowing smiles, and then the pressures of everyday living make themselves felt and it's back to business. It's a blessing none of us are here to see how very little anyone gives a damn when we die.

I passed Rosario Soldano's medical section and the payroll department, the plant safety unit, and the public relations office. Then I reached Kenji Tomita's office and slowed down. I checked my watch. It was twenty minutes after six, and most of the Gamble employees had gone home. A junior executive too old for his job, who had been working late in the mistaken belief that he could score points with his supervisor, was hurrying from his office, shrugging himself into a raincoat. I nodded as he passed me, trying to look as if I belonged there, and listened to his footsteps on the cold tile floor of the corridor. Then I turned the corner and confronted a door marked MEN. I was one of those. I pushed it open and went inside.

It was a three-staller, with three sinks and two urinals on the other side of the room, and a floor covered with the kind of diamond-shaped bathroom tiling that had been popular in the thirties, when the building was constructed. I stepped into the far stall, hung my jacket on the hook provided, and sat down on the john to wait. A stall in a public rest room is not my idea of a pleasant place to pass the time, but I wanted to make sure everyone was gone before doing what I had to do. I didn't want to explain to plant security why I was breaking into an executive office. I passed some of the time studying the graffito on the inside of the stall door facing me; it was a detailed black ink drawing of a disembodied vagina, faithfully rendered. Beneath it in block letters was a two-word suggestion.

At about six thirty-five someone came in, used a urinal, hawked and spit into it, and flushed. Then he washed his hands, dried them on three paper towels, and left. Business as usual in the men's room.

At five minutes past seven I timidly emerged from the stall. I went to the sink and washed my hands. I don't know why, perhaps it was a conditioned reflex. I dried them on some paper towels, put on my jacket, and went back out into the hallway.

I retraced my steps until I was in front of Mr. Tomita's office. Once more my gaze swept the corridor until I was satisfied that I was alone, and then I tried the door. I knew it would be locked. Fortunately I had my set of lock picks with me. I had put them in my pocket along with my .38 police special before I'd left the house, remembering from my scouting days the virtue of preparedness.

Office locks aren't nearly as complicated as those used in most private homes, and it took me about two minutes to spring the mechanism. I went inside.

I passed the secretary's desk and proceeded into Tomita's inner office. His desktop was cleared of everything except a pen set, a leather-bound appointment book, and a console telephone with more buttons than a policeman's tunic. I briefly scanned the appointment book, but nothing of significance caught my eye.

A bank of steel filing cabinets, twenty-four drawers in all, stretched along one wall. They were all locked too. I looked in the desk drawers in vain for a key and then went at them with the lock picks; they proved to be harder to open than the office door. By the time I felt the pick connect and turn, it was nearly eight o'clock and I was bathed in perspiration.

There were personnel jackets by the hundreds in there, all so carefully filed that I found the ones I was looking for immediately: Agatha Rusk, Rama Magdi Khali, and Kenji Tomita himself. None of them told me anything I hadn't known before, except vacation dates, salary rates, and efficiency reports. Agatha Rusk's evaluations were glowing, praising her efficiency, loyalty, and follow-through abilities, all signed by Tomita and Jason Gamble. Her salary was $33,500 a year; she was worth a lot more. Kenji Tomita was pulling down $88,724 per year, and Khali had been making $97,425, plus bonuses and incentives adding up to another $23,000. Khali's evaluation spoke of his engineering skills and his dedication, but noted that he was often demanding and abrupt with subordinates. "Rama needs to work on getting along better with those who work for him," was the conclusion. Again, signed by Gamble and Tomita.

In another drawer, this one containing the records of former employees, I found the work history of Peter D'Anjou, spanning the eleven years he had been with the company. The earlier evaluations, positive in the extreme, were signed by someone named Orrin Klemmer, and when I looked him up I found he was the man who'd held Khali's job up until a year ago. He had retired with a full pension, $54,000 annually. Not a bad paycheck for sitting on your ass in the sun.

The last evaluation in Peter D'Anjou's jacket, dated ten months earlier, had been signed by Khali. They were all rave reviews, and none of them mentioned D'Anjou's supposed womanizing.

I replaced all the personnel files and began rummaging through the other drawers. I came across plant maintenance records, purchase orders for equipment and office supplies, environmental impact reports. Apparently Kenji Tomita just about ran the joint.

The fourteenth drawer was difficult to open; when I managed to drag it out I found that something was stuffed under the files, keeping the drawer from sliding freely. I dug down between the Pendaflex folders and came up with a fat manila envelope, looking as if it had recently been opened and reclosed. I could see where the flap had been torn away and then resealed with postal-approved packaging tape. There was no way I could open it and seal it up again neatly, and I thought for a long while about replacing it in the bottom of the drawer and going on with my search.

But my curiosity got the better of me. It usually does. It's gotten me into a lot of trouble over the years, but it also makes me fairly effective in my work. I opted for recklessness and ripped the tape off the flap of the envelope.

Inside were three duplicate sets of shipping records showing that fifteen hundred barrels of crude oil had been shipped from Gamble Petroleum to Vista Number One in September of the previous year. The bill of lading had been signed by Kenji Tomita, director of plant operations, and the receipt had been initialed R.M.K. I guessed that stood for Rama Magdi Khali.

Bound in light blue legal covers were articles of incorporation stating that Donald Stack was the owner of sixty percent of Vista Petroleum, a California corporation. David Grayco owned ten percent, and the other thirty was divided equally between two other partners. Rama Magdi Khali was one. The other was Kenji Sueo Tomita.

There was also a diskette in a plain white envelope. A label had been affixed to it: CONFIDENTIAL.

I didn't feel secure enough here at Gamble Oil after hours to turn on Tomita's computer and read the contents of the diskette. I'd take it back to my own office and do it there on the used computer Jo Zeidler had shamed me into buying eight months before from a now defunct business academy that was in the process of quickly liquidating its assets. But if it contained the data I suspected it might, Nanette Amptman would be off the hook and Joe DiMattia would have his killer.

That would have been the easy way. But I have noticed on more than one occasion that things don't often fall like that for me. I usually do things the hard way—not by any conscious choice on my part, but because there are always other people with a penchant for standing between me and the easy road, arms akimbo, hell-bent on sending me down the bumpy road.

Such a person was Kenji Tomita, who now stood in the doorway of his office. He wasn't smiling.

"You are trespassing, Mr. Saxon," he said.

21

"Furthermore," Tomita continued, "you have something that does not belong to you." He took two steps into the room, leaving the door between his office and his secretary's open. He was wearing a brown three-piece suit that might have been purchased in the boy's section of a local department store. "You'll give it back, please?"

"I don't think so, Mr. Tomita."

"It is stolen property."

"I wasn't the first one to steal it," I said. "But we'll let the police decide. This will keep an innocent person out of prison."

He cocked his head like a sparrow. His expression was benign, interested. "And how is that?" he said.

"Because it proves you were part of a massive swindle. You signed the shipping order that sent fifteen hundred barrels of oil to Donald Stack at Vista Number One. He'd pour the oil into the well at night and pump it out the next day."

"What does this have to do with your insurance company?" Tomita said.

"I'm not with an insurance company, and you know it."

"Then I don't understand your concern."

"Bear with me, Mr. Tomita," I said, and he bowed politely. I bowed back. "Donald Stack knew that if a watered-out well like Vista Number One started producing that much oil, Jason Gamble would get suspicious and demand an inspection. As soon as the shaft was drilled, he simply stopped pouring the oil back into the well, and when the well dried up, he sued Gamble for ten years' worth of production. That's how he was able to guarantee David Grayco a return on his money."

"Very good, Mr. Saxon."

"Wait, it gets better. The job of chief engineer opens up at Gamble Petroleum, and Khali moves right in to keep an eye on things over there. In the meantime, Gamble knows he's been reamed but he can't prove it. So he stages a break with Pete D'Anjou and, as far as the world knows, fires him. But D'Anjou is still on Gamble's payroll and becomes a spy over at Vista Number One, while Khali in the meantime is spying on Gamble. Wheels within wheels. Has an interesting symmetry, doesn't it?"

"Classical," Tomita agreed.

"Just about the time D'Anjou gets the goods on Vista, someone—you or Stack or Khali—gets wise to him. You were all in it together, anyway. You decide you have to get rid of him before he reports what he knows back to Gamble, and your three-million-dollar-a-year sting goes down the drain. So Stack gets himself an alibi and Khali goes visiting. D'Anjou let him in, of course. And Khali wraps one of D'Anjou's silk scarves around his neck. Then he steals this diskette from D'Anjou's home." I waved the envelope at him. "I'm sure that when I get it booted up it will show Pete D'Anjou's complete report, with documentations of everything, including these shipping orders and receipts. I imagine one of these copies is the one Khali took from D'Anjou's files."

Tomita nodded. "You are so sure of your facts, Mr. Saxon. I wonder how?"

"Khali was very concerned with maintaining the traditions of his homeland," I said. "Wore a turban, didn't drink alcohol, which had to set him apart from most of the people in the oil business around here. He even kept a pet snake in a glass case in the living room, just to remind him of the good old days back in India. It only stands to reason if he were going to kill someone it would be in a traditional way.

Ever hear of thuggee, Mr. Tomita? That's where we get our English word 'thug.' It was an East Indian cult of about two hundred years ago that worshipped a lady named Kali, the Hindu goddess of destruction, and offered up human sacrifices to her by strangling unsuspecting pilgrims with a handkerchief. Careless of Khali to do it that way, but as far as anyone knew he hadn't even seen D'Anjou for more than six months and there would be no reason to suspect him. And then when I happened to see Nanette Amptman leaving the murder scene, everything fell together for you. The police called it a crime of passion, they were more than satisfied with their suspect, and it was all over with."

"Sadly we did not count on your involvement."

"I'm sorry I spoiled everything for you, Mr. Tomita. Let's see, fifteen percent of thirty two million dollars would be . . ."

"A considerable sum, I assure you."

"Yes. It's no wonder I made you nervous. The first one to spook was Don Stack, when I came around to his oil well last Saturday. That's why there's such tight security around Vista Number One. So he sent Jim Shay around to scare me away, and when that didn't work—now, this is where it gets a little vague. Khali got scared, didn't he? This wasn't an oil swindle for him anymore now, it was murder. He panicked, threatened to run, and you went to his apartment and killed him Sunday. From the way the knife was sticking in his neck, it was obvious the person who put it there was much shorter than he."

Tomita laughed.

"I'm amusing you?"

"To a large extent, Mr. Saxon."

"What I can't figure is how you got in and out without the doorman spotting you."

Tomita smiled. "The apartment is owned by Gamble Oil, Mr. Saxon; it is one of five we have here in Los Angeles. As the director of operations I have a key, and to the downstairs garage as well."

"Neat. And then I was the only one left who was making

218

you nervous. So you came to my home Sunday night, meaning to kill me, too. Except I must have startled you by leaving the house late for my little drive in the rain. You followed me to El Tercero and ran me off the road. Careless of you, Mr. Tomita. You should have stayed to finish the job."

"It was a loud crash, Mr. Saxon. I feared it would bring the police."

"Cops don't like to go out in the rain any more than anyone else."

"Your deductions have been impressive," he said. "You have only made a few mistakes."

"Such as?"

"Poor Mr. Stack is a criminal and a swindler, but not a very good one. He could never have proceeded as he did without my help, and Khali's. And he did not know that Mr. Don-Jew was still working for Gamble. I discovered it quite by accident when I was going over the accounts and noticed several payments, off the books, to Mr. Don-Jew. I informed Khali, and we decided that Mr. Don-Jew had to be . . . disposed of. Quickly. Mr. Stack had no knowledge of that, before or after. He would not have permitted." He allowed himself another wry smile. "You westerners persist in the belief that Asians have less regard for human life than you."

"I believe you have a high regard for your own life, Mr. Tomita."

"That, as they say, is a different story."

"Am I to consider this a confession?"

"Consider whatever you wish," he said.

I didn't like that. It was too easy. I had the feeling he had a few more tricks to play. I said, "Perhaps you'll come along and repeat this story to the police?"

"I think not," he said.

I reached under my jacket and brought out my police special. "I think so."

His eyes widened a bit behind his shiny glasses; then his shoulders slumped and he sighed. "I did not think you had a gun, Mr. Saxon." And formally, ever so politely, he bowed.

And then, too fast for me to counter it, much less stop it, he pirouetted and his foot whipped out against my wrist and sent the gun spinning across the desktop and onto the floor. He whirled around on the other foot and kicked again, his shoe connecting with the side of my head, and I went tumbling over the desk after the gun, the telephone coming down on top of my head, red lights exploding behind my eyes. The little fucker was a martial artist, and a good one.

I landed face down in a heap between the chair and the desk, the fallen gun digging into my chest. I tried to get up but Tomita kicked me in the small of my back, and I sprawled forward again, momentarily paralyzed by incredible pain shooting up my spine and blossoming out into my legs, arms, and shoulders like a skyrocket exploding in mid-air. I writhed like a scorpion zapped with bug spray, unable to coordinate my movements as he bent and took the envelope from the floor where it had fallen. I lay still for a few seconds, mainly because I had to, my hand buried under me groping for the gun. I sensed him standing over me and glanced over my shoulder as he stepped back for another kick, one that would undoubtedly kill me.

I shifted to one side so my hand was free, and then I rolled off my side with the gun in my hand and shot him in the left arm, shattering the bone between elbow and shoulder and leaving the arm dangling uselessly. He screamed. The bullet's impact made him stagger backward, and he caromed off the corner of the desk and twisted into the center of the room, falling to one knee. He looked up at me, his eyes wide with fear behind the thick glasses, and then he scrambled to his feet again and ran out of the office.

I grabbed the edge of the desk and attempted to stand erect, but my muscles didn't seem to work very well, my legs as rubbery as a vaudeville drunk's. Every inch of me hurt, and there was a numbing sensation in my extremities that made me very nervous. Finally I hauled myself to my feet and stood there, trying every way I knew to make my knees lock, and working my jaw to make sure it wasn't dislocated. I wasn't certain; it hurt too much. When I was able to breathe without causing twinges of agony all through my body, I turned and started after Tomita. I found I was limping like an old man with rheumatism.

I lurched out into the empty corridor. On the tiled floor of the building was a thin trail of blood leading off to my right, and I followed it, bouncing from one wall to the other like a pinball. The trail stopped at the door to fire stairs, and I opened it and went in. The gun was warm in my hand, smelling of cordite. It's a lousy smell, one that I hate: the smell of bad news.

I could hear him below me. I pounded down three flights of stairs, each step jarring my entire body. Then a door opened and closed and the only sounds in the stairwell were the ones I was making, my heavy, uneven footfalls and my tortured breathing. I got to the bottom, where a solid metal door barred my way. I wrenched it open and found myself outside in the dark at the rear of the building. I was thankful for that. If Tomita had gone down the front way, the security guard in the lobby would probably have stopped me—and not gently, either.

I stripped off my jacket in spite of the cold; it was too ungainly to allow me the freedom of movement I needed. I looked around through the fog in every direction. Visibility was poor to zero, and I strained my eyes to pierce the gloom. Finally I saw Tomita's small silhouette heading out across the parking lot. The blue arc lights were shining off the tops of the cars, turning night to twilight. Mr. Tomita was running unevenly, almost drunkenly, his left arm flopping at his side. But his kick to the spine had insured that I wasn't exactly running like an Olympic sprinter either. I hobbled off after him.

He ran toward a chain link fence at the far end of the lot. Beyond the fence I could hear and sense rather than see the oil wells pumping. He slipped through an opening in the fence and disappeared into the darkness of Gamble's oil field, and it took me almost a minute to reach the gap and go in after him. The lamps that brightened the parking lot didn't reach here, but every so often I would see him move through a pool of light cast by the illumination of the individual wells, the pumps bowing precisely as he ran by them. I didn't know where he was heading, and I don't think he did, either. He seemed disoriented and confused. A bullet wound can do that to you.

He was too far away for me to get off a good shot, but I don't think I would have fired at him in any event. I don't like to shoot people unless I have to, and I didn't think I had to. Eventually Mr. Tomita was going to run out of room.

I lost him for a moment. It made me nervous, not knowing where he was. I didn't know how familiar he was with the terrain, but certainly he knew the oil field better than I did. I was carrying a weapon, but he had one, too, as formidable as mine. The wound in his arm had not disabled those lethal feet of his, and if he caught me unawares from behind, my gun would be as much use to me as sweat socks to a dolphin.

I came abreast of one of the wells. The smell of oil was rich and thick and made the membranes in my nose sting, bringing tears to my eyes. There were people who worked around that odor all the time—I didn't see how they could stand it. I stood there in the light for a moment, peering into the infinite gloom as the fog swirled in front of me like movie special effects. I thought I detected some movement about a hundred yards away near the farthest oil well. It could have been only a trick of light and mist, but I limped toward it, not really sure I wanted it to be Mr. Tomita. He was a tiny man, sixty years old and bleeding, but the pain in my back, which had now spread down into my abdomen and thighs, told me he was even more dangerous than a gorilla like Jim Shay. He could kill with his hands and feet, for one thing. For another, he had nothing left to lose.

I reached the place where I thought I had seen him. The ground was mucky and wet, the dampness seeping through my shoes to my socks. The fence surrounding the well bore a sign reading GAMBLE #31, with a date beneath it, and the noise of the machinery hummed behind me, metal against metal, as the head of the pump dipped and rose. And then I saw him, crouched down inside the fence behind the well. The sleeve of his jacket from the bicep to the cuff was soaked a dark red, and perspiration drenched the rest of him. In his hand he clutched the envelope that would send him to prison for the rest of his life.

"Give it up, Mr. Tomita," I said, pointing my .38 at the widest part of his little body. "You have no place to go."

He stood upright and came toward me. I didn't have to worry about a karate kick, as the fence was between us, but he was smiling at me, a benevolent and peaceful smile. Something about that sent a chill racketing through me. He stopped about six feet from me, the pump bobbing behind him. I could hear the creak of the machinery as it turned, the slush of a mixture of mud and rock and water slurping through the Kelly. He held the envelope out at arm's length, almost as though he were teasing me. Then he dropped it onto the wet ground, and the plopping sound made me jump. He smiled again and bowed slowly, ever the stickler for tradition. Then he turned around and moved quickly, amazingly so for a wounded man of his age, and ducked under the machinery near the shaft. I cried out his name in helpless horror, and with my face pressed to the links of the fence I watched as the heavy head of the pump came down and smashed in his skull.

Deprived of the traditional ceremonial sword, Kenji Sueo Tomita had committed *seppuku* in a less appropriate fashion.

22

I hate ladders. I especially hate aluminum kitchen stools with a set of steps that pull out. But Kim and Marvel and I had picked the tree out of an open-air lot in Mimosa Beach that afternoon, and there wasn't much point in just letting it sit there in the Ledbetter living room, so we'd sent out for Chinese food and then begun the ritual of trimming the tree. The big white angel had to go on the top, and I was the tallest, so I got elected. The sharp, fragrant needles scratched my face and hands as I reached past them and put the topmost vertical branch of the Scotch pine up the angel's skirt and then pulled down to anchor it there.

"A li'l to the left," Marvel said. He was standing just behind me, his hands on his hips, critically surveying my performance. Every job needs a foreman, and Marvel had volunteered.

Kim had opened the cardboard boxes and removed the newspaper wrappings from the glass ornaments and little wooden Santas and horns and gingerbread men and was festooning the branches of the tree with them. Billy was over by the picture window, trying to make something of the hopeless tangle in which we'd found the strings of Christmas lights. A Yule log crackled on the hearth, the two bowls of eggnog, with and without rum, were on the coffee table, and Christmas music emanated from the stereo. Marvel and I had gone two out of three falls regarding the volume at which the music was to be played, and a compromise had been effected.

It was only the eighth of December, but Kim is one of those people who loves the holidays so much, she puts the Christmas decorations up almost as soon as the Thanksgiving dishes are done. Her grandfather usually humors her. And that was all right with me.

Just about everything Kim Ledbetter did was all right with me.

"I got a call from Jason Gamble this afternoon," Billy said, frowning at the light cord. "Thought you might be interested."

I teetered on the step stool and grabbed one of the thicker branches for support. "What's up?"

"You won't like it."

I minced down the steps backward. "Probably not, but you're going to tell me anyway, aren't you?"

"He says his lawyer talked to Don Stack's lawyer. Stack is going to give back every cent."

I picked up my cup of eggnog. "Why wouldn't I like that?"

Billy separated one strand of lights from the rest and laid it lengthwise across the floor. "Because Gamble has agreed to drop all charges."

Kim said, "Do we have to talk business?" but we both ignored her.

I said, "You mean Stack is going to walk?"

"Appears that way."

I shook my head and plopped down on the sofa to recuperate from my task. "Doesn't seem right, somehow."

"Oh, he's gonna get a wrist slap from the Department of Commerce. A hefty fine. And they're gonna close him down."

"What happens to Grayco?"

"Not much. He rolled the dice when he invested his money in the first place. He's already made a few bucks out of it, but basically he's seen his last payday from Vista Number One."

"Let's hear it for the Department of Commerce," I said, toasting. "Champions of truth, justice, and the American way."

"And the Amptmans?" Kim said.

"Ah, the Amptmans," I said, swirling my cup around so that the eggnog made the clear glass sides opaque. "The lovebirds are going into relationship therapy to see if they can put the pieces of their marriage together."

"He comes aroun' me," Marvel muttered, "ain' gonna be no pieces left."

"I imagine they'll stay together for the sake of the children."

"What children?" Kim said.

"The Mercedes, the Volvo, the house, Pacifica Properties, Seaward Development. People like that don't love other people, they love things. If they break up, each has to give some things away, and that would be more than they could bear. There'll be another Pete D'Anjou in Nanette's future and in her pants, and the next time George will look the other way and keep on playing Monopoly with real buildings to help heal his broken heart. They'll work it out. People like that always do."

There was an uncomfortable silence. Cynicism has no place at a Christmas party. I felt as if I'd just condemned Tiny Tim to death.

"Look at this one, Marvel," Kim finally said, holding up a clear glass ornament with a snow scene inside it. Marvel was not impressed. She put it on the tree, high up and in the front where it would show. "This one is my favorite."

She came to the coffee table to pick up her unspiked eggnog and I pulled her down onto my lap. "This is too much like work," I said. "Let's neck."

She slapped at me without rancor and went back to the ornaments. I said, "You don't want to talk business, you don't want to fool around—gee!"

"You really didn't think Jay Gamble was going to take him down, did you, son?" Billy said.

"Stack? He tried to nick Gamble for thirty-two million bucks. If it were me, I'd be peeved."

He laughed. "That's 'cause you don't understand oilmen. Hell, it's not your fault, you got to be born to it."

I smiled, glad to be let off the hook.

"There's one well that produces for every nine wildcat wells drilled. The rest of 'em are nothing but holes in the ground. When a fortune rides on your guts and your instincts like it does in oil, you tend to get kind of crazy sometimes. That's why oilmen are the biggest bunch of rogues you can imagine. Hell, old John D., Paul Getty, all of them that got big rich, they lived in their fancy houses and endowed museums and foundations and all, but scratch off that veneer and they're pirates. Just like Jesse Gamble. And Don Stack."

"And just like you, Billy," Kim chimed in. She broke open a package of angel hair and began draping it over the tree between the ornaments. It didn't really look like snow.

"Gamble knew Stack was skinning him somehow or other," I said, "and Stack knew he knew it. It was a game, then. A goddamn game."

"That's it," Billy said. "No sense you getting all exercised about it." He plugged in the strand of lights, and all of them glowed except two. He pulled the plug out of the wall and took some loose bulbs from a battered grocery sack to replace the defective ones.

"Three people died, Billy."

"That's the problem," he said. "Peter D'Anjou was a talented boy, but he was all schoolbooks and test tubes and theories. Oh, they're fine in their place, but it takes a real oil man"—he looked over at Kim and beamed with grandparental pride—"or woman, to put it all together. Those other two, they came over here with a lot of smarts, all right, but not oil smarts. You don't kill somebody, not even over all those dollars. That's not the way

227

we do it over here. You ever go to the movies when you were a kid?"

"Sure," I said, "that's why I got in the business."

"The Westerns—*High Noon, Red River, Shane,* Joel McCrea and Randolph Scott. There's a code, even for outlaws. You don't throw down on a man first, you don't kick him when he's down, you always back your partner, and you're never silly enough to sit with your back to the door or draw to an inside straight. That's kind of how the oil business is, son. That's where it started a hundred years ago, Texas and Oklahoma. And guys like Gamble and Stack and Ledbetter, we like it that way and we still play by those rules. Oh, the conglomerates rattle their sabers and set the prices, sure, and the Arabs throw their weight around and spend their money on real estate. But when it all settles down, it's the real oil people who are gonna keep calling the shots in this country. 'Cause we're the ones with the heart, and heart wins out over petrodollars every time. Remember when Gable and Tracy settled the ownership of a billion-dollar oil field by tossing a coin in *Boom Town*? That's the way it really was. And still is. You're a generous winner and a gracious loser, and if you play it any other way, sooner or later you're going to get stomped on."

"You make Stack sound like some folk hero," I said.

"Well, he is. The last of the rogues."

Kim dragooned Marvel into hanging a few ornaments on the tree. He did it a hell of a lot more pleasantly than if I had asked him. Kim had a strange and mysterious hold on Marvel, perhaps stemming from her knowledge of James Worthy and the Lakers, but he did just about anything she asked him to. He had even started picking his shoes up and throwing them in the middle of the floor in his own room.

"And I'll tell you something else that may surprise you."

"What's that, Billy?"

"Somewhere down the line Don Stack is going to come up on something big. A new field nobody knows about yet, maybe in South America, virginal and just waiting for the bite of a drill bit. So rich with crude that you can smell it, you can taste it in the wind. And when Stack needs a few bucks start-up money, when he's looking for a partner, Jason Gamble will be one of the first guys he asks. And he'll get it too. 'Cause that's the way they're made."

I didn't say anything. I went to the tree and began stringing the strand of lights around it, trying hard not to get two green ones or two red ones too close together.

"If we're lucky," Billy said, "we'll be in on it too, or one like it. Kim and me. Lord Jesus, wouldn't that be something else, the two of us together on a big strike? And it'll happen, just as sure as God made little green apples. It's the crude in our veins, son. What we're made of. You can't fight it."

I looked at Kim and she dropped her eyes. It appeared that our situation was going to be stalled, sooner or later. That we had different life-styles was not news, we'd known that when we started, but we'd ignored it, as people often do when they are in the beginning of things, when the fire burns so brightly that it draws the eyes to its merry flames and away from the realities. But she had her priorities and I had mine, and here under the Christmas tree, with Bing Crosby pah-rum-pah-pum-pumming on the radio, we were both having trouble envisioning a relationship carried on between the west side of Los Angeles and some yet-to-be-discovered oil field in Bolivia.

She looked up at me almost defiantly, her china-blues almost too big for her face. I could see the fine tracery of veins beneath her fair cheek. It was hard to believe they carried crude oil to her heart, but Billy had told it true, and there was no use fighting it. It was what it was, and it was fairly obvious that one of us had broken the rules—the code—and had begun nurturing expectations.

I plugged the lights in, and our faces were set aglow in several different colors. Marvel broke into a big grin at the first Christmas tree he'd ever helped decorate. It was a big deal to him—the parties, the presents, the music and the glitter and the goodwill toward men that he'd never really been a part of. The magic of a kid's Christmas was coming a bit late in life for Marvel, but he was eating it up. That, at least, I felt good about.

They were the kind of lights that winked on and off in sequence so that you couldn't ignore them if you wanted to. It seemed oddly fitting.

It was pretty festive, all right. 'Twas the season.

"Joyeux Noël," I said.